Praise for
Nicole McLaughlin

"Nicole McLaughlin had a new fan by chapter two!"
—*New York Times* bestselling author
Erin Nicholas on *All I Ask*

"Nicole's fun, sassy stories and sexy heroes are not to
be missed!"                    —*USA Today* bestselling
author Julie Brannagh

"A wonderfully fresh voice in contemporary romance—
sweet, sexy, and immensely satisfying."
—*New York Times*
bestselling author Lauren Layne

NO LONGER PROPER
ANYTHINK LIBRA
RANGEVIEW LIBRA

D1019630

Also by Nicole McLaughlin

*Maybe I Do*

...TY OF
...ARTES]
...KY DISTRICT

# Maybe This Time

## Nicole McLaughlin

St. Martin's Paperbacks

**NOTE:** If you purchased this book without a cover you should be aware that this book is stolen property. It was reported as "unsold and destroyed" to the publisher, and neither the author nor the publisher has received any payment for this "stripped book."

This is a work of fiction. All of the characters, organizations, and events portrayed in this novel are either products of the author's imagination or are used fictitiously.

MAYBE THIS TIME

Copyright © 2018 by Nicole McLaughlin.

All rights reserved.

For information address St. Martin's Press, 175 Fifth Avenue, New York, NY 10010.

ISBN: 978-1-250-14000-5

Our books may be purchased in bulk for promotional, educational, or business use. Please contact your local bookseller or the Macmillan Corporate and Premium Sales Department at 1-800-221-7945, ext. 5442, or by e-mail at MacmillanSpecialMarkets@macmillan.com.

Printed in the United States of America

St. Martin's Paperbacks edition / March 2018

St. Martin's Paperbacks are published by St. Martin's Press, 175 Fifth Avenue, New York, NY 10010.

10  9  8  7  6  5  4  3  2  1

To my beautiful friend Jennifer, for being one of the coolest people I've ever known.

# Acknowledgments

It's hard to believe that this is my ninth published book. Doesn't seem possible, and it wouldn't be if it weren't for a team of amazing people. First of which is my friend and agent, Sarah Younger. You're the best out there and I'm so grateful for you. Holly Ingraham, my fantastic editor. Thank you so much for adopting me! Jennie Conway, thank you for everything you do and for being so on top of it. I'm amazed. Titi Oluwo, you've been so fantastic. Marissa, Justine, Brittani, DJ, and anyone else I may not know of, you are all so wonderful. Everything you do behind the scenes is so appreciated and I'm so grateful for each of you. The beautiful covers of this Whiskey and Weddings series are thanks to Lesley Worrell and I couldn't love them more.

Of course I always have to thank my family. All of them! My sister-in-law Tracy, who is my consummate cheerleader and amazing friend. My sister, Lauren, who is busy cooking my future nephew!! My mother,

Denise, for being the best. My husband, Michael, for being my best friend and biggest supporter—I love you. And my three boys, Sean, Branden, and Blake, who I love so much I can hardly stand it.

# One

*Twelve years earlier*

Apparently, blondes *did* have more fun. Or at least got more attention, Jen Mackenzie thought as she made her way down the main hall of her high school. Three guys had already made lewd comments, she'd received one request for her number, and several girls had given her dirty looks.

And the day was only half over.

The first tardy bell sounded as she took a left toward the history and social sciences wing of Green Hills High School.

"Looking good, Jen," the best friend of the most popular guy in school said. Did that make him the second-most popular guy? Jen didn't hang around with—or give two shits about—popularity. It wasn't for her, so she just gave him the finger and kept on walking.

He laughed in response. "Anytime you want."

She rolled her eyes, but smirked. She could appreciate a guy that could take it as well as he gave it. Jen was no stranger to male attention. However, she wasn't used to it being so blatant. Not at school anyway, where she was normally an outcast. Or the kind of girl guys propositioned in secret. But the previous week she'd performed the role of Sandy in her high school's musical rendition of *Grease*. Apparently dyeing your normally dark hair blonde, proving you could act and sing, and donning tight-as-hell pants, could turn an obscure emo girl into an overnight sensation. Now the catcalls were loud and proud. Who'd have thought?

Although she was smart enough to know none of it was genuine, not even a jaded and bitter soul such as herself could deny the instinctive pleasure this new attention brought her. It wasn't that she'd wanted to be a nobody . . . necessarily. It was just so much easier to not care. Case in point: She was already feeling the pressure from this newfound attention. The blonde hair had to be part of the appeal, and yet, there was no way her mother would give her the money to maintain it. The director's sister did hair, and so she'd let Jen come to her shop and get a head full of platinum highlights for free. But a few weeks from now she'd be the girl with the nasty dark roots—a clear reminder to her peers that she was not one of them. With a sigh, she picked up her pace as her stomach gave a tiny moan of protest. *Don't you dare humiliate me, stomach.*

She'd purposely not eaten lunch for two reasons. One, she didn't want to risk spilling anything on her top, and two, to ensure she didn't have bad breath for this hour. And okay, probably a little bit because her lunch account was negative nine dollars. At ten, they held the right to refuse you, depending on the mood of the cashier, and Jen wasn't willing to risk suffering that humiliation. Not again. Asking her mom for lunch money was only successful when she was in a good mood. Otherwise she'd get the "if you want to eat lunch every day, then get a job" speech. But a job would not allow her to attend rehearsals. A dilemma, but they didn't call them starving artists for nothing. Someday her talent would pay off.

As Jen approached the door to her fifth-hour Government class, she slowed, trying not to appear over-eager. Normally, that would have come naturally. She hated this class. Mr. Timmons was a bore, and she hated the texture of his hair, which looked like a toupee but supposedly wasn't. All she could do was stare at it all hour to try to see if it moved in conjunction with his head. Incredibly distracting, and several times she considered just raising her hand and asking if he'd just give it a good tug so everyone could finally focus on the three branches of government.

Today, however, she was nervous and excited. Popping a piece of gum in her mouth, she entered the class as the second bell rang, the reason for her anxiety staring back at her from the far row.

TJ Laughlin.

Just the sight of him made her nauseous and tingly. And did he just shift in his seat and look away in disgust? Was he annoyed? The seating arrangement had just changed at the end of class yesterday. Maybe he wasn't happy, considering he used to sit next to a group of his friends.

"Hey, Jen," a second-tier popular girl named Renee said from her seat. "Cool hair."

Jen glanced at her, trying to analyze if it was a sincere compliment. Unable to tell, she replied, "Thanks." No smile. Better to play it safe and not look foolish.

Making her way to the table she was now sharing with TJ, she pulled out her chair and sat down. He said nothing, but his left leg was bouncing nervously beneath the desk. Her first instincts must have been right.

"Feel free to request to move to another seat," she said under her breath.

His leg froze as he looked at her. "Why would I do that?"

He almost looked pissed off. She glanced down at his leg. "Either you have to take a piss, or I make you uncomfortable."

He let out a huff of a laugh and shook his head. "You have no idea."

That was a vague answer. Before she could demand he clarify, Mr. Timmons was beginning his droll lecture. TJ, having always been a perfect student, wouldn't appreciate her talking to him during class. Nerd. Except he was a hot, rich nerd. The kind of guy who would never want anything from Jen but what she could give him in fifteen minutes in his car. She was no prude, but she wouldn't give any guy the satisfaction of looking down on her any more than he already did.

Mr. Timmons went on about Congress, and it wasn't long before Jen was leaning back in her chair and doodling in her notebook. Anything to take her mind off how good TJ smelled, or how his forearm muscles constricted as he furiously took notes. He was left-handed, and she liked watching the way his wrist curled in as he used his pen. Almost like he was writing upside down.

"The way you write looks messed up," she whispered.

His hand stilled as he turned to look at her. "I'm left-handed."

She gave him a long look. "No shit." She sat up, scooted her chair forward, and leaned on the table, looking at him. She whispered. "Does that mean you jerk off with your left hand?"

"What the . . ." He turned away, as if to be sure no one overhead her. Redness bloomed on his cheeks and down his neck.

Jen smiled, biting her bottom lip as he faced her once more.

"Why would you ask me that?"

She shrugged. "Just curious. There's no shame in jacking off, TJ."

He gave her a side-eye. "I didn't say there was."

They stared at each other for a long moment until his eyes finally roamed over the blonde waves framing her face. "You gonna dye it back?" he asked, surprising her.

"I don't know. Should I?"

He lifted an eyebrow. "Doesn't really matter. But the blonde isn't you."

She wasn't sure what he meant by that, but she assumed it was because her normal dark brown hair was drab. Just like her. Jen wasn't meant to be a sweet, beautiful, upbeat, Sandy kind of woman. In fact she'd auditioned for Rizzo, thinking she was a shoo-in. She felt like she was made for the role. But the minute she'd got done singing, the director had stood up, clapped, and said, "I did not expect that voice to come out of you. But I think we have our Sandy." Nobody had been more shocked than Jen, and probably most of the student body. And she still hadn't decided if his initial reaction was a compliment or not. She was leaning toward him being a stereotyping jerk, but she did appreciate the part.

Jen looked away, trying to convince herself that TJ's comment about her hair didn't sting. From anyone else, it probably wouldn't. There was no explaining her thing for him, but she knew it went beyond the fact that he was beautiful to look at. They had four classes together this semester, and she often found his eyes glancing away from her, which made her look at him more, always hoping to catch him staring back. It made her feel a little insane and obsessed.

Maybe she was tired of his judgment and subconsciously wanted to convince him that she could make him want her. Stupid her should realize that boys didn't want girlfriends who talked about pissing and jacking off. They wanted a lady. If only they could see those "ladies" in the locker room. They were all crude, even the popular ones. In fact they might be the worst.

Mr. Timmons stopped in front of their table and handed them each a worksheet titled FROM BILL TO LAW. "Feel free to work together," he said. He probably thought Jen couldn't handle the work on her own. Jerk.

"Don't feel obligated," she muttered, pulling a pen out of her purse.

TJ scooted his seat to face her a little more. "I don't, but it would be stupid not to work together and get this finished faster. It's front and back."

Jen sighed, covering up her relief. "Fine."

It didn't even take them fifteen minutes to get through the entire thing, and she had to admit, he was a good partner. Didn't try and answer all the questions first. That surprised her.

"You really know this stuff," TJ said, stuffing his pen into the backpack on the floor at his side.

"I'm not stupid."

He gave her a long look. "Will you cut it out with the attitude? I never said you were stupid. But considering you drew pictures of fairies all through the lecture, it surprised me how much you knew."

She stared at him, wondering how he'd managed to see what she'd been drawing. Wondering why he'd been interested. Shrugging, she put her supplies away. "I find government fascinating and also infuriating enough to hold my attention. I read the chapter last night."

When he didn't respond, she glanced up at him. God, he was so handsome, his green eyes sparkling, light-brown hair sweeping over his forehead just right. Even his eyebrows were perfectly placed and groomed. Was that natural or did he maintain them? She wanted to ask, but didn't, because his lopsided smirk was suddenly throwing her off.

"What?" she asked.

He opened his mouth to speak, but they were interrupted by Evan Peterson, Green Hill South football star and ladies' man. "Hey, you two."

Jen looked up to find him leaning on their table. It was only a few minutes until the bell rang and Mr. Timmons was busy with something at his desk, so several students had left their seats to socialize.

"What's up, Peterson?" TJ said dryly. Jen knew the two guys were friends, so TJ's irritated greeting surprised her. Evan was kind of cute in the rugged jock kind of way, but sooo not her type. Or in her league. He'd recently broke up with Adeline, a varsity cheerleader and total rich bitch. Could anything be more cliché?

Evan smiled at Jen. "Great job last week. I think you had every guy dreaming of you in those tight pants this weekend. You should wear them to school."

"Jesus, dude. Shut up," TJ said.

Evan looked at him, confused. "What for? That's a compliment." He turned to Jen. "Right? Shit, I never even *go* to the musicals, but after I heard about how amazing you were, I had to. Didn't disappoint."

Jen wouldn't mind slapping the dickhead in the face, but for some reason she just gave him a tight-lipped smile.

He took her silence as agreement and leaned in closer. "I was kind of wondering. How would you like to go to the dance together next Saturday?"

Jen's shock was further intensified by the way TJ froze beside her. His bouncing leg once again halted. And had she seriously just been asked out by one of the most popular guys in school? Why did it make her feel a little excited? Maybe because she'd been watching these handsome yet self-absorbed asshats walk these halls for almost four years, looking straight through her the entire time? Probably also because in those four years she'd never been invited to a dance. Which reminded her.

"Isn't this a Sadie Hawkins dance?"

"Yes. It is." TJ's voice was low and stern beside her. She glanced at him, but his eyes were glued to Evan. "Which is why this is stupid."

Jen looked at her potential date. He just shrugged. "Didn't want to take the chance. After last week, you're a hot commodity. Feel free to ask me instead. Laughlin can keep a secret."

Jen glanced back at TJ, who finally met her eyes. Why did he look mad? Maybe they were all going as a group and he didn't want her around? The thought pissed her off. No, she was not popular or rich, but she had every right to hang out with whomever the hell she pleased.

She turned back to Evan. "Maybe I will ask you. Better stay on your toes."

He gave an awkward and obviously stunned laugh. "Alright then, I will. Can't wait," he said before walking back to his seat.

Jen and TJ were both quiet in his absence, so she finally picked up her backpack. The bell would ring any second, and she'd be off to Acting 2. Her favorite class. Drama Club and the performances were the only reason she didn't just drop out of school already.

"You really gonna ask him?"

She glanced over to find TJ staring at her, his own backpack over his shoulder.

"Do you have a problem with that?" Maybe he'd be honest. Her theory was that she was hyperaware of his constant judgement because she herself was so focused on him. He must sense that she had a ridiculous crush on him, and he was trying to subconsciously send her "no fucking way" signals. She knew other students looked down their nose on the weird poor girl, too, but TJ was the one she *felt* it from. It must be annoying for his friends to be asking her to join their social events.

"Yeah. It does bother me," he said, his eyes narrowed, brow furrowed. He breathed in hard and blew it out through his nose before glancing up at the clock.

Jen stood there fuming. Screw this guy. There was no point in being attracted to such an asshole any longer. She *would* be asking Evan to the dance. Maybe it would finally send hot rich boy the message that she was not beneath him.

Yep. Blondes totally had more fun.

# Two

*Present day*

Standing in her mother's tiny apartment kitchen, Jen Mackenzie squeezed her eyes shut as she logged onto the bank app on her phone. She muttered a quiet prayer. *Please not yet. Please not yet. Please not yet.*

Holding her breath, she opened one eye and peeked at the screen. A heavy sigh of relief escaped her lips as she quickly scanned the list of debits and determined the car payment she'd paid online yesterday hadn't yet posted to her account. Her pitiful bank account remained in the black another day. Constantly checking her bank app was an anxiety-laced game she'd been playing more often lately, ever since she'd lost her job at Maple Springs Community Theater, which had finally closed due to federal funding cuts.

She hated being broke all the time, but until her Broadway dreams came true, or that sugar daddy quit evading her, it was probably her destiny. But at least today she could get some gas in her car and make it to work. Tonight she'd leave the Stag with tips from the bar, and Monday was payday, so if everything worked out as planned, she should be all good before that bill posted to her checking account. Score a point for head-barely-above-water Jen.

Realizing it had been a half hour since her mother went into the bathroom to shower, Jen walked down the hall and tapped on the door. "Everything okay, Mom?"

"I'm fine. I had trouble shampooing my damn hair."

Jen frowned. She'd thought her mom had seemed a little stronger today when she'd shown up for her daily check-in. Clearly, after watching her mother battle cancer for the past year or so, she'd lost all perspective of what the woman looked like on a good day. Considering she'd given up her favorite hobbies—drinking and smoking—when she received her diagnosis, one would have thought her mother would feel better. Like a new person. But although Jen was so proud of her mom for making that lifestyle change, sometimes she wanted to bring her a bottle of vodka from work. You know, just to see her smile again. Or stop being a total bitch.

So far, Jen had refrained from being the ultimate enabler. For now.

Instead she took the brunt of her mother's frustration with life. Checking on her daily even though she was ungrateful, bossy, and irritable. Some days the woman didn't even have the strength to get out of bed, and while Jen had urged her to discuss depression with her doctor, she didn't think it had happened.

It wasn't that she and her mom had experienced an ideal mother-daughter relationship up until this point. Quite the contrary—except for when things were going well in Diane's life. But Jen had secretly hoped the diagnosis would inspire a change in their tumultuous relationship. So far, no dice.

"Do you need help?" Jen said to the closed door.

"No. Said I'm fine."

Leaning against the wall in the hallway, Jen felt guilty for being annoyed. She hated the self-centered feelings she sometimes had regarding her mother, but as much as she wanted the woman to make a full recovery, caring for her was difficult. After a lifetime of bitterness toward her selfish mother, it wasn't always easy to be the bigger person. It was downright difficult. But just as her mother had found the will to give up smoking and drinking, Jen had decided her contribution would be that of head cheerleader. Her constant attentiveness wasn't earning her any thank-yous, but she wasn't being told to lay off either. Deep down she knew her mother was grateful—they just didn't really know how to love one another.

But Jen was trying, by showing up every day, driving her to the doctor when it was needed, making her food. Being present and kind, even when it was brutally hard and she was emotionally and physically wrung dry. She could only imagine how her mother felt—considering it was her poor body that was under attack—but sometimes Jen just wanted to stand on the side of the highway and hitchhike herself out of this life.

Glancing down at her phone, she realized she'd been there longer than she'd thought. She pushed off the wall and leaned into the bathroom door once more. "Okay, well, I need to get to work. You going to be okay?"

"Of course I am," a slightly irritated voice answered.

Jen looked up at the ceiling and bit her tongue. *Sorry for worrying about you.*

The door opened, releasing a puff of steam into the air. She backed up as Diane Mackenzie stepped into the hall. Jen instinctively glanced away before her eyes could land on the woman's satin robe. The way it clung to a flat—almost concave—chest. The same chest that used to fill out a Circle H gas station uniform polo to the point of straining the buttons. It wasn't that Jen was repulsed by the sight of her mother's double mastectomy, it just made her achingly sad.

And scared.

Fear of injury or sickness had always been a problem for Jen. The sight of blood or a trauma, or even just hearing about someone's accident made her feel lightheaded. Then there was the panic of her own health. She'd finally forced herself to stop doing internet searches for the statistics of the heredity of breast cancer. The problem with that was, while she could stop looking, she couldn't erase the previous information from her mind. It could hit her out of nowhere, and then repeat in her brain like an earworm of "We Are Family" after a night bartending a wedding. *Having two relatives with breast cancer is more concerning if they are on the same side of the family.* Bad news for Jen—her mother and her aunt were survivors. For now, anyway. So statistically speaking, it didn't look good, and she couldn't help thinking that her D cups gave cancer a lot of space to take up residence.

As she followed her to the bedroom, Jen noticed her mother's hair had grown a little longer, finally covering

the tops of her ears. It had grown in grayer than before she'd lost it. Diane hadn't said, but Jen knew she
hated that. If they'd had a normal mother and daughter
relationship, Jen might have suggested she try styling
it, to make her feel more like herself. But as it was, she
couldn't imagine making the offer. And it was possible the idea was stupid, since her mother's hair had
been down her back before the chemo. Something
Jen had always thought silly for a woman in her forties.
But when it had all begun to fall out in thick clumps,
leaving her mother crying on the shower floor, Jen
had quickly realized how a person's hair—a woman's
especially—was wrapped up in their identity. Their
self-confidence. Even their sexuality.

Now that she looked again, the short wisps around
her mom's ears suddenly didn't seem like something
to celebrate but more like a reminder of what she'd lost.

After finishing up her last round of chemo in May,
they'd been hoping for some positive news. But three
weeks ago, testing had revealed an elevated white blood
count, which then led to an MRI, and of course they'd
found another small mass underneath her armpit,
because neither Jen or her mother could catch a break
in life. Diane had barely reacted. Almost as if she'd
known it was inevitable. Her lack of sadness, outrage,
fear . . . any emotion at all, had terrified Jen.

Assuming she'd be ready to start fighting with another round of chemo, Diane had shocked Jen when
she'd chosen instead to do a clinical trial of two new
medications that had until recently been used only in
Europe. Sure, they'd had some good results, but Jen was
still furious about it. There was too much unknown. So

far, the side effects appeared to be fatigue and depression. Or maybe those were just the side effects of dying.

"Do you have plans today?" Jen asked, trying to take her mind off her renewed frustration.

"I do. Terri is going to come by with dinner. Bringing a movie."

"That sounds nice. You haven't seen her since she took you to your last appointment, have you?" Jen leaned against the door frame. Terri was the only one of her mother's friends she liked. Probably because she'd always been happily married and not as inclined to party like Diane and their other friends. The woman had also been a godsend the past year, helping take Diane to appointments, to pick up her prescriptions, and whatever else they needed help with.

"Not in a week or so, no." Diane pulled some underwear and a soft tank-style undershirt from her top drawer. There was no longer much need for bras, and Jen had gotten rid of them before they'd even come home from the hospital eleven months ago. Her intentions had been good, but she still didn't know if she'd made the right call by doing that. Her mother had never mentioned it, so she hoped that was a good sign.

"Can I do anything for you before I go?"

A heavy sigh preceded her "No, Jen. I'm just fine."

"Just fine" was her mom's favorite phrase. Jen had heard her say it a million times, as an answer to a million questions throughout her life. *You'll be just fine. We'll be just fine. It'll be just fine. Everything will be just fine.* Jen had learned one thing: living a *just fine* life was pathetic.

"I'd like you to be *good* for once, Mom. Consider lying if necessary. Just to give me some peace of mind."

Her mother turned and stared at her. "You know . . . you don't need to check in on me all the time," her mother snapped.

Jen pushed off the doorframe, ready to leave. She forced a deep breath and then replied in the sincerest tone she could muster. "Yeah, well, I think I'll keep doing it whether you like it or not."

"Then don't complain about my response." Diane tied her robe and jerked the belt tight.

"Noted. I'll keep being the best daughter ever, and you continue to have a chip on your shoulder." Jen waited for a snarky reply, almost pissed when one didn't come. It had been a while since the two of them had engaged in a good yelling match. Maybe they were due for one, but Jen refused to be the one to start it. "Well, I'll probably be late tonight. It's the uncasking party."

That seemed to rouse a genuine smile from Diane. "Give the guys my love."

The "guys," in Jen's life, were her three bosses at the Stag Distillery, Dean, TJ, and Jake. And in classic Diane fashion, they had earned her mother's love just by being handsome men.

"I will. They'd have liked you to come tonight." Dean had insisted that Jen take an invite home to her mother, who had at first been excited to go. That is until this new mass had been discovered.

"I know, but they understand."

"They do. They just like to see you."

"I'll come visit them soon when I feel better," she said. The *which will probably be never* remained unsaid.

"Okay, well, bye, Mom. Have fun with Terri."

Her mother just raised a hand in response. Jen rushed through the dark living room to the front door, and took a deep breath as she stepped outside. She would never stop checking in and worrying about the woman, but it was always a relief to leave. Walking down the sidewalk, Jen turned to head up the metal and wood staircase. She and her mother both lived at the shitty Shady Meadow apartment complex in Maple Springs, Kansas, just a five-minute drive from the downtown square. And its name did not lie, because it was shady alright. The management did the bare minimum to keep the place maintained, and many of the residents were on a first name basis with the local cops.

Jen lived on the second floor of building C, her mother on the first of building B, right next to the parking lot and the mailbox, which had proven pretty damn annoying once or twice. Notably the last time Jen walked out with a guy one morning and her mother was standing there in a robe holding her Bed Bath & Beyond mailer. That had earned her a long, judgmental stare. Ironic, considering men had always been her mother's third weakness, coming in after booze and cigarettes.

Dropping her keys on the sofa, Jen headed to her own tiny kitchen—identical to her mother's except that it was flip-flopped—to grab her jug of distilled water. Saturday was plant-watering day, so she went from pot to pot checking on her babies, talking gently to them as she touched their soil and then watering those needing it. She currently had eight plants, down one after losing Fey a month prior. Some asshole had stolen the fern off her miniature deck, and Jen still hadn't recovered from it. Who steals a fern?

She'd discovered her love of plants when her mother had her mastectomy and the owner of the convenience store she worked at sent a calathea to the hospital. Diane had seemed unmoved by the gesture and in too much pain to care for it, so Jen had taken it home.

It hadn't taken her long to realize how comforting—and surprisingly therapeutic—it was to care for something else, especially something that couldn't talk back. Slowly she added to her collection when she had a few dollars to spare, and now she practically had a greenhouse in her little apartment. She loved it. Not only were the plants peaceful, but she loved the way they softened the look of her crappy place. It felt more fresh and alive.

Once all the living things had been cared for, Jen headed to her bedroom to finish getting ready for work. She swapped her shorts for her favorite denim skirt and then gently maneuvered her fitted gray Stag tee over her half-up hairdo, which she'd sprayed into submission just an hour before. Jen had a bit of an obsession with makeup, and she could easily waste away an entire Saturday watching video tutorials online.

She'd recently purchased a new red for her lips, although she really shouldn't have. But hey, it was from the drugstore, she was bad with money, and thus could convince herself that even she deserved a splurge now and again.

Moving her head from side to side, Jen inspected

her eye shadow and liner. Perfect. As were her brows, if she did say so herself. Growing those puppies back in was one of her biggest personal accomplishments over the past five years. Pretty frickin' sad for a woman who'd just turned thirty and had one day hoped to have her name in lights.

Standing in the doorway of her tiny closet, Jen stared down at her collection of cheap shoes. It would be a long night, but she wanted to feel a little cute, so she chose her Mary Jane–style athletic slip-ons.

After grabbing her purse, she headed out the front door and down the stairs. She couldn't help throwing a quick glance at her mom's front door—still closed, drapes shut—and then walked to her ten-year-old F-150 pickup. Twenty minutes later she had a quarter tank of gas, her favorite purple energy drink in her hand—another shouldn't-have purchase—and was heading inside the Stag Distillery on the corner of Hickory and Sterling in Maple Springs.

Stepping inside, she was greeted by a chill rushing over her skin and the familiar yeasty scent of the distillery building she'd been working in for the past several years as a bartender and now also temporary receptionist. At first glance it appeared no one was here. The front desk in the lobby where she sat Monday through Friday was empty, so she checked Dean's office. Empty. A little further down the hall she checked TJ's, her heart accelerating. *Stop it.* Empty. And since Jake usually ran late, she didn't bother checking his office or the meeting room.

Someone had to be here, considering the party started in less than two hours. She headed for the old freight elevator and pulled open the metal cage door before stepping into the car.

"Hold up," a deep voice called out from the back room. Jen froze. Of all the people to encounter first, it would of course have to be TJ.

Sometimes she still couldn't believe that after crushing on him all through middle and high school she ended up working for his company a decade later. When she'd applied for the bartending job several years ago to supplement her income at the community theater, she'd had no idea TJ was one of the owners. Dean, a co-owner, had hired her on the spot because they had started booking weddings at breakneck speed and were desperate. She'd happily accepted and started the same night, despite her only experience being a lifetime of watching her mother and her friends drink. Turned out that had worked just fine, and she'd learned the rest from Google searches on her phone when needed.

She could still remember that following weekend when TJ had come in and they'd seen each other for the first time in almost a decade. Her first thought—after catching her breath—had been that he'd barely changed. Still handsome as all get-out, just older, more muscular, and with a shorter, more modern haircut. The butterflies in her stomach had performed the same dance at the sight of him as when she was still in a B-cup bra.

There'd really been no mistaking the what-the-hell-is-she-doing-here look on his face that day. But as much as she'd wanted to, she couldn't hold that against him because there was no doubt she'd been wearing the exact same expression at seeing him. And for the past several years they'd maintained a civil—albeit slightly tumultuous—working relationship. Mostly because she enjoyed pushing his buttons.

Before he got on the elevator, Jen quickly took a guess at what TJ might be wearing today. Khaki slacks with a light-blue button-up, or gray slacks with a white button-up. It was always one or the other. Belt, sleeves rolled up at the forearms, top button undone revealing a hint of his neck. God, he was so predictable it was maddening. In fact, she was almost getting tired of giving him shit because the material never changed. Then again, part of the problem was that he looked so damn good in those preppy outfits.

Jen stood waiting, holding the gate, listening as his footsteps sounded on the tile as he headed in her direction.

"Thanks," he said as he stepped onto the platform and pulled the elevator door shut.

Jen swallowed, her mouth going dry at the shocking site of him this afternoon. Quickly finding her voice, she lifted an eyebrow and decided to throw him a bone. It was a day of celebration, after all. It was the least she could do for a sort-of friend. "You look rather *GQ* this evening."

He glanced down at himself as the metal gears of the old elevator jerked to life. "Thanks. I have to admit, I wasn't sure what to wear tonight." The boyish grin on his face when he lifted his gaze back to hers had her feeling a little melty. Not entirely unusual for her in this man's presence, although she hated to admit it, even to herself. Plus, she didn't often see his smile. Not directed at her, anyway.

She shrugged. "I think you did okay. The jacket is nice."

"Thank you. It was a gift from my mom." He touched the lapel, glancing down at the fabric. He glanced up at her through lowered lids. "I'll await your ridicule for that."

Jen feigned insult, putting a hand on her chest. "I can't imagine what you're talking about."

He just shook his head. Yes, she gave him shit. But she wouldn't tonight. Besides, it was no surprise that he was the pride and joy of clan Laughlin, and tonight his mama made sure he dressed the part. His dark denim jeans were so perfectly fitted to his hips and thighs, Jen wondered if he'd had them specially made. He still sported his signature brown belt, paired with—wait for it—a blue-and-white-checked button-up. Something she'd never seen on him before, and while it almost should have been tacky, it was perfect. But the best part was definitely his mom's gift, the navy dress jacket, and there was no doubt it had been tailored. That service alone probably cost more than her rent. But lord, it was worth every penny. The sight of his broad shoulders and firm biceps made her mouth water. She looked away.

Of all the men she'd encountered in her life, why did the fantasies in her twisted head always fall back on this one? It didn't make sense, her weird thing for him. She'd known him for so long, had seen him go through his awkward pubescent phase and he her *many* awkward phases. Shit, she was *still* trying to figure out who the hell she was. Right now, she was knee deep in "almost middle-aged, broke woman trying to look put together." But tonight, TJ was perfectly polished sexiness. Now her fantasies would never get a reprieve. Damn him.

"Excited for tonight?" she asked, changing the subject.

"Yeah. I am. Five years is a long time." He was referring to the bourbon and whiskey they'd first barreled five years ago when he and his two partners Dean and Jake had first started their distillery business. Tonight, they'd finally share their signature offerings with the public.

"Good things come to those who wait. Or some trite bullshit like that," Jen said.

TJ chuckled. "Hopefully they say it because it's true."

"I'm sure it is. This will be great. I'm happy for you guys."

His left eyebrow lifted, and she realized she'd not been the only one surprised at her pleasant words. She and TJ had a default mode: awkward. It was a combination of her giving him constant verbal jabs, and him being annoyed with her. She couldn't help herself, he was so damn stuffy and self-righteous. TJ Laughlin had been judging her since middle school, and so she'd made it her personal mission to remind him that she was her own woman and she didn't give a shit what he thought. *How's that going for you, slick?*

"This is a big night for you too, Jen," he said, this

time surprising her. "You're an important part of this company."

Hmm. She wasn't sure where to go with this conversation as she stepped off the elevator. He followed behind her, shutting the metal gate with a loud click. The two of them didn't usually have such pleasant and benign interactions, so he was probably expecting her to reply with a snappy comeback. A test maybe. She wouldn't give him the satisfaction of being right. She'd already complimented his outfit for goodness' sake.

With a smile, she said, "Thank you, TJ. That really means a lot."

His eyes narrowed the slightest bit, but she just turned and headed toward the far end of the event space—her domain.

The massive wooden bar where Jen slung fancy cocktails held up the east end of the room and sat perpendicular to the giant fireplace centered on the north side. This event space on the second floor of the Stag was gorgeous. Wooden floors and beams, floor-to-ceiling windows overlooking the square, and a massive and intricate handmade antler chandelier. Complimenting that was a giant stag head over the huge fireplace. There was no denying the three male owners had been instrumental in styling the space, and somehow they'd managed to pull off rustic and elegant at the same time. Big and spacious, yet cozy and intimate. And that was the reason it was such a popular wedding venue and had made the guys a lot of unexpected money, considering they'd never planned on being in the event business when they'd first bought the building. But it had worked out, giving them much-needed additional revenue while their main liquor offerings aged in barrels in the giant storage building across the alley.

Up until recently, they'd only been selling their unaged spirits, which had been very well received over the past five years. They had a lot of customers chomping at the bit to get a taste of what would come out of these barrels tonight.

Jen immediately got to work behind the bar, taking stock of what was there, making note of what she'd need to go get from storage. Tonight would be fun. They'd created several new cocktail recipes to highlight the signature products, and she couldn't wait to serve them.

While this was called an uncasking party—and they would ceremoniously open a reserved barrel—they'd officially opened the rest of them two weeks ago in order to be ready for distribution next week. It had been crazy hectic at the Stag, planning this evening, bottling, tasting, finalizing orders, on top of the work for their wedding clients. The guys had worked their asses off over the summer, and that didn't even include the personal drama that they'd all been dealing with. Everyone deserved to enjoy themselves this evening. Even stuffy old TJ, Jen thought, as she caught sight of him from the corner of her eye. Something she tended to do from time to time. Or constantly.

She watched as he arranged bottles of Stag Signature Bourbon on the display near the fireplace that had been set up the day before. It all looked nice, various old crates stacked on top of one another.

Someone—probably Charlotte, Dean's new girlfriend, who was very creative—had inserted some mason jars of dried wheat and rye and some ears of corn to represent the varieties of alcohol they produced. However, the way TJ was just shoving in the bottles was completely ruining the aesthetic.

Jen shook her head and walked over. "I hope you don't decorate your own house."

He glanced over at her and then back at the display. "What's wrong with it?"

Reminding herself that she was giving him a reprieve tonight, she changed her tune and gave him a tight smile. "You've given it a good try, but I think it would look better if you lined them up just so." She rearranged the last four bottles he'd set up in a nice row, staggering a few in front. "See how much better that looks?"

He lifted an eyebrow and let out a manly sound of agreement. "Thanks," he said quietly. "That does look better."

"See, having me here isn't as bad as you think it is." She turned to walk away, but he grabbed her hand, shocking her. Their eyes met as she jerked back.

"Why do you always do that?" he asked, still holding on to her hand.

"Do what?" She swallowed.

"You know what, Jen." His voice was low and controlled, but she could hear the frustration in it, as if her pleasant attitude had confused him and he was just waiting for a moment to return them to their normal. "You like to imply that I don't want you here. It's bullshit. You know I want you here."

*Okay.* That was not their normal. "Maybe I have low self-esteem," she joked, feeling a little overwhelmed. And his fingers were still burning into her skin.

He glared at her. *"Please."*

She smiled in reply, trying to make light of the conversation, and not be offended by his sarcastic tone. Just then she heard heavy footsteps coming up the back staircase followed by a concerned feminine voice echoing. He let go of her hand at the sound and they both turned toward the back stairwell door.

"Everything will be fine." The voice was Charlotte's. Jen recognized it immediately. "She knows what she's doing. Let's just enjoy this evening."

Dean entered the room first, his face full of fury, and Charlotte bringing up the rear with a smile on her face as soon as she spotted them. Odd. Was everyone participating in Opposite Day around here? Dean was usually super laid back. Took a lot to ruffle his feathers, although Jen had accomplished it a time or two just because she couldn't resist a direct challenge.

"Has to be about Alexis," TJ muttered, referring to Dean's younger sister.

Jen nodded her agreement as they both watched Dean stride purposefully toward them across the big room. He and Charlotte held cardboard boxes of what appeared to be table centerpieces. When Charlotte set her box down on the closest table, Jen could see the worry in her eyes. She tried lightening the mood.

"Hey, lovebirds. These are pretty," she said, picking up one of the centerpieces. It was similar to the decorations on the crates TJ had been arranging, a large glass bottle full of wheat and silk sunflowers. Very Kansas.

"They're left over from Alex's wedding." Dean said, his words clipped with anger or frustration. Maybe both.

Jen bit her bottom lip, regretting her words and not knowing what to say in response. Dean's younger sister was in the army. She'd been deployed for several years, and over the past few months Charlotte and Dean had been planning a wedding for her. They'd chosen everything: the cake, the DJ, even the meal. Had things gone as planned, Alex and Nate had only to show up during their short leaves and get hitched. Except things hadn't worked out quite that way. The wedding was supposed to have taken place last Friday, but about a month before, Nate had been killed in a helicopter accident on deployment in the Middle East.

Setting the glass jar on the table, Jen smiled. "Well, they are lovely. How nice that they can still be enjoyed."

Dean didn't respond, just began unloading his box, but Charlotte piped up. "I agree. And Alex was relieved that they could still get used. This was the perfect event."

Nate's death had shaken them all at the Stag, even those that had never met the man, like Jen. But obviously Dean had been devastated. He'd practically raised Alex, and as soon as he'd heard the news, he'd flown to Georgia—where Nate was from—to meet his sister and her fiancé's remains. They'd buried him there with his family, and Alex had spent the past four weeks grieving, understandably so. Jen knew that

Dean had been struggling to see his sister go through so much pain, but the one bright side of the past few months was that he and Charlotte had finally come together through the process. Finally, because Jen had been a spectator to the two of them dancing around their obsession with each other for a while.

Jen smiled at Charlotte, who reciprocated, but the other woman's expression was still forced. TJ hadn't taken his eyes off Dean, no doubt trying to assess what he should say to his friend.

Charlotte placed a gentle hand on Dean's arm. "I'm going to run back out to the car and get all my gear. I'll be back."

Dean nodded silently. Charlotte turned to Jen. "Could I ask you for a hand?"

"Oh, sure. Of course." Jen jumped at the chance to flee the awkwardness in the room, but more important, she wanted to get the scoop. The two women headed down the back staircase, through the area that held the supplies and the access to the distilling room, and out to the back alley.

"What is going on with him?" Jen asked as they made their way to Dean's SUV. Charlotte sighed before she opened the door to the back seat.

"Alex just informed us this afternoon that she is going ahead with her deployment to Italy."

Jen considered that for a moment. "Okay, that does suck. But hadn't that been the original plan?"

"Yes," Charlotte said, as if relieved someone finally saw reason. "It *was* the original plan for her and Nate after the wedding. It was part of the reason we'd been planning their wedding, their short time at home before leaving. She'd reenlisted and requested to go there so they could be together. But for some reason Dean had assumed Alex wouldn't still go alone."

Charlotte leaned into the backseat and then handed Jen a black bag of camera gear. Charlotte was a photographer—the catalyst for her and Dean meeting since she shot so many weddings at the Stag. Jen admired Charlotte immensely for owning her incredibly successful business, and also for just being one of the funniest, kindest women Jen had ever known, and it had occurred to her more than once that she might even get along well with Charlotte outside of work.

"So, he's upset that she's leaving or that she's leaving alone?"

"Both, I think." Charlotte reached for one camera body, then a second, before shutting the back door with her butt. "He's scared. It's always worried him that Alex is in the military, but he's afraid for her to go back as a grieving widow of sorts."

"Maybe it's what she needs. To return to normalcy. Get away. I mean, Italy sounds like a pretty awesome place to heal. And the military is what she does. I'm sure she can handle it."

"That's exactly what she said, and I agree with her. He's just being an overprotective big brother. He'll get over it, he just has a bad habit of thinking he knows what's best. I'm trying my hardest to break him of it," Charlotte said with a sigh.

"Good luck with that," Jen replied, hefting a bag farther onto her shoulder.

Charlotte laughed quietly, and then her brows furrowed. "I just hate that it happened today of all days. This was supposed to be a good day for him."

Jen followed Charlotte back into the building. "Yeah, not great timing. When does she leave?"

Charlotte glanced at Jen. "Monday."

"Yikes. So soon. Is she coming tonight?"

"That had been the plan and I hope she still does," Charlotte said, her voice going quiet as they headed into the building. "He was kind of a dick back at their place when she told him. Made her cry. I know that's the biggest reason he's pissed right now. He's mad at himself as much as he's upset about her leaving."

"Another thing you need to break him of," Jen said. "You're reminding me why I avoid relationships."

Charlotte stopped on the third step up to the second floor and turned, her expression pensive. "It's true. It's work. But . . . it's worth it. You know?"

"I'll take your word for it." Jen's lips quirked. The fact that she liked Charlotte so much was really saying something because Jen didn't usually have a lot of friends. Especially female friends. Acquaintances, party buddies, sure. But true secret-telling kinds of friends? She couldn't even recall the last one. How many times had her mother reminded her that most women were spiteful and couldn't be trusted? And yet, for some crazy reason, Jen could see herself trusting Charlotte.

The only thing making her hesitate was guilt. Once upon a time when she'd first started working at the Stag, she and Dean had hooked up. *One time.* They'd been drinking one night after a late and very stressful wedding and each saw the other as an available warm body. It had been stupid and meaningless, and while she didn't necessarily do regrets, Jen had never had any desire to repeat it. She was certain that Dean felt the same way.

The incident had really been of no consequence, until now. She wanted this friendship with Charlotte to develop, but the closer they became, the more Jen felt the need to come clean. But then that would quickly end the relationship, wouldn't it? It was a moral dilemma that Jen usually didn't suffer from, but in this scenario, *she* would be perceived as the woman who couldn't be trusted, and the thought made her feel like shit.

"One more thing before we go up," Charlotte said, her brow furrowing. Her sudden change in demeanor had Jen's arms feeling weak. Or maybe that was the heavy-as-hell camera bag she had in her arms.

"Yeah?"

"I wanted to tell you before she showed up. TJ has a date coming. Some woman he's been going out with for a few weeks."

The stairs suddenly felt as if they'd turned to a metal slide under Jen's feet, and her body went warm and tingly. Not the good kind. And not because of the heavy bag. No, this was the warm prickly feel of her body screaming *Danger! Abort the situation.*

She managed to play it cool. "Well, good for him. I didn't know he was seeing anyone."

So much for trust, but right now Jen couldn't stomach the sympathetic look on Charlotte's face. What the hell tipped her off to make her think Jen cared if TJ had a date or not?

And also, how had Jen not known TJ was seeing someone? Oh yeah, because she and TJ didn't communicate well. The last person he would discuss his relationship status with was her. The person who always made fun of him for having no love life and for being a prude. Ironic.

"Charlotte, seriously, I don't know why you're concerned." *And this is why you don't have friends.*

The other woman shrugged. "Well, I wasn't really, but Dean's kind of convinced you guys like each other. Don't tell him I told you that. I'm only sharing because, in case he was right, from one woman to another, I didn't want you to be blindsided tonight."

Jen sucked in a breath. Okay, that was nice. "I appreciate that, Charlotte. I really do. But no, it's fine. I'm happy for him. And I can promise you, there is no way TJ likes me. I live to piss him off."

"Are you sure? I mean, we're totally friends, Jen. I won't tell anyone if you do like him," Charlotte whispered before turning and making her way up the rest of the stairs.

"And by 'anyone' I assume you mean anyone who isn't Dean?" Jen said to Charlotte's back. She hoped the other woman could discern the amusement in her voice.

Thankfully, Charlotte smiled over her shoulder. "Well . . . only if it came up."

"Which it would."

They stopped at the top of the stairs before entering the main room. There were other voices now. Probably the caterers, so they wouldn't be heard.

"But seriously. If you need anything tonight, let me know. Okay?" Charlotte said before walking into the main room. Jen blew out a breath and followed. Damn. She hadn't lied to Charlotte. Not completely. Dean was wrong if he thought TJ had any interest in *her*, and she'd never given him any reason to think she had feelings for him.

But if that was true, then why did the thought of seeing TJ with another woman suddenly make her sick to her stomach?

# Three

TJ was sweating.

Surely two hours into a party was appropriate for the host to get a little more comfortable. After leading Brooke—his date—to the edge of the room, he peeled off his jacket and tossed it onto the back of a chair. He liked the jacket his mother had gotten him—and had felt obligated to wear it—but it was like wearing a portable sauna. It was late July for god's sake, and although they had the air-conditioning cranked, this was a hundred-year-old brick building. They were on the second floor, and there were easily two hundred people mingling in the room. Some things modern technology could not compete with.

"I like this shirt," Brooke said. She slipped her fingers under the front placket, her nails sliding against the skin of his stomach. "You look so handsome tonight."

"Thank you," he said, rubbing her arm lightly. He glanced down at all five and half feet of her and forced a smile. He was a hair above six foot one, so standing side by side—even with her in tall-as-hell heels—he felt like a giant. It was a bit annoying for some reason.

"How long do we have to stay? I'm kind of in the mood to get you alone." She grinned up at him, suggestion in her eyes, but TJ was not feeling it tonight.

"Sorry. This is kind of a big night. Plus I need to stay and help clean up."

"I know it's a big night. But that calls for a celebration." Brooke smiled up at him.

"Uh-huh. And that's what we're doing here," he said, suddenly peeved by her indifference to the situation. "I don't want you to feel obligated to stay, though." Did that sound like a request for her to leave? Would it bother him if it did? Because he could almost use a break.

"I can wait for you," she said smiling.

"Thanks," he patted her arm again, noting that she hadn't offered to help clean up *with* him. Just 'wait.' It wasn't her job, of course. But still.

They hadn't discussed if she was coming home with him, or he with her, but he already had a feeling he'd be too tired to give her what she was looking for. God, he was pathetic. With a sigh, he let his gaze linger on the bar once more. Something he really should quit doing, but he was a glutton for punishment. Always had been when it came to the woman they employed to pour their drinks and temporarily run their front desk. He was pissed to see she was still talking to the same guy that she had been talking to for fifteen minutes now. Not that he was counting.

"That bartender . . ." Brooke followed his gaze. "What's her name again?"

"Jen." TJ looked back down at the woman plastered to his front. Wasn't she a little overwarm? It would really help his body temperature if she stepped back. "Why do you ask?"

"She is so sweet," Brooke said. TJ held in a response of surprise. "I wasn't really sure what to expect when I saw her, but oh my goodness, she's adorable. And so funny."

"Hmm." TJ rubbed Brooke's arm absentmindedly while he processed what she'd just said. "What do you mean 'when you saw her'?"

Brooke grinned, her nose wrinkling a bit. Instead of reciprocating, he glanced to the woman in question as Brooke went on, sounding a little defensive. "You know . . . tattoos, lots of makeup. Black hair. I don't know."

Yes, Jen had a sleeve of tattoos three quarters of the way down her left arm, but they weren't of skulls and crossbones for god's sake. They were feminine. And yes, she wore a lot of makeup, but . . . she always looked attractive, and shit, he'd stopped noticing what hair color she had, as many times as it had changed over the years.

TJ knew he was now frowning at the bar when Brooke angled herself into his line of sight. "Hey, I'm sorry. I didn't mean to upset you. I'm sure you guys are friends since she works for you."

She sounded sincere, but this suddenly felt like a trap. He should have just let the statement go without comment. There'd been no mistaking what Brooke had meant, even though he hadn't liked it. Jen had always favored a certain look and it brought to mind storm clouds, hard angles, and darkness. From her midnight hair to her black fingernails, she resembled a gothic Cinderella. Yes she could be potently snarky, but Brooke was right, Jen was mostly sweet—to everyone but TJ. Even though he was certain it was often a ruse. And he guessed in his date's defense, that was her point: Jen's outside appearance didn't match her outgoing personality. But when *he* looked at Jen, all he could see were curvy hips, plump red lips, and colorful tattoos of flowers and fairies. She was . . . an enigma.

"I know you didn't mean it like that," he said, although he wasn't completely convinced. "But yes, Jen has been our employee for a while and she's been going through a rough time. We're all a little protective of her."

The wary eyes looking up at him were the gaze of a woman trying to decide if she bought his level of concern or not. He knew that, so he squeezed her arm again in reassurance, hoping the subject would be dropped, because if there was one thing he didn't want to discuss with the woman he was dating, it was Jennifer Mackenzie.

She seemed placated by his touch, so TJ let his gaze slide over the room. They had a great turnout for the uncasking. He'd shaken plenty of hands and received hundreds of slaps on the back, and shockingly his parents had come. They were currently sitting with the mayor of Maple Springs. His mother was no doubt throwing back more than her fair share of free cocktails while his father pretended that he'd been in support of this business from the get-go. TJ had lost count of the times his father had called the distillery "the stupidest idea I've ever heard" and had asked "Why *make* whiskey when you can buy Johnny Walker at the liquor store?"

Nothing like unwavering support from the man you should have considered a role model. Instead, his father was the last man on Earth TJ desired to emulate in any way. No, he aimed to make money honestly by working hard and playing fair. And to be loving and faithful to his wife and children if he ever managed to get that lucky. That last part was feeling less and less likely every year he got older.

"She told me she's known you since middle school," Brooke said, still talking about Jen. TJ forced himself not to raise his eyes to the ceiling and sigh. Now he really felt sweaty. Why wasn't she dropping this topic?

He glanced down at Brooke. She was a beautiful woman, with a petite yet muscular stature, sandy-brown hair, and bright-green eyes. They'd met through a mutual friend a couple of months ago, and had now been out six times. Slept together three of them. She was attractive, kind, educated, and employed. All good things. So why did he suddenly feel like he was suffocating?

"We did. In fact, we went to middle and high school together."

Her eyes widened. "Were you guys friends?"

"No, not really." Which was the truth. "In fact, we did a government project together once and she was pissed at me the entire time."

Brooke grinned. "Aw. She doesn't appreciate your genius like I do." She went up on her toes, so naturally

TJ leaned down to let her kiss him quickly on the cheek. As he stood back up, his eyes shot to the bar just in time to see Jen watching. She gave him a tight-lipped smile and went back over to chat with the same asshole she'd been talking to before.

"That's too bad she's been having a rough time, but the fact that Jordan Bodisto is so into her will hopefully get her in a good mood," Brooke said with a grin.

TJ forced his body not to stiffen. "Oh yeah?" he asked, going for merely amused interest. But inside he was fuming. A Bodisto had a lot of nerve showing up to their uncasking after giving them the shaft for the past five years. He let his eyes travel back to the bar. Jen was laughing at something the guy talking with her said while she made drinks for those in line. How had he not recognized Jordan? They'd grown up frequenting the same country club for years. He'd put on about thirty pounds of muscle and his hair was a lot shorter. "You sure that guy's Neil Bodisto's son?"

"Of course I'm sure. Most women would be thrilled to have his attention for so long. I have a friend who went out with him once." Brooke wiggled her eyebrows. "According to her, he could take any woman out of her funk."

*Okay.* What was she getting at with that comment? And why did TJ suddenly feel like he'd put his jacket back on? A thin line of sweat trickled down his back. He swallowed hard and pulled himself together. "Well, good for her then."

He spied a catering server approaching, so he took the opportunity to unpeel Brooke from his body and step forward to grab himself another Maple Springs Mule he didn't need. To his gratitude, Jake, one of his co-owners and long-time best friend, joined them. Hopefully Brooke would drop the subject of other men rocking Jen's world in bed.

"Can you believe this turnout?" Jake said, a huge grin on his face.

"I'm so proud of you guys," Brooke said, giving Jake a big hug. Seemed like an odd thing to say considering she hadn't been around for ninety-nine percent of their business growth, but TJ remained silent. It was a nice sentiment, and she'd known Jake a while, since they'd gone to the same high school.

Brooke untied herself from Jake and looped her arm through TJ's again.

"You talk to Dean yet?" Jake asked, a concerned look suddenly on his face.

"Earlier. I think everything's good for now." TJ gave his friend a look that let him know they shouldn't discuss their friend's issues any further. For some reason, he didn't want Brooke asking any questions. She knew about the death of Alex's fiancé, of course, since she and TJ had just started seeing each other when it happened, but the subsequent issues were none of her business. And if that wasn't a red flag about how he truly felt about a relationship with her, he wasn't sure what was.

"Well, he should feel good about this turnout tonight," Jake said, thankfully taking the hint.

"Yeah." TJ shifted focus, trying to think about the many positives of the evening. "Everything has gone great. Food's good, signature drinks have been well-received. I've gotten a lot of positive responses on all the products in general tonight."

"So have I," Jake said. "And did you notice Neil Bodisto sent his son? I talked to him for a while. Asked him when Shakers was going to finally open an account with us. He laughed it off. Acted a little cagey if you ask me."

TJ nodded, still annoyed to find out that the man talking with Jen was a Bodisto. Neil and his sons Jordan and Jonas owned Shakers. A very successful cocktail centric bar and grill chain that had more than ten locations throughout the Kansas City metro area. The original store—which was at least forty years old—sat opposite the Stag on the square. TJ, Dean, and Jake had assumed that Shakers would be a shoo-in to carry locally crafted spirits in their bars, but they'd shocked them all by declining. They'd then had the balls to turn around and try their hand at making a white whiskey of their own. Obviously, it had failed, because you didn't go into the business of making alcohol just to prove you could. Your heart had to be in it. TJ, Dean, and Jake had just laughed it off, although it had secretly pissed TJ off. But the guys at the Stag weren't going to beg anyone for their business. Not even a local institution, so it was interesting indeed that Jordan had come this evening.

"I didn't even know we'd sent an invite to Shakers," TJ said.

"Yeah, on a whim I hand-delivered it to Neil myself," Jake said, looking smug. "Smooth move of his to bow out, but send his son. Probably wanted intel on our operations."

"Did he take the tour downstairs?" TJ asked. They had their newest employee, John, giving quick tours of the distilling room.

"Not sure."

"Hmm. I'd given up on them," TJ said.

Jake shrugged. "I sort of had, too, but I'm glad to see him here. I'm definitely following up with him next week. How awesome would it be to get an account with them?"

TJ nodded, taking a drink as he watched the man in question laugh at something Jen said. Maybe now that the Stag had proven itself with five years of business, Neil—Jordan's father—had resigned to the fact that the distillery wasn't folding. The senior owner had been a fraternity brother of TJ's father, and as much as it pained him, TJ always wondered if his father had asked Bodisto not to work with them. It was sad to consider your own dad capable of such a backhanded thing, but not much about James Laughlin surprised TJ anymore. He had some odd philosophies on life. TJ wouldn't put it past him to think he was helping his kid out, by making him work for it.

"Well, gentlemen, you'll have to excuse me while I run to the ladies' room," Brooke said, giving TJ's arm a squeeze before walking off.

Once she was gone, TJ caught Jake's smile from the corner of his eye. "What's so funny?"

"Still can't believe you're dating Brooke Anderson."

Jake and Brooke had gone to school at Green Hills North High, a town over from Maple Springs. TJ had gone to Green Hills South, but he and Jake had become friends through Little League, then competitive sports, and eventually gone to the same state university. Now here they were running a company together. Still best friends despite their differences. One of which was that Jake had no shame when it came to the ladies.

"She was untouchable in high school," Jake said. "Every guy I knew wanted a piece of that. I bet it's amazing."

TJ gave his friend a long look. Yes, they were best friends, but he had no desire to betray a woman's trust in that way. And for fuck's sake, they were grown men.

"Oh, come on," Jake whispered. "You're not going to tell me if we all pined in vain?"

"We are not having this conversation."

Jake just growled in frustration. "You and your high-brow morals. It's not like you're serious about her."

"What does that mean?" TJ asked.

It was Jake's turn to give a long look. "Seriously? She's not the one. Not *your* one. I'm sure you wish she could be, but it's not there. I figured you were just in it for the sex."

Was he in it for the sex? Maybe. Before Brooke it had been a while. TJ looked back out at the crowd. Across the room he watched Dean wrap his arm around Charlotte's waist, who then smiled up at him as they chatted with guests. Despite the pain he'd endured with his sister and the death in their family, Dean had never appeared more content since TJ had known him. And the guy had secretly had a thing for their most popular photographer for a long time. Years. Now here they were, finally making it work.

Jake stepped a little closer to TJ and spoke under his breath. "Listen, sorry, that was kind of an asshole thing to say. Brooke's great. But as your friend, I hate to see you get any deeper into this relationship without even telling Jen how you feel."

TJ refused to meet Jake's gaze. "As my friend, that's horrible advice."

"Bullshit. I mean . . . what if, man? *What. If?* You don't know unless you try."

TJ blew out a breath and finally glanced at his friend. "Not a good idea."

"Why the hell not? Jen's sweet when she wants to be."

"She's a pain in the ass."

"But she could be *your* pain in the ass. You've had it for her for a long damn time."

"Be quiet," TJ hissed.

"Man, I get the fear. I mean . . . *I* have no desire to settle down right now, but I think you do, and I hate to see you do it with the wrong person because you're hung up on some stupid shit. I don't even know why you hold back."

"A gut feeling." And a healthy but irrational paranoia that he may be as shitty of a husband as his father was. If his own brother was any indication, the apple hadn't fallen far for one Laughlin offspring, so why not two? And as much as TJ hated it, he wanted his dad's respect, and James Laughlin would take one look at Jen and consider her prime side-piece material. The thought made TJ sick to his stomach.

"I love you, dude, but you can be stubborn as hell,"

Jake muttered. "You need to pull your head out of your ass and just see what happens."

Before TJ could reply, the sound of the elevator across the room caught their attention, and a woman walked out.

"Holy hell," Jake whispered. "Is that who I think it is?"

TJ's eyes widened as he took the vision in. Alex, Dean's little sister, was dressed in a short, tight dress, her hair swooped up off her neck. There was a bit of uncertainty in her eyes as she glanced around. The look of a person hoping to see someone she knew quickly so she didn't feel alone. TJ wondered if this was the first time she'd put makeup on since coming home with Nate's body. Poor girl. But TJ had to admit, she looked gorgeous.

TJ glanced over to find Jake's eyes wide. *Oh hell no.* "Listen, you should take *my* advice when I suggest that whatever you're thinking . . . I promise it's a really bad idea."

Jake's eyes jerked to his, instantly glowering. "Damn, Laughlin. Give a guy some credit for Christ's sake," Jake said, sounding truly hurt by the comment. "I know she just lost her fiancé."

TJ sighed, feeling like an ass. "I know. I'm sorry. Just . . . be careful. Dean would destroy you."

With an annoyed shake of his head, Jake headed toward the elevator and TJ watched relief wash over Alex's features as she saw his familiar face approach. She wrapped him into a hug, they chatted for a bit, and then Jake led her to the bar. TJ scanned the crowd looking for Dean once more, wondering what his take on the exchange would be. So far, he appeared not to notice. Ah well, how much trouble could Jake get into since Alex was leaving on Monday for Italy?

Yeah, on second thought, that didn't make TJ feel much better.

He continued to watch them as they ordered drinks. Alex smiled. Then laughed. She took a highball glass that Jen passed across the bar. Laughed again. It was nice to see her smile. TJ had been over to Dean's once not long after they came back from Nate's funeral, and hell, it had been bad. Worse than bad, and understandably so. Alex had been asleep on the sofa, tucked into a tiny ball, her face a swollen mess from crying, messy hair glued to her cheeks. Tonight, she was a different person. There was still a shadow behind her eyes, but she was a world away from the woman he'd seen several weeks ago.

Feeling eyes on him, TJ's gaze shot to Jen who gave him an eyebrow raise and a subtle nod to Jake and Alex who were now both laughing. Well, shit, if Jen was concerned, maybe he should keep a closer watch. TJ grabbed his jacket and headed over to the bar. Brooke intercepted him on the way there, her fingers linking with his.

Together they approached Jake and Alex, the latter of whom gave TJ a hug in greeting. When she pulled away, he introduced Alex and Brooke to each other.

"Great dress," Brooke said.

Alex looked down at herself and then smiled before responding. "Thank you. I borrowed it from Charlotte. I don't think I've worn a dress in over a year, to be honest." Her expression faltered a bit. "Well . . . except for Nate's funeral, but that doesn't really count I guess." A sad smile followed.

"We're so glad you came tonight," TJ said, not wanting any discomfort for her.

"I wouldn't miss it. And this is such a great turnout for you guys," Alex said.

"Isn't it? Most of the credit goes to your brother for being such an amazing distiller."

"Yes, I haven't seen Dean yet," she glanced around, sipping her drink.

Everyone got quiet. TJ really hoped they would make up tonight, if Dean hadn't already called to apologize. When TJ had spoken to the guy earlier, he was half afraid Dean was going to break down from the guilt he felt over how he'd responded to her deployment news. TJ knew how protective his friend was of his little sister, and knew it had gutted him when she'd lost her fiancé. It was hard to comprehend a loss like that. To love someone so much only to have them ripped away from you in such a tragic way. Almost made it seem like maybe just playing it safe in a relationship was the way to go. Caring about someone was just too risky.

He'd add that to the list of reasons he was keeping his distance from Jen.

# Four

Jen was grateful she had the handsome man—what was his name again? Oh yeah, Jordan—to keep her company tonight at the bar. Talking to a hot guy made it much more tolerable to witness TJ's tiny cheerleader girlfriend paw all over him.

And it still grated that she was the last to know he'd been seeing someone. TJ *never* dated. Well, he probably had gone out on a date in the last several years they'd worked together, but she'd never heard about it, and he'd certainly never gotten serious with anyone.

But God, if Jen had ever tried to guess his type, it probably would have been this woman exactly. Sophisticated, beautiful, toned calves, cute little nose, pricy handbag. Blah, blah, blah. She'd already known he was predictable, so why was she so irritated?

Jen smiled at Jordan as she handed him another Stag Signature Bourbon and Coke. "It's nice to have someone to talk to while I work," she said.

He smiled at her. "I seriously doubt you hurt for male attention."

She liked that he was a straight shooter, like she was. The fact that he was tall and had large biceps didn't hurt either. She bet he played football in college. Was he her type for a serious relationship? Not a chance. Especially since relationships were for squares. But he could be fun for a night or two.

"Okay, you're right. I get my share of male attention. But it's nice to have attention I feel inspired to return," she said.

His lips quirked. "Glad to hear you feel that way."

Jen's eyes narrowed in on TJ and his date, who stood with their backs to her not five feet away from Jordan, talking with Jake and Alex. As his date's hand slid down his back toward his perfect butt, Jen felt her insides clench. She couldn't take her eyes off the perfectly manicured fingers, the way they began to curve down, apply pressure.

"TJ," she called out without thinking. He jerked around, effectively forcing the woman's hand to fall.

"Yeah?" he asked, almost coolly. No surprise, he was easily annoyed by Jen. Always had been.

She nodded her head at Jordan, who had turned slightly on his bar stool. "I thought you might like to meet Jordan Bodisto. Owner of Shakers."

Jordan turned fully and stuck out his hand the same time TJ put his own out. "Absolutely. Nice to meet you, man," TJ said, turning on the charm. Did they learn that in good-ol'-boy finishing school?

"Likewise. Sorry it's taken me so long to stop in."

TJ gave his world-class smile. "No problem. We're glad you came by." He turned to tiny cheerleader who was smiling at the two of them. He faltered as he spoke, his eyes flashing quickly to Jen. *Interesting.* "This is, uh, my date, Brooke."

Jordan shook her hand. "Pleasure to meet you, Brooke."

"Pleasure is all mine," she crooned. Jen mentally gagged.

Jordan looked past Brooke to the rest of the group, so Jake—who had obviously already spoken with him—introduced him to Alex. Once everyone had said hello, Jordan glanced at Jen and grinned. "You guys have got quite a good thing going for you here. I wasn't sure what to expect, but this building and your setup is amazing."

"Thank you. We've put a lot into this. All three of us," TJ replied. "It's nice to finally have all of our products out for distribution."

"Yeah, and they're really good." Jordan nodded at Jen. "Your fantastic, and very enticing, bartender has made sure I tried everything. I may become a customer just to have an excuse to come over and see her."

Jen faked embarrassment and batted her eyes as she swapped out her lemon pan on the bar. "So many pretty words," she said on an exaggerated sigh. Jordan winked at her, his expression full of amusement. He thought she was entertaining. And she was, damn it. When Jen's eyes cut to TJ, he had one eyebrow lifted, the other one narrowed. Jen wrinkled her nose at him, because she was a mature adult. And because she was so sick of him judging her.

TJ cleared his throat. "So, does that mean we've enticed you into offering Stag products at your bars?"

Jordan chuckled. "That I can't promise. My father likes to have input on all those decisions."

"Yeah, about that. I've always been curious as to why he's chosen to give us the shaft for the past five years," TJ said.

Everyone got quiet, eyes bobbing back and forth between the two men. Jen stared at TJ, a little shocked at his aggressive comment. He was normally diplomatic to a fault.

Jordan took another sip of his drink and then turned fully. "I honestly have no idea why my father does what he does or doesn't do." He shrugged. "I just do my job. But I plan on putting a good word in for you guys next time we talk."

If Jen had to guess based on that response, Jordan and his father didn't have the most loving relationship. She could understand that, but TJ—the prodigal son—probably couldn't. When her eyes cut to him, he was nodding.

"Understood. And I appreciate the good word," he said.

"Tell you what I *can* do. Repay your hospitality. We have a band coming out next Saturday evening at Shakers on the square. Drinks are on me if any of you would like to come by."

"Oh, that would be so fun," tiny cheerleader said, smiling up to TJ. "We should go."

Jen continued to restock her garnish station, but she could tell by the look on TJ's face that he wasn't so sure about the idea. However, the others in the group seemed interested. Except Alex, who quietly mentioned she wouldn't be in town.

"What band?" Jen asked as she grabbed a couple of limes to slice.

Jordan looked back at her, leaning on the bar. "Four Deep."

"No kidding?" Jen said, surprised. She cut her lime in half. "Anthony Carmichael is a friend of mine. We went to high school together. TJ also," she said, nodding at him. He didn't reply, just stared back at her.

"Sounds like you need to be there," Jordan said, his voice low and suggestive.

She grinned at him. "I could possibly be persuaded," she teased, before going back to her slicing.

"She has to work Saturday night," a deep voice interjected. "Sorry."

*Sorry? How dare he speak for her.* Frustrated, Jen shoved her knife down on the lime to make her next wedge, only for it to slice right into the fatty base of her pinky finger. She sucked in her gasp, dropped the knife, and instantly curled her hand closed. The lime juice bit into the wound, pain zinging through her finger. Her heart began to pound in her ears, whooshing in her head, and she wobbled as she turned to face the back of the bar.

She vaguely heard a voice behind her, but the pain and dizziness had her tuning everything out. Acting on instinct, she walked quickly down the length of the bar, out the end, and headed straight for the small hallway at the back of the room that housed the restrooms.

Without knocking she tried the women's door only to find it locked. Glancing down she saw a drop of blood on the floor. "Oh God," she whispered. She turned and tried the men's bathroom. Open.

A large body came up against her side and she dazedly looked up to find TJ's face, full of concern. "Let me see it," he insisted.

"No," she whispered. Her body suddenly felt cold and listless. Jen considered herself tough as nails when it came to most everything, or at least she tried to appear that she was. But she did have a kryptonite. Injury. Mainly the kind that arose out of tragedy, and usually included mangled limbs, gashes, blood, or all of the above. Just the thought of it could send her into panic mode.

"Come on," TJ said, leading her into the men's bathroom and straight to the sink. He grabbed her hand, but Jen held it closed tight, not wanting to see the results of her stupidity. She knew how to use a knife, and she'd let her emotions make her careless. Because of him.

"Open up. I have to see how bad it is," TJ said, gently prying her fingers apart. They were covered with blood that was now dripping into the sink, swirling down the drain with the water. Jen swayed on her feet, but TJ quickly grabbed her around the waist with his free arm. "Jen, it's okay. Just let me see."

Finally, she let him open her hand fully, but she looked away, squeezing her eyes shut. "This is your fault."

"Jesus," he muttered. "How do you come up with that?" He led her hand under the faucet and the minute the water hit it Jen gasped and yelped in pain.

"If I want to find someone to work for me next Saturday, that's my business."

She heard him sigh as he held her hand under the

water. "It's not so bad. A little deep, but a clean cut. I'm going to use soap."

"No! It will sting."

"Hush. Focus on how pissed you are at me. That should keep your mind very busy."

That almost made her smile, until the soap hit her cut. She yelped, but he held her steady.

"Deep breath, Jen. I've got you." He put her hand back under the warm water.

"It's okay," she said quietly, still not looking at the cut. TJ however pulled it up so he could look closer. "Can you just get me a Band-Aid?"

"No, but I can drive you to the hospital to get stitches."

Jen's eyes went wide. She shook her head. "No. No, no."

He turned off the sink and grabbed a wad of paper towels. "Yes. Right now."

"You said it wasn't so bad. That it was a clean cut."

"I did. But it's not in a good spot on your finger. It needs to be stitched closed. It gapes."

"Oh God, no, don't say that," Jen moaned.

"You don't do blood, huh?"

*Why the hell was there a hint of amusement in his voice?* "Shut up," Jen said, starting to pant. She was still lightheaded. How much more awful could this be? If she didn't focus, this would turn into a full-blown panic attack—and she'd had some doozies.

She sucked in a deep breath and blew it out slowly while TJ patted her finger dry and assessed it a little more as he cradled it in his own hand. She continued to breathe, and also watch his face as he stared down at her injury. His eyelashes were so long this close, and his upper lip was just slightly poutier than the lower one. He pressed the paper towel against her cut again and then he glanced up, locking eyes with her.

They'd never ever stood this close before. So close that she could see the tiny strands of brown that surrounded his pupils like wavy rays on a sun you drew when you were a child. God, they were intense. And perfect.

"Everything okay?" a feminine voice asked from the doorway.

TJ stepped back a foot. "Yeah. But she's going to need stitches."

Brooke gave Jen a friendly look of pity. "Oh no! I'm so sorry."

Jen's tight-lipped smile probably wasn't that friendly, but she really couldn't care less under the circumstances. Her finger still throbbed and stung, and for some reason Brooke's presence made the pain intensify. "No big deal," Jen said. She looked at TJ. "Guess you'll have to close the bar down for me."

His eyes narrowed. "No, I'll drive you. You shouldn't go alone." He looked over at Brooke. "I'm sure it won't take long. Do you mind?"

Brooke looked shocked, but she quickly collected herself. "Of course not. Come over after?" She pleaded, her eyes cutting to Jen.

"Sure. Okay," TJ said.

"You really don't have—" Jen started, but TJ cut her off.

"I'm going to tell Dean and Jake what happened. Meet you in the alley in five?"

"Fine."

"You okay to walk?"

Jen glared at him. "I didn't cut a leg off."

He nodded, stared at her for a fraction of a second longer, and then before Jen could protest further, she watched him place his hand on Brooke's lower back and lead her out the bathroom door and back toward the party.

Jen risked a peek at her cut, but the minute she saw the raw inside flesh exposed she squeezed her fist closed again. The pain surged once more. In that moment, standing alone in the men's bathroom with a gash in her finger, Jen felt helpless and afraid. The worst part was that she wasn't quite sure which was more painful. Her finger, or the fact that TJ was seeing a beautiful woman he would go home to tonight. He would touch her. Probably have sex with her. Probably already had.

Jen shook her head. Of course they'd already had sex, why wouldn't they? She needed to let this go. Her jealousy had already caused her to act foolishly.

"Oh, sorry—"

Jen opened her eyes to find the mayor of Maple Springs standing in the doorway looking flummoxed to find a woman having a bloody meltdown in the men's restroom. "No, sorry, my fault." Jen smiled and stepped toward the door. "I was just leaving."

He stepped out of her way, and Jen headed toward the bar. Jordan was waiting for her. "You cut yourself?" There was concern in his voice and she smiled up at him.

"I did. I'm not usually so clumsy. Guess TJ's driving me to the ER. I need stitches."

"Damn," his eyes narrowed. "I've had bartenders do that before. You want me to take you?" He looked eager to do it for her, and for a second she considered letting TJ off the hook.

But she didn't want to. Also, it would be uncomfortable to go with a man she'd just met. "No, but thank you." She smiled. "I enjoyed talking to you this evening."

The handsome quirk of his lips, and the way he stepped closer to her, almost made her forget about the throbbing in her finger. For a moment. "Not as much as I enjoyed talking to you," he replied. "Promise you'll come next Saturday. Even if it's late. The band doesn't get started till about nine anyway. I'd like to see you again."

"I'd like that, too. And I'd love to hear Ant play. We used to do theater together. It's been awhile."

"Theater, huh?" He smiled. "I can see that."

She wasn't sure if that was a compliment or not, but she just laughed it off. He gave her a wink, and walked toward the elevator just as Jen caught sight of Charlotte rushing toward her.

"TJ said you cut yourself. Are you okay?"

"Yes, yes. I'm fine. Or I will be, after I get it stitched up."

Dean came up behind Charlotte. "How'd it happen?"

"I was just being . . . careless I guess."

"You sure you're okay with TJ taking you?" Charlotte asked, giving Jen a knowing look. "I've gotten all the important photos of tonight. I can take you."

"No. It's fine. But I appreciate the offer." And she did. It was a friendly thing to do, but she couldn't deal with the pain and her conflicted feelings about her friendship with Charlotte at the same time. Plus, she couldn't deny feeling excited about alone time with TJ. So silly of her.

"We'll shut down the bar for you tonight." Dean interjected. "Most people are winding down anyway. You just get home and rest after you get fixed up."

Jen smiled at Dean. "Thank you. I appreciate it."

After grabbing her purse and awkwardly arranging it on her arm so she could continue to hold the paper towel against her hand, Jen hurried down the stairs. She quickly cut through the back room and out to the alley.

TJ had pulled his shiny white Camaro up to the stoop, and when Jen walked out he got out of the car and opened the door for her.

"Wow, romantic," she said in a flat voice.

"Quiet. It's the least I could do since you're maimed."

Jen couldn't hold in her smile as she angled her body and fell into the car. Literally, since it was so close to the ground. "Good grief, this isn't a pain in the ass to get into or anything," she said sarcastically, pulling each leg into the vehicle. "Didn't you have to take Brooke home?"

"She met me here."

*Okay.* As soon as she was situated, he shut the door. Jen used the few seconds to glance around and inhale the scent of TJ, a spicy cologne, and leather seats. He had the AC blasting, the stereo on low, and there was a pack of gum in the console cup holder that sat between them. Jen picked up and read it. SWEET MINT. So that's what TJ would taste like.

She dropped it back into the cup holder just as he opened the driver's door.

"Seat belt," TJ said sternly, as he sat down.

"Yes sir." Jen went to reach for her belt with her right hand, then realized that without the help of her left, she wasn't going to be able to do it. She turned to look at him. As soon as their eyes met, he realized her predicament and leaned to the side to help her.

"Can you pull it toward me?" he asked.

Jen yanked it down and passed it off to him, then scooted her butt over so he could reach in between her and the console to lock her in. His hand brushed her outer thigh as he pulled it out.

"Thank you," she said quietly then turned to look out the window.

"Hey," he said. Jen looked over at him. "You okay? Are you in a lot of pain?"

"Not too bad if I keep a fist. Just throbs. That lime juice seemed to have soaked into my bone."

He winced, nodded, and pulled out onto the main street. They drove in silence for a few minutes as he headed for the hospital on the edge of town. The sun was just starting to touch the horizon. She glanced at the dash to see it was just past nine o'clock. He wouldn't get back to Brooke until late, no doubt. Nothing at a hospital was ever speedy.

"Sorry to ruin your evening," Jen said.

"You didn't ruin anything." His voice was low and quiet, almost hard to make out over the whooshing of the air conditioner.

"Feel free to just drop me off."

"Jen, I'm taking you and staying. Accept it."

She felt relieved to hear him say it, but still felt a little awkward. "I know tiny cheerleader wasn't happy about you ditching her to do this."

When Jen heard his quiet chuckle, she turned to watch him, his lips quirked, eyes creased with amusement.

"What?" she asked.

He angled his head enough to give her a typical TJ eyebrow lift. "Tiny cheerleader?"

"Oh please. I saw her calves and her white-strip smile. Tell me she wasn't one?"

He was silent, just shook his head.

"I knew it!" Jen said. "God. I swear I can read you like a book."

"And what does that mean?"

"It means I knew exactly what your type would be."

"You have no idea what my type is." He sounded so sure, but Jen was skeptical.

"Obviously I do, and tonight I was proved right. You want someone adorable and . . . posh. I bet she has an Instagram page full of herself posing in her outfit of the day just for the fun of it."

He shook his head again. "What does 'posh' even mean?"

"Nicely dressed. On trend. And accessorized with a stick up the ass."

"Ah. I see. And should it offend me that you assumed my type was a woman with a stick up her ass?"

Jen shrugged. "Probably. But that's your cross to bear."

"It isn't actually, because you're wrong. And Brooke is a very nice woman."

Jen scoffed. "Whatever. She's judgmental. I could see it in her face. You don't need that in your life."

"And you're not? You just accused her of having a stick up her ass *and* being a cheerleader."

Jen glared at him. "*Yeah*, and she was! Is it considered judgmental if you're right? I call that perceptive."

"Christ, you're something else," he said on an awkward laugh.

What did he mean by that? And why the hell could she not just stick to being nice this evening? He always brought out the worst in her. Called to every deep insecurity she'd ever had. Why was she surprised that he judged her so harshly?

No one spoke for a minute, but Jen hated awkward silences, so she thought of something else to say. For conversation's sake, of course. "So, then what *is* your type?"

TJ's eyes widened, his head jerking over to her then back to the road. "I don't know."

"Nope, try again. You were adamant a minute ago that I did not know your type, so then you must have an idea."

TJ let out a deep sigh and leaned his right elbow on the center console. It was such a masculine position, his right hand resting leisurely on the bottom rung of the steering wheel, left arm stiff and gripping the top. It made her insides tingle.

"Okay, I guess my type is . . . attractive, obviously. I'm only human." He glanced at her nervously, as if asking for her approval.

"Fair," Jen rolled her hand with a flourish, encouraging him to go on.

"I guess I want someone outgoing. Creative. Strong and . . . not afraid to be herself or speak her mind. Funny. Caring. Hard-working. Compassionate."

Intrigued, Jen shifted in her seat to stare at him. "*Hmm.*"

"Hmmmm, what?" he asked, turning on his blinker. They were almost there.

"I'm just surprised."

"Yeah, well, maybe you don't know me as well as you thought you did."

"It's always possible. But I doubt it."

"You're pretty cocky, Jen Mackenzie," he said as he pulled into a parking spot.

"Am I? Noticed 'cocky' wasn't on your type list."

He stared at her. "Maybe I just forgot to mention it."

She stared back at him, a little stunned. There were those sunrays in his eyes again. She glanced away and used her good hand to unclick her seatbelt. By the time she had the door handle, TJ was there, pulling it open, lending a hand to pull her up out of the low-sitting seat.

As they walked into the ER, she felt his hand settle low on *her* back this time, and her legs nearly give out. TJ *never* touched her. Ever. So why was he tonight? Because she was in a helpless position, being injured? That still didn't explain him grabbing her hand earlier before the party.

Once she was checked in, they sat down in the waiting room together. Thankfully there weren't that many people there, so she hoped that meant it wouldn't take too long.

"I hate hospitals," Jen said quietly.

"Yeah, I hear ya," TJ replied. Their arms were

brushing and his left leg was bouncing up and down, a bad habit of his. "You've probably been in them too often lately. With your mom and everything."

"Yes." Jen blew out a breath.

"How's she doing? I'd hoped to see her this evening."

"Yeah, I would have liked her to come. She needs to get out of the house. I'm tired of her being so depressed."

"I'm sure the past year has taken a lot out of her. She's lucky to have you."

"I guess. I'm not always the sweetest daughter, but I've tried."

He gave her a half smile. "Maybe you two are too alike."

"God, I hope not." But she had a feeling he may be onto something whether she liked it or not. Jen breathed in deep, feeling incredibly overwhelmed. Her mother's health, job, and financial stress, and now she had stitches to look forward to. These days life just felt like one sucker punch after another.

"Things have just been really shitty lately." She heard herself whispering.

TJ turned to her, his leg halting. "How come? If this new receptionist gig is too much—"

"No, I like that job even if it is temporary," she said. He looked relieved. "The biggest problem right now is my mom. They found another mass." Jen squeezed her sore hand tighter around the wad of bloody paper towels.

"Are you serious? Why didn't you say anything?" TJ sat up straight and leaned into her.

Jen shrugged, a feeling of helplessness coming over her.

"Damn, Jen. I'm sorry. I feel like you guys can't catch a break. How is she taking the news?"

"Not well. I know it's why she's been more depressed than usual. I mean, it's been rough since she was diagnosed, but she'd done okay with the surgery and the treatment. Remained pretty strong and seemed optimistic. It's different now. I can just . . . feel that she's giving up."

"I'm sure she'll get back there. Your mom seems tough. She's probably just processing."

Jen shrugged and twisted at the paper towel. "Maybe."

"What's the next treatment?"

"Well, they gave her a couple of options. I really wanted her to do another round of chemo. It had worked the first time. But she didn't want to. Instead she chose to do a clinical trial."

"Okay. Well, good for her. Maybe it will work."

Jen shifted in her seat, looking at him. How could he not take her side? "And maybe she'll get loaded full of placebos. I mean, seriously, TJ. Chemo has helped people thousands of times. This trial is not a sure thing."

"None of it's a sure thing, Jen. Thousands and thousands of people have also died after chemo. Maybe it really didn't work considering there's a new mass. This trial might be just the thing she needs. There are new advances in cancer treatment every year."

She flopped back in her seat and wiped away a shocking tear, overcome by the well of emotion that sprang up in her heart. She was always so good at pushing the pain deep, masking it with the hustle of daily life and a consistent diet of denial. Why were her walls crumbling now—and in front of this man? "You're supposed to just agree with me to make me feel better," she whispered, hating that he could probably hear the tears in her voice.

"I want to make you feel better by being here beside you, Jen," he said.

*Oh God.* She sucked in a noisy—very telling—breath. Damn him for saying something so sweet and perfect. Jen turned away from him, willing her eyes to dry. But instead, TJ reached over and wrapped his arm around her back, locking in on her shoulder and pulling her into his chest.

"Jen. Come here."

He tugged and she turned, and just like that, she gave in. *Oh no.*

Jen had never fallen from any substantial height, but she now knew the feeling, her body tumbling through air, solid ground nowhere in sight, her limbs loose and tingly, and her lungs in her throat. When the sensation passed, leaving her with an odd feeling of safety in his arms, the dam broke so hard and fast there was absolutely no time to brace herself. The fact that he was so warm and solid, and his shirt smelled so good and TJ-ish, only had the tears coming faster. This time when she inhaled, the tiniest sob escaped, completely humiliating her in his presence. And yet, it only made her want to cry more. Hold on tighter. Pretend she was in a bubble of safety, even though she'd never really understood what safety felt like.

This had to be it.

Thankfully, her soul instinctively recognized it and didn't ask her mind for permission before settling in and sinking into his body. Her injured hand was gently held up by the chair rest between them that was biting into her ribs, but she couldn't find it in her to care as her right hand settled on his upper abdomen. She clinched his beautiful checked shirt in her fist and he responded by leaning his head down to rest against hers as he whispered murmurs and hushes into her hair.

They sat like that for a few minutes, her silently crying and in complete shock at the unexpected turn of events. She was going to chock this up to the trauma of the past hour. Past year, maybe past life. Truth was, Jen had never learned to rely on anyone. Or let go, because letting go was dangerous. But damn this right here felt amazing.

TJ's body shifted beneath her, but she didn't budge. Wasn't even certain how long they'd been sitting like that. When she cracked her eyelids open she saw he had set a box of tissues on his knee, well within her reach. Jen snatched one and used it to wipe her nose. "Thank you," she said.

Without lifting her body or her head, she glanced around them to find a toddler with a nose full of boogers turned backward in his seat and staring at her from the next row over. The sight was so unexpected and jarring, she shot up straight and grabbed another tissue to wipe at her eye.

"God, I'm sorry. I probably look like a mess." She wiped her other eye, noticing the mascara and eyeliner coming away on the tissue. *Great.*

"Look at me," TJ said.

Jen hesitated, but then did as he asked. His lips quirked with slight amusement, but he pulled another tissue from the box and while he held her chin with one hand, the other wiped at the corner of one eye. Then the other.

"There. Now you're good as new."

"I'm sure that's not true," she said, dabbing at her face once more. As gentle as he'd been, there was not a chance in hell her eye makeup had budged. She appreciated the gesture just the same.

"Why are you being so good to me tonight?" she asked, while nervous energy radiated through her body.

He angled his head back a bit, obviously considering her question. "I've always been good to you, Jen. You just don't always notice."

Her heart skipped a bit at his words. That was certainly not true. Once upon a time he'd hurt her deeply. He just didn't know it.

A nurse called her name from across the room.

"Are you coming with me?" She suddenly felt panicked. "I've never had stitches before."

"You'll be fine." He immediately stood and held out his hand for her. "But I won't leave your side." She took his hand, and they proceeded together.

An hour ago, she might have given him a smart-ass reply to that, but now, she was just grateful he was here.

# Five

Jen knocked on her mother's door the next morning. She'd tossed and turned the night before after TJ dropped her off. He'd walked her to her door, said good night, but then quickly retreated. He was probably weirded out by how needy she'd turned out to be the first time he'd chosen to be nice. Nobody was as shocked as she was.

She knocked again, a little harder this time. "Mom? You awake?"

Cursing under her breath, Jen turned to run back to her place to grab her key when the door opened behind her. Making her way back to the apartment, Jen found her mother looking as if she'd just awoken from a coma.

"Room service," Jen said, holding out a strawberry protein smoothie.

Her mother reached out and took the cup. "Thanks."

She left the door open and walked to the sofa. Rolling her eyes, Jen followed, shutting the door behind her. Taking in the room, she noticed it was still a little messy, just as it had been yesterday afternoon. Not a good sign, considering her mother had company.

"How was last night?"

Diane took a drink of her smoothie and then looked up at Jen with a blank expression. "What do you mean?"

Jen lifted her arms at her sides. "You and Terri. What did she bring for dinner?"

"What happened to your finger?" Her mother nodded at Jen's wrapped pinky.

"I cut it at work. No big deal. I asked you a question." Jen sat down in the recliner. It was ugly as sin, but gosh it was comfortable.

Diane took another swallow of smoothie. "What kind of milk did you use in here?"

"Almond. Just like every other day," Jen said, leaving out that she'd used half water since she'd run out of the milk. Still better than nothing, and apparently didn't stop her mother from gulping it down. When had she eaten last?

"I don't like almond milk," Diane said, wrinkling her nose down at the glass.

"Funny, you always finish it. Why are you just now saying something?" Jen felt like screaming. Yes, her mother was battling cancer, and discovering a new normal after giving up her two vices, but the attitude was beginning to be too much.

"I guess I didn't want to complain." Diane took a final big swallow and set her empty cup down on the side table before leaning back on the couch.

"Sure, that sounds just like you," Jen said sarcastically. "Maybe I'll try cashew milk next time." But not until she got paid.

Diane fluttered her hand in the air. "Just stick with the almond. Whatever."

Holding in a lot of choice words, Jen blew out a breath. "So," she prodded once again. "Tell me about last night."

Her mother shrugged. "I wasn't really up to it so I canceled."

"Why would you do that?" Jen felt deflated at the news. How long was she going to go on helping a woman who didn't want to help herself? "Terri is one of your best friends and she's done a lot for you lately. It would have made you feel better to spend some time with her."

Diane's head jerked in Jen's direction, her eyes narrowing. "You honestly think hanging out with my healthy best friend makes me feel better?"

Jen pursed her lips. "Yes, I do. You've known Terri since you were in high school. She knows everything that's going on so you don't have to pretend with her. It would have done you some good."

Diane shook her head and looked away. She was still in her robe and her hair looked clean but ratty. Jen figured she'd never even bothered dressing after her shower yesterday.

"What can I do to help you feel better?" Jen asked. It had taken a lot to get the words out of her mouth, but she was tired of this moping.

Two sad eyes turned her direction. "Bring me a pack of cigarettes."

Jen glared at her. "You don't mean that."

"It's tempting. I'll tell you that much." Diane leaned

back on the cushion. "I mean why am I worrying about my lungs if I'm going to die anyway?"

"Don't say that, Mom."

Diane jerked up. "Why not? Tell me why I didn't beat this. Why did it come back?"

Jen sagged in her seat. "I don't know."

Diane's eyelids fell shut and her head dropped back to the cushion once again. "I'd been fighting my ass off. I was optimistic, eating right, exercising. Gave up all the good things in life for fuck's sake. I was doing it all. Women beat breast cancer all the time. Why not me?"

Jen stared at her mother. The woman who had raised her. Taken care of her—in her own messed up way. Some years were better than others. Diane Mackenzie hadn't always realized her boyfriends were dickheads quite soon enough, but she eventually did. The rent often didn't get paid and they'd get evicted, but Jen never starved. There were kids who had it way worse off than she did.

"I haven't given up, Mom, and it makes me angry that you obviously have."

"Well, you'll never be as angry as I am."

"You're right." Jen stood up, suddenly furious. "So why don't you just keep on being mad and bitchy. If you're gonna die, you're gonna die. No need for us to be kind to each other in the process. Why start now, right?"

Her mother looked shocked at Jen's outburst. "That's not fair. You're not the one dying."

"But I'm the one losing a mother. You're not even

dead and you're gone. Is it too much to ask that I'd like to have just a tiny bit of decent time with you? It's not fair that you're going through this, but honestly, Mom . . . you're being selfish acting this way."

Jen watched the woman stare off into the distance for a long moment before she finally just leaned back into the chair. It was no use. They'd never been super close. Never understood each other. If Jen had dreamed up any illusions that staring down death might cause her mother to have any epiphanies, she was in for disappointment. She knew this. But it still stung.

"I'm dying, Jennifer," her mother said quietly. "They told me this time it was more aggressive; the tumor was bigger. And my body is still trying to recover from last time. I know I'm not handling it well, but don't think for one moment that I'm not thinking of you. Don't you think I hate that you'll be alone?"

Jen froze. This she hadn't heard before, and suddenly she felt as if she couldn't breathe. So her mother was worried about her, knew her days might be numbered, and yet she still couldn't bring herself to show her only child any love or appreciation.

Taking a deep breath, Jen blew it out slowly and then spoke in a steady voice. "Why don't you share more with me what you're thinking? Your fears? And why are you worried about me being alone?" It was news to Jen that her mother even stopped to think about Jen's well-being. Her entire life she'd basically taken care of herself. Diane had never been the typical mom who did things like parties, teacher conferences, and clothes shopping.

Diane gave her a long, irritated look. "You're thirty years old. Single. Live in a shitty apartment."

"Exactly. Thirty years old is an odd time to start worrying about whether your daughter knows how to take care of herself. Besides, your apartment's as shitty as mine!"

Diane lifted her hands out to the sides. Her voice took on Jen's least favorite tone: critical sarcasm. "Oh I know, I've failed you as a mother. Please remind me again and again. I didn't pay for singing lessons. I couldn't come to all your performances. I'm the reason you have man issues. I know all of that, Jennifer. You've told me before."

Jen's lips pursed in fury, but she refused to be baited into this conversation. Here she thought they might finally have a bit of a heart-to-heart.

"Have you ever stopped to consider what I've gone through as a mother, Jen? You weren't always kind to me either. You have never liked to be close, didn't seem to want me to help you in any way, or be around you. You're like that with all people. The guys you *do* bring home aren't good for you. You know that. But you don't like to *feel* anything, Jen. You can be cold sometimes. And that's not all my fault."

Well. So much for opening up and sharing their feelings. Jen spoke quietly, trying to keep her hurt and anger in check. "Wow, Mom. You've never told me you thought I was a misguided, cold-hearted bitch before. If I'd only known I was just unfortunate enough to be born that way. I guess I was under the illusion it was the mother's job to initiate the closeness. I'm sorry

I ever thought my childhood had anything to do with how fucked up I am."

She stood up again, and this time she headed for the door and opened it. Before she walked out, she turned back. "Just so you know, cold and unfeeling daughters don't bring their ungrateful mothers strawberry smoothies."

Slamming the door behind her, she headed for her apartment, holding in tears. Nobody deserved this kind of shit, not even from their dying mother.

Monday morning, TJ sat in his office listening to the slapping of Jen's sandals on the old wooden floors in the main area of the Stag. Since he was a pathetic idiot, he could picture her feet clearly, just as he could any other part of her body. Her toenails were painted in one of two colors: black or bright red. She had a tattoo of three little hearts running up the side of her foot, and a tiny puckered scar on the back of her left ankle.

Yep, definitely pathetic. Even more so because he'd yet to have the balls to go out and face her today, which was killing him. He wanted to see her. Check on her finger. Make sure she'd kept it clean and dry, and that it didn't look infected.

But a part of him feared Jen's backlash from Saturday night. The two of them had adopted completely new roles when they'd stepped into that hospital. Jen had let her guard down, which he knew, once she reflected on it, would piss her off.

He'd seen Jen cry one other time, although she had no idea. It had been during a wedding—the father-daughter dance—and he'd glanced behind the bar to catch her wiping a tear from her eye. It had been beautiful and intimate, and he'd never forgotten it. He knew that crying in front of him was something she would regret.

But they'd both given up a piece of themselves to each other. In his case he'd been vulnerable by letting her see that she was important to him. What she made of that, or how she'd interpreted it, he didn't yet know. But one thing was certain, TJ had reveled in taking care of her. Holding her while she'd cried, which had been so unexpected and raw, he still had trouble believing it had happened. And then, of course, holding her hand while her wound had been scrubbed clean and stitched up.

"Look at me, Jen," he'd said in the ER while the doctor prepped his needle. TJ was nearly certain she'd cut off circulation in his hand for five minutes, but there'd been no letting her go as he spoke quietly to her. "I'm right here with you."

She'd nodded at him, eyes shining, a look of fear but also trust in her eyes that had nearly undone him. How long had he wanted Jen to turn to him? Need him? And not as the man who signed her paycheck—he knew she needed that from him, but he wanted more. Wanted to be the man she turned to, to take care of her.

But he had two problems. One, it had become glaringly obvious that he needed to end things with Brooke. Regardless of what happened with Jen, it wasn't fair to continue with things as they were, knowing he wasn't in it for the right reasons. In fact, last night had made him feel like his father, which he hated. Using a woman was not okay, and although they'd been keeping it casual, Brooke was starting to hint at exclusivity, and he needed to end it before he hurt her.

His second problem was Jen herself. As much as he wanted her, she didn't do need or trust very easily. Exactly why he was inclined to keep his distance today. If he walked out there and picked up where they left off at her doorstep Saturday night, her walls would go up so fast his head would spin.

Tapping his pencil on the desk, TJ listened as she answered a phone call out at her desk. Her voice was light and friendly. She laughed, and he caught his lips quirking at the sound of her happiness.

For years Jen had been the primary-event bartender. But about a month ago she'd started a temporary position as their receptionist and bridal consultant, in addition to bartending on the weekends. When she'd asked to fill in for Tara while she was on maternity leave, it had been an easy yes for TJ, and thankfully for Dean and Jake also.

And Jen had slid into the job with such ease, it was going to be hard to let her go when Tara came back in a couple of months. Not that Tara wasn't great, she was, but Jen was just electric when she dealt with people.

He got up and walked to his office door so he could hear her voice as she spoke on the phone.

"Oh my goodness, that is a beautiful idea. I've never seen it done here in the Stag but I know we can accommodate you. I will make sure that's all set up on your date myself. I can already tell your wedding is going to be amazing," she said.

TJ almost laughed. Who would have thought snarky and opinionated Jen had a gift for customer service? Then again, she'd been tending bar and schmoozing for tips for years. She was also an actress, so the more he thought about it, the more it made perfect sense.

"Of course, I totally understand. And like I said, this is totally doable. I'll get everything we just discussed typed up in your contract and email it to you. Oh, and I'll shoot this invoice and receipt over today. Perfect! Thanks so much, Anna. Okay, bye."

He wondered what she was cooking up. Jen had been surprising all of them by taking it upon herself to reach out to a few area vendors they didn't work with often or hadn't yet, to form relationships. She'd even set up a little tour and tasting for curious vendors the week before, and about twelve people attended. TJ was impressed with her business sense, which he would not have guessed she'd had in her. And it was so darn adorable to watch her get excited when she told the guys about all that she was accomplishing.

If there was one thing Jen lacked, it might be modesty. If she felt like she'd done something worth celebrating, she was sure to let him, Dean, and Jake know. Twice if she felt it necessary. And they didn't mind, because she was Jen and her occasional self-celebrations were part of her personality. It was charming.

At least *he* thought so.

Her footsteps sounded again, and this time he knew they were definitely heading his direction so he turned, rushed back to his desk, scooted around the wood, and slammed down into his seat. He cleared his throat—just in case, although she could be going to talk to Dean—and ran a hand through his hair.

The minute she came around the corner, she fell against the doorframe, crossed her arms over her chest, and glared at him.

"I've been here over an hour. You haven't come to check on me."

TJ raised an eyebrow. His heart was pounding. Was he breathing heavy? Taking a breath before he replied to this loaded statement, he picked up his phone, hit a random app, closed it, and then looked back up at her. "I wasn't aware you were waiting on me."

Jen rolled her eyes, dropped her arms, and then walked across the small room and up to his desk. He watched quietly as she picked up a tiny Stag shot glass that sat to the left of his computer monitor. Her pinky stuck out as if she didn't want to bend it, but he was pleased to see a clean injury beneath her four little stitches. He watched her dump several quarters he'd put in the shot glass at some point into her hand and then drop them back into the glass. He just watched her in silence.

"Well, my finger is doing fine. Thanks for asking," she said, holding up the stitched pinky, but not meeting his eyes.

"I'm glad." He steepled his fingers and leaned back in his seat, eyes roaming over her body as she snooped through the items in his pen holder. Today she had on tight jeans and a flowy striped top that was currently dipped down enough to reveal the tiniest hint of her black lace bra. The sheer sleeves allowed him a peek of the fairies and vines on her shoulder and arm. He was always imagining what she'd look like bare beneath him. He would love nothing more than to trace those vines and find out exactly where they lead.

Still sifting through his collection of pens and pencils, she pulled out one of his favorites, clicked it a couple of times, then held it up. "I'm taking this to my desk."

"Don't lose it."

She held it up, analyzing it. "Is it expensive?"

"For a pen, yes."

"You could tell me no."

"I could."

She smirked at him. They both knew he was not going to tell her no. "Seems like a waste of money," she said, clicking the pen a few more times.

"I like good pens."

"Not a surprise. You're geeky like that."

TJ's lips pursed. Yes, she'd known him during a few of his . . . less than cool years. Seventh and eighth grade were particularly rough, but he knew she was trying to egg him on with that comment. He was not falling for it.

"Use that pen for a day and tell me you don't agree that it's worth it."

She raised her eyebrows. "Challenge accepted. But you must realize that most people can't afford expensive pens no matter how wonderful they are."

He paused at that, unsure of how to respond. Yes, he was very aware of his privilege in life. Was grateful for it and tried to use it for good. The last thing he wanted her to think was that he looked down at her.

"How mad was tiny cheerleader last night?"

The change of subject caught him off guard, but he appreciated not having to address her previous statement. He propped his elbow on his armrest, cradling his chin between thumb and forefinger, as he watched Jen walk around to the side of his desk—closer to him—and began straightening his things. She tapped a stack of papers into a neat pile, moved the calculator, and set the cocktail of the day calendar Tara gave all of them for Christmas last year to the correct date. He'd almost forgotten it was there.

His chair squeaked as he pivoted to face her, and in his mind, he fantasized about parting his knees and drawing her down into his lap. She'd never come in here before just to talk, and certainly never gotten so close, or so . . . familiar. Every time she touched something on his desk, it felt intimate.

"I didn't go back to Brooke's Saturday night, if that's what you're wondering."

She shrugged. "None of my business. Just curious if she was upset it took you so long."

Truth was, she had been a little miffed, and hadn't even tried to hide it. He really couldn't blame her, considering he'd bailed on her to care for another woman, and she'd implied just that in a not so subtle way when he'd called her that night. But in his defense, Jen was his employee. She'd injured herself on the job. If someone needed to give her a hand, why shouldn't it have been him? But yeah, he was going to have to end things with Brooke. Soon. "It was nothing I couldn't handle."

Her eyes cut to his. "So, she *was* mad."

"A little, yes. But don't feel bad."

She gave a little shrug. "I don't."

Typical Jen. TJ just laughed and shook his head.

"I mean," she started as she walked around the front side of his desk and rested the edge of her butt against the wood not three inches from his knee. TJ swallowed. "It's not like we did anything wrong."

"True." He forced his eyes off of her thighs, so close he could touch them without any effort at all. "I think for her it was more disappointment that we hadn't been able to be together."

"Hmm. Probably. You still could have gone over. It was only eleven when you left me."

But it had been a quarter after eleven when he finally got the strength to drive out of her complex parking lot after sitting in his car talking himself out of going up and kissing her good night like he'd wanted to when he walked her to her door. Something about last night had changed things between them, and part of him had wanted to just test it out. See if she was feeling what he was. Thank God he'd talked some sense into himself. Besides, the last thing he wanted was Jen to turn to him out of a need to assuage her frustration and grief. He wanted her to want him for him. Which would likely never happen, so either way he'd made the right decision.

"I guess I didn't really feel like it after that. Taking care of you is exhausting."

"Please. I'm the least high-maintenance person."

"You think?" He smirked, wondering if she truly believed that.

"I *know*. No one has ever had to take care of me."

He looked up at her, and the certainty on her face made his heart ache. "What about Diane?"

Jen just laughed and looked at her fingernails, which were currently painted a soft pink. Interesting. He'd never seen her in that color before.

"I mean, sure, she changed my diapers, fed me, and kept me alive once upon a time. But the minute I could fend for myself, I did. I don't mind."

TJ bit at his bottom lip, trying to decide what to say. The only thing he could come up with was *Let me take care of you*, but he could only imagine how well that would go over. "And now you're taking care of her."

"Crazy, right? I'm not even sure if she wants me to."

"Of course she does, Jen," he said.

With a heavy sigh, she pushed off the desk, and TJ just barely kept himself from reaching for her hand.

"Anyway. Thank you again. For the other night. Driving me to the hospital."

"You're welcome. The hand feeling okay?"

"It stings a little when I move it a certain way, but it's fine. Still can't believe I did that."

"I'm surprised you did, too. I've watched you cut fruit a thousand times," he said, instantly wondering if that gave too much away. He often watched her, even if she didn't realize it.

"Yeah, well, I won't be cutting it for a week or two. By the way, I asked Tony if he could bartend Saturday for me. He said yes. You okay with that?"

TJ's lips pursed. Yes, she was told it would probably be best not to bartend until the stitches were out, but he knew Jen. If she'd wanted to work, she would have. This was about getting off so she could go to Shakers Saturday night. He stood up and slowly walked toward the door where she stood.

"You'll have to let John know. He's on for this weekend's wedding, and he's still new to it." John had only been hired a few months earlier as Dean's distilling assistant, and as if things around the Stag weren't already interesting enough, he was also Charlotte's ex. Thankfully, so far things seemed to be working out just fine between the two distillers. "Might be nice if you were there for backup."

She frowned. "I think he can handle it. He literally just has to be in the building. Plus, this wedding has a planner."

A planner did make their job a lot easier as they oversaw just about everything. Clearly there would be no changing Jen's mind. She was going to Shakers whether TJ liked it or not. "Fine. Whatever. But just let him know."

"You going that night? I don't know if you remember, but Ant went to high school with us."

"Yes. I do remember." TJ also remembered the guy playing the lead in *Grease* opposite Jen as Sandy. Which meant he'd gotten to touch her. Spend lots of time with her. Sing and dance with her. Kiss her. And although TJ had never desired to act or sing in his entire life, he'd been insanely jealous of Anthony Carmichael.

"Then you know how amazing he is. Should be a good show."

"That's why you're going then?" he asked, taking a small risk that he might appear over-interested.

"Partly. Free drinks and a potential hookup also sound fun." She grinned, and TJ died a little inside. It certainly was not the first time Jen had referenced her sex life so brazenly, but today it hurt even more.

He turned and headed back to his desk. "Yeah, I don't know if that's my scene or not."

"Oh come on, TJ. Don't be a party pooper. I want you to go, too."

Stepping behind his desk, he looked at her. "And why would that be?"

She put her hands on her hips. "Because. You need to get out more. For me. It will be fun."

"I'm sure you'll have plenty of fun without me."

"Well . . . yeah. But I want you to come."

Why was she insisting? She'd just admitted to wanting a hookup with Bodisto, and TJ wasn't really interested in a front-row seat to them flirting with each other. The thought made him sick. And furious.

But she was asking, and he was not strong enough to flat out say no. "We'll see. Okay? Just . . . leave it at that."

# Six

"I'll just take a side salad with ranch," Jen said to the server at Sylvia's Café, a new restaurant on the square. It was Wednesday afternoon and she was dining al fresco on the patio with Charlotte.

"Oh no, get more than that. You have to be starving." Charlotte put up a finger to the woman in the Sylvia's polo shirt. "Can we have one more minute?"

The woman nodded and walked away. Charlotte leaned in. "Get the Chicken Avocado Club. It has peppered bacon made from a local butcher. It's so good."

Jen made an uncertain face, as if this were even an option worth considering. If she wasn't careful with her money for the next two weeks, she wouldn't make it until payday. As things stood, she wasn't sure how she was going to pay the credit card bill due Friday and a couple of other bills she was already behind on. "I'm really fine with the salad."

Charlotte gave her an annoyed look. "Jen, I don't know if I can live with myself if I don't make you try this sandwich. It's my treat today."

Jen's eyes widened. "No way. That's not necessary." It had never even occurred to her that anyone would treat her to lunch.

"No, I insist. My idea, my treat. Besides, we're celebrating you booking four weddings this week. That's amazing. Dean said that's the most ever in one week since they started."

Jen picked at the corner of the menu. She usually had no problem being enthusiastic about her accomplishments, especially around the guys at work, but she wasn't usually concerned about looking like a jerk. For the first time in a long time, Jen wanted this friendship thing to work out with Charlotte, and nobody liked a bragger. So she just nodded.

"Yeah, I was pretty excited."

Charlotte laughed. "I heard. Dean told me how after number four you sent all of them an email full of Beyoncé GIFs."

Jen smiled. "I totally did that. There's a lot of testosterone in that place."

"No kidding. They love having you though. Dean's been so impressed with all the things you've been implementing," Charlotte said.

That shocked Jen a little. Not that they liked having her there, but that Dean would be compelled to talk to Charlotte about her accomplishments. It made Jen feel incredibly guilty. How was she going to continue to be friends with Charlotte on a lie? They were just getting to know one another and Jen had already broken girl code in retrograde.

"I like the job a lot. Sucks that the position is

temporary. It will be hard to go back to just bartending when Tara comes back."

They were interrupted by the server again, and Charlotte took it upon herself to order two Chicken Avocado Clubs, two salads, and two fresh lemonades. She glanced at Jen for approval, so she just nodded her head feeling a mix of appreciation and a bit of embarrassment. Taking a gift made her feel like she must appear needy, and that was the last thing she wanted.

"So, what if Tara doesn't come back?" Charlotte asked. "That's a real possibility. I can only imagine how hard it would be to leave a newborn with someone else so I could go back to work."

There was obvious longing in Charlotte's expression, and Jen couldn't help wondering if she and Dean were thinking about having children. There was at least a decade age gap between them, so Jen figured they would probably need to get right to it. But she wasn't going to pry. They weren't that close yet. Maybe never would be.

"I don't know what would happen if Tara chose not to come back. As it is, she's planning to. But even if she didn't, that doesn't mean they'd offer me the position."

"Of course they would. You're obviously amazing at it. Not everyone has a knack for sales and customer service type of jobs."

"Yeah, I don't know. It just comes easily to me I guess." Which was true. *Imagine that.* "I've never considered any other career besides working in theater. I think I still dream of teaching acting or of opening up my own company for children. It's always been part of my identity."

The previous year, the Maple Springs Community Theater, where she'd worked for the past three years teaching voice and assisting in productions, had lost its funding and was finally forced to close several months ago. Jen had adored that job, and the loss had devastated her, not only emotionally but financially. It wasn't like she'd made great money, far from it. But it wasn't like she had a college degree, so she'd been content to make subpar money doing something she loved.

Tara going on bed rest and leaving the Stag guys without a receptionist long before they'd expected was just an easy opportunity for Jen. No interviewing necessary—thank goodness because she sucked at it. Although going in and asking the guys to let her have the job had nipped at her pride a bit, she'd done it, and even she was surprised at how much she'd been enjoying the work.

"I can see you opening your own theater company," Charlotte said. Jen wished she felt comfortable enough mentioning how much those words meant to her, but just smiled. "But there are other things you could do in the meantime, I'm sure. Maybe find a summer camp to work at. Or help with some high school productions. If you love theater that much, you'll find something."

Jen hadn't tried brainstorming on that lately. She'd been too busy trying to keep her head above water and her mother alive, but Charlotte's words sparked something inside of her. "You're right. I could consider some various things. In fact, I should start looking around, put feelers out. Sometimes I get tunnel vision when it comes to things like that. Thanks for the push."

"That's what friends are for," Charlotte said.

Jen smiled as their food was placed in front of them. It was definitely the best lunch she'd had in a while.

They'd been back from their lunch date for a little over an hour, and Jen still hadn't seen Charlotte come out of Dean's office.

Five more minutes went by. Ten. *What are they doing?*

She probably didn't want to know.

Finally the door opened, followed by the sound of Charlotte's happy laugh. Jen watched as Dean followed his girlfriend through the main room of the Stag, toward the front door.

"Thanks again for lunch," Jen said from her desk.

"It was so fun. We'll do it again soon," Charlotte said. She then gave Dean a final kiss and left.

He watched her walk away for a moment and then walked over to Jen's reception desk and leaned his arms on the high counter.

"Charlotte said you guys had a good time today."

"We did. It was really nice of her to ask me," Jen said. Before he could reply, she put up a hand. "Listen, speaking of which . . . we need to discuss something."

Dean lifted an eyebrow. "What?"

"I need to tell her." Jen looked at him, knowing by the look on his face that he knew exactly what she meant. He glanced to the main part of the room, toward the front door, and then back at her. Obviously checking to see if they would be heard, so she lowered her voice and continued. "I have to do it, Dean. It's eating me up inside. I like her a lot, and I know she's probably going to hate me once it's out, but I can't go on with the guilt."

Dean's lips quirked. "I understand your feelings, and I'm sure she'd appreciate them. But she already knows."

Jen's mouth dropped open. She was . . . shocked. "What do you mean?"

"I *mean*, I told her. When we decided to make things official, I told her. I had to."

"So . . . today . . . she *knew*?"

He nodded. "She knew."

Jen had no clue what to do with that knowledge. Her entire life she'd been working with the belief that women would judge you, stab you in the back, and turn on you in a hot second. Forgiveness, understanding . . . those were things she didn't have a lot of experience with.

"Wow," she said, suddenly feeling emotional. "She's been so nice to me."

Dean chuckled. "She's a nice person."

"Yeah, but . . . that takes a big person."

He shrugged. "Maybe. But I told her it was a long time ago, that it didn't mean anything, and there wasn't a chance in hell it would ever happen again."

Jen's eyes narrowed. "Jesus. Be careful or you might leave me with a shred of pride."

Dean smiled. "You know you feel the same way."

"Fine, you're right. But she wasn't mad even for a minute?"

"Well, yeah. Or . . . I guess you could say she wasn't

happy to hear it. She definitely hadn't seen it coming, but we talked about it. Both of us know that adult relationships come with adult baggage. I mean, her ex fiancé works with me for Christ's sake."

"God, yeah. You're right." Jen furrowed her brow at him. "You two are weird. But I like you together."

His grin was about the most genuine she'd ever seen on Dean. "Not as much as I do." When he began to walk away, she called his name. "Yeah?"

"Does uh . . . anyone else here know?"

He walked back over to the desk. "No. I've told no one else, and I have no plan to. But if *you* feel the need to tell anyone, I understand and respect that. Just ah . . . give me a heads-up. Okay?"

She scoffed. "Why would I feel the need? I was just curious."

Dean raised an eyebrow. "Whatever. You can keep telling yourself that."

# Seven

Jen hadn't gone to check on her mother today. It was Saturday, so she'd given herself a day off from negativity and despair. Plus, she still hadn't bought anymore almond or cashew milk. Instead she'd cleaned her tiny apartment, tended to her plants, gone for a walk, and lain by the pool. Basically, every free activity she could think of.

She continued her self-care as she got ready for the evening. That included a bath, shaving all the things, spending a lot of time on hair and makeup, and even fresh nail polish. Black, to match her dress. Several times over the course of the day she'd considered just staying home, but she'd promised everyone she was going to Shakers this evening. Jordan had even stopped by the Stag yesterday to say hi and make sure she was coming. And even Charlotte had texted earlier to see what Jen was wearing. Total woman stuff, which had Jen feeling amused and awkward.

The thing that kept eating at her was having to see TJ with his girlfriend again. He'd left work early yesterday and she'd overheard him telling Jake that he was going to her place. It made Jen want to scream, which was ridiculous because they had nothing going on between them. It was just plain jealousy, and that was one of many emotions she preferred not to dabble in.

After grabbing her purse, Jen locked up her apartment and headed down to the parking lot. She hesitated on the first floor by the mailbox, glancing over at her mother's unit. The flashing lights of the TV filtered through the curtains.

Blowing out a breath, she continued to her truck. Everything was fine. She deserved a day off from worrying. And arguing. If nothing else, her mom was a big girl, she had a phone, and she damn well knew how to use it.

A few minutes later she pulled into the square in downtown Maple Springs only to find that most of the parking was taken. Not a surprise, between the wedding going on inside the Stag, the band at Shakers, and the couple of restaurants open. Jen decided to park in the alley behind the Stag and couldn't help noticing a certain white Camaro some ways down.

She needed to get TJ out of her head. A bit of a challenge considering she would be seeing him soon. Tiny cheerleader would probably be hanging on him. What if they got drunk and made out? *Ugh*. That might be more than she could handle, she thought, as she walked across the green.

The sky was light blue and red as the sun set. People milled around, heading to and fro, and she stepped carefully up the curb and through the grass. She'd worn her favorite pair of strappy booties that showed off her toenails, which she'd also painted. It felt nice to get done up, something she hadn't done in a while, and she felt pretty, even.

Once she was out front of Shakers, she panicked a bit. Normally she would not have minded walking in alone, but this felt . . . different. Anxiety was taking over, and she hated it.

Pulling out her phone, she shot Charlotte a text. *"You guys inside?"*

She paced back and forth a bit, waiting. What if they weren't there?

*"Yes! Head straight back. We have a table."*

With a sigh, Jen stepped inside. She hadn't been inside of Shakers in years. On a Saturday night it was more bar than grill, so the odor was a mix of fried food and the cologne of desperate men.

It was pretty packed as she glanced around the room. The left side was still mostly people dining, but the entire right side was crowded with bar patrons. There were three or four pool tables near the door, a long bar along the far wall, and a stage and dance floor in the back. Currently the band's set was up, but the members were not onstage.

Jen decided to just head to the back as Charlotte instructed, hoping she'd spot them. The music playing over the speakers wasn't too loud, but the place still felt overwhelming in the way a bar on the weekend does. Jen angled her neck to scan the room ahead and smiled when she saw Charlotte waving, but before she could get there two strong arms wrapped around her waist, pulling her back against a hard wall of man.

On instinct she revolted, turning, ready to give someone a dressing down—this wasn't the first time she'd experienced this type of behavior from a man—and found Jordan smiling down at her. His arms were still locked around her waist, but she decided not to be angry even though it was a little forward. Okay a lot. But he did look handsome.

"You're finally here," he said in her ear. "And you look so sexy tonight."

"Thank you," she said. Jen didn't blush, but she was a little taken aback by his comment for some reason. It was just so unexpected. Her friends were already here. Were they watching? Was TJ watching?

"Your friends are this way." He nodded toward the stage and grabbed her hand.

Jordan led her through the crowd and up to a big round table, where, sure enough, Dean and Charlotte, Jake and some random woman, and of course TJ, were sitting. He was lounging back in his chair, a foot casually propped on one knee, his fingers squeezing a beer bottle while he stared back at her. Her first thought was that he looked a little hazy. How long had they all been here? Her guess was long enough to get a good buzz going. The next thought was, why was TJ alone? An empty chair sat between him and Charlotte with no sign anyone had recently vacated it.

"Sit. We've been waiting for you," Charlotte said, grabbing her hand and pulling her away from Jordan and toward the empty chair beside TJ.

"I didn't mean to keep you all waiting, but now the party can start," Jen teased.

Jordan leaned down to speak in her ear. "I've got to

do a few things, but what can I bring you to drink? Anything you want."

"Anything?" she asked playfully. He nodded. She considered her options. "Even Glenlivet and water on the rocks?" She asked, knowing it was a top-shelf choice.

His eyes widened and his face lit up with amusement. "Yes ma'am."

"This dress is so great," Charlotte said when Jordan walked away. "I could never pull off something like that."

"Thanks." Jen had splurged on it last year. She loved that it showed off all her tattoos, which covered her entire arm and shoulder from the top of her left breast all the way down to her elbow. "It's one of my favorites."

Charlotte's smile and kind comment reminded Jen of the conversation she'd had with Dean earlier in the week. She hadn't seen Charlotte since then and it was still hard to believe that she knew that Jen had once had sex with her boyfriend. After deliberating, Jen had decided maybe it was best if she didn't say anything about it. What good would it do if the two of them had already hashed it out as a couple? Obviously, she was choosing to still be Jen's friend. Hopefully it wasn't to spite her later.

*No.* She couldn't think like that. Diane's words and paranoia had to get out of her head.

She turned to her left. "Hey," she said to TJ.

"Hello." TJ sat up straight in his chair and scooted closer to the table. Was that to be closer to her? His eyes darted to her shoulder, and she waited for him to make a smart-ass comment about her ink.

Instead his eyes met hers. "You look beautiful to-night."

Her eyes widened in surprise. "Thank you."

When he went back to his beer and didn't look at her again, she was annoyed. He didn't get to just compliment her without an explanation.

"You riding solo this evening?"

He stared at his bottle. "I am."

"Why?" The conversation of their friends and the ambient noise of the bar gave them a bubble of privacy. Leaning on the table, he turned his head to look at her. His eyes were a little bright, but he wasn't wasted. She doubted TJ ever got wasted, but he'd definitely had more than one beer.

"I ended things."

Never mind. He might possibly be full-on drunk. "No more tiny cheerleader? Say it isn't so," Jen teased.

They stared at each other for a long minute, neither speaking. Suddenly a hand came between them, cutting off their gazes, and set a glass down in front of her. "Scotch and water for the lady."

"Thank you," she said, giving Jordan a polite smile.

"You need another beer?" he asked TJ.

"No thanks."

Jordan leaned on the back of Jen's chair. "One of my bartenders is late, but as soon as he's here, I can join you."

"I'll be waiting," she said with a smile.

He walked away after giving her shoulder a squeeze. Feeling eyes on her, Jen shifted in her seat.

"How drunk are you?" she asked TJ.

"I'm not drunk."

That was obviously debatable. "Why don't you like him?" She asked the brooding man next to her. Was he just feeling the effects of a bad breakup or was she imagining the possibility that he could be a little jealous? Foolish of her to get her hopes up, but he *had* just called her beautiful.

"He's too forward." He took another swig of beer.

"What's wrong with that? A lot of women like a forward man. No games. Lay it all out there. Leaves no room for misinterpretation."

"Maybe. If you're looking for a casual hookup."

She shrugged, swirling the ice in her glass. "I'll assume you weren't trying to offend me with that comment."

"Of course not. I didn't mean to imply anything about you."

She cocked her head. "Then why did you say it?"

"Well . . . in my experience, when a guy comes on that strong from the get-go, he has a specific endgame. And it isn't taking you home to his mother."

Jen bristled. Bingo. As much as she wanted to deny it, he was just about right.

"At least *he* plies me with quality whiskey." She held up her glass as TJ glared at her.

"Low blow, Jen. Really low. Don't let Dean hear you say that."

"It's adorable that you care so much about a man's intentions with me. Problem is, sometimes a woman has the same endgame in mind. I understand if that concept is a little too progressive for you."

His beautiful eyes bored into hers. "I have no problem with casual sex. None. I've been known to have it myself from time to time. So, get it out of your head that I'm judging you . . . or being a misogynist . . . or whatever else you've convinced yourself of."

"Fine. I won't. But you could tell me why you're acting like a jerk."

He stared at her for a moment and then leaned a bit closer. "Maybe I don't like it . . ." He hung on that last word as if about to regret everything that may come after it. She waited with bated breath, their eyes locked. "When a man comes on to a woman I want for myself."

Time stood still as he spoke the words. The blood in her veins rushed to life as every nerve in her body fired simultaneously. This was the moment she'd been waiting for. TJ Laughlin to want her. And it felt . . . amazing. The sudden heat in his eyes was so intense she could catch fire. Yeah, he'd definitely had a few too many beers, because this was so unlike him. He'd probably regret it tomorrow, and if the fact that instead of waiting to hear her reply he'd gotten up and headed for the restroom was any indication, he already did regret it.

Glancing around the table, Jen realized that none of their friends had been a witness to what had just gone down between them. They were still talking and laughing as if her entire world hadn't just flipped on its side.

This past week, things between her and TJ had shifted. The way he'd stared at her last Saturday during the uncasking, and of course the way she'd cried in his arms. Her sudden comfort in just walking into his office to talk, and his not so subtle jealousy about

Jordan. Something about their interactions was too bizarre not to be something, and usually *something* translated into sexual tension.

So here they were. He'd broken up with his side piece so he could have casual sex with Jen with a clear conscience. What a good boy.

Question was, could she just have casual sex with TJ?

TJ frowned as Jen finished her third scotch and water and headed back to the dance floor. Did she really have to choose such a potent drink?

She'd been up dancing with Charlotte and Jake's date several times while her band friends played on-stage. It was strange to see the couple of guys they'd gone to high school with. Anthony, of course, and some other guy who TJ couldn't recall the name of but recognized.

"You okay?" Jake asked, leaning toward TJ. When the girls had left the table to dance, Dean and Jake had moved closer so they could talk.

"What do you mean?" TJ replied, taking a drink of water. He'd decided to sober up after flat out admitting to Jen that he wanted her a couple of hours ago. Still couldn't believe he'd done it, but damn, watching Jordan put his hands on her had brought something primal and ugly to life inside him. Acute jealousy, and he'd wanted her to know it. Even if he had panicked at her immediate lack of response. He wasn't even sure what he'd wanted her to do or say.

"You know exactly what I mean," Jake went on. "Bodisto's been all over your girl."

"I don't have a girl here tonight," TJ said, being a purposely ignorant dick.

Jake shook his head. "Dude. Make a move. You broke up with Brooke for a reason. Now no one will get hurt. You have absolutely no excuse."

TJ looked at his friend. "Someone will definitely get hurt."

"You don't know that."

"I'm pretty damn sure." When he'd come back from the restroom, she'd already been up to dance, and still hadn't said anything to him. A clear sign that she had no intention of acknowledging his admission.

Jake shook his head. "You're starting to piss me off, Laughlin. I've put up with your pansy-ass bullshit for years, but this has gone on far too long."

TJ gave him a long glare. "You breaking up with me? And here all this time I thought we were both getting what we needed out of this relationship."

Jake grinned, putting a hand to his heart. "When you love someone, let them go. But if they come back to you, it's because they don't have the balls to *finally* hook up with Jen."

With a dramatic sigh, TJ let his shoulder blades hit the back of his chair. For the thirtieth time in the past hour, he sought her shape in the crowd. It didn't take long—his eyes were trained to zero in on dark hair, sexy curves, and red lips. She was smiling up at Ant, singing along to some late eighties cover song, hands waving in the air.

The song ended, and the crowd applauded. Four Deep was a good band, no denying that, but TJ was feeling restless and highly agitated. Yes, he'd secretly wanted her to reply to his announcement of desire for her by getting up and dragging him out of the bar and back to her place. He needed to work on his expectations.

And that was when he heard it. The bass guitar clumsily trying to pick out a very familiar tune. One he hadn't really heard in years if he recalled correctly, but had sat through several nights in a row back during his senior year of high school.

Once the bass caught the tune, several people began to cheer wildly, finally recognizing it. The rest of the band joined in, and TJ looked at Ant, who was pointing at Jen.

That's how he knew for sure that his memory had been correct. This was a song from *Grease*, that Anthony and Jen had sung together.

"That beautiful woman right there," Ant said into the microphone, still pointing at Jen, who was frantically shaking her head no. "That's my Sandy."

TJ heard Jen holler over the crowd, her voice so damn loud, "No fucking way, Ant!"

"What's happening?" Jake muttered. Even Dean had leaned forward and was looking at TJ in question. Why did they all turn to him when it came to Jen? Stupid question. He knew exactly why.

"They did *Grease* together in high school," TJ said loudly over the crowd's sudden enthusiasm.

"I thought I recognized this song. You think he wants her to sing?" Dean asked.

"Looks like it," TJ said, his body humming with anticipation.

"Think she'll do it?" Dean asked.

"Shit, I hope so!" Jake said. "I love it when Jen sings."

So did TJ. Too much. She sang around the building, while she bartended, when she walked in the door. But it was usually to herself. She wasn't flamboyant in her singing ability. But he knew better than any of them what she was capable of.

He could remember going to see Jen in that production of *Grease* like it was yesterday. And yes, he'd gone alone. Every single night it was open. Just to watch her sing her heart out as Sandy. God, he could still close his eyes and picture her. Jen was an insanely gifted woman, with the most beautiful, clear singing voice he'd ever heard. And as much as he loved having her as an employee, it was a shame she wasn't on a stage somewhere.

And then she was.

"*I've got chills*," Anthony crooned into the microphone, doing his best Travolta, which funny enough sounded nothing like the singing voice he'd been using for the past hour. TJ watched in shock as Ant dragged a reluctant but laughing Jen onto the stage. The women on the dance floor went wild. Glancing around quickly, TJ noticed most everyone in the building had come into this side of the bar to watch. When Ant angled the microphone stand toward her lips, she rolled her eyes, but then leaned into the shiny metal, her cherry lips parting.

TJ stopped breathing.

And then she sang. So clear and pure, it was like going back in time to a point in his life where his obsession with her kept him up at night.

Something came over Jen in that moment. TJ had watched it before and it was just as magical twelve years later. It didn't matter that she had a healthy buzz going, she obviously knew every word, and was so beautiful as she strutted across the stage. She playfully shimmied the edges of her dress off her shoulders, and the entire bar lost their shit around them, clapping, cheering, and catcalls filling the air.

Reluctance now tossed aside, Jen ate the crowd's enthusiasm up, and as her and Anthony's voices harmonized, many of the patrons began to sing along with them. It was absolutely mesmerizing to watch her move, her hips swaying, and body naturally performing a dance routine it knew by heart even over ten years later.

TJ couldn't look away. He vaguely heard Dean speaking to his left, something about how amazing she was, but there was no focusing on anything but the radiant woman in front of him.

Suddenly she was starting right at TJ as she sang the next verse in a suggestive tone. TJ felt Jake elbow him but didn't have the time to acknowledge it. There was no way she could see him with the lights on her face. He was almost certain. She looked away and pressed her finger into Anthony's chest, the two of them grinning at each other. TJ had been so damn jealous of that guy in high school. Just the fact that he got to spend so much time with Jen during practice and then during the four performances was enough to make TJ consider theater. He hadn't, of course. For one thing, he didn't have a creative or talented bone in his body. Plus, his parents would have wondered what the hell was wrong with him, never mind the shit his friends would have given him. But the thought had crossed his mind. He'd had a problem then.

He had a problem now. And that beautiful problem was currently wearing a tiny black dress, shaking her ass onstage, singing show tunes for a crowd that was loving it. Even Bodisto was grinning like a dumbass from the far side of the stage. He looked completely infatuated, and TJ couldn't even blame the guy. He did hate him for it, though.

Jen held the mic out toward the audience like a pop star, and the whole room sang at the top of their lungs. Glancing quickly around the table, TJ realized even Jake was mouthing the words. TJ was dumbfounded. And so taken with her it was nearly painful. No one could charm a room like Jen when she was singing. It was why she'd become the most popular girl in high school almost overnight when she'd played this role—causing his friends to finally notice the girl he'd been noticing for years, which had infuriated him.

He caught sight of Charlotte and Jake's date in the crowd. They were into it, singing into each other's faces. The entire bar was completely loving this. Of course they were. The nostalgia of the song probably had a lot to do with it, but still.

Jen was . . . Jen.

Electric. Beautiful. Talented. And yeah, Anthony and his band were good, too. But Jennifer Mackenzie was magic.

When the song was over, the applause was nearly deafening, and TJ found himself on his feet, clapping and grinning as she actually blushed onstage.

Something he'd never seen her do. She smiled, taking in her ovation, biting her bottom lip. Turning, she held her hand out to Anthony, he reciprocated by giving her a worshipping bow.

She gave a shy little wave and bowed, and then Bodisto rushed over to help her down the stage steps. Funny, she hadn't needed his help getting up there. TJ's jaw clenched as he watched the dickhead wrap his arms around her and pull her into a hug so hard it brought her feet off the floor. He whispered something in her ear that made her laugh, and in that moment, TJ knew the jealousy he'd felt as a teenager, or when she'd first entered the bar, was nothing compared to what he felt right now. But just like with his friends back in high school, he couldn't help thinking, *Before you saw her light up a stage, I already knew how special she was.*

Jordan led her back to their table, and as soon as they arrived, Jake and Dean both proceeded to tell her how impressed they were. In fact, several bar patrons circled around praising her. For nearly ten minutes they all sat and watched her converse with strangers about how impressed they all were. TJ hadn't watched Jen smile this long in ages. If ever. Finally, she could address their group without fans butting in, but TJ hated that the shuffle of chairs had her across the table from him. Still standing by Bodisto.

"That was the most amazing thing I've ever seen," Charlotte said, now seated at the table. "I was dying."

Jen smiled. "Thanks. It had been a while. I didn't even get to warm up."

"As if you needed it," Charlotte said.

TJ watched as Jordan casually placed his hand on Jen's lower back, sending fury spiraling through TJ's limbs. All week he'd had the smallest inkling that maybe—just maybe—this wasn't one-sided anymore. He didn't know if she felt more comfortable with him after their ER visit, or maybe she was just lonely and needed some attention. But something was different, so much so that he could not accept the idea of her going home with that meathead tonight.

He stood up without thinking. "Jen, can I talk to you outside a minute?"

Her eyes landed on him, and he didn't look away, but he could feel his friends glancing between the two of them. They all went oddly quiet.

"What about?" she finally replied, her tone classic Jen condescension.

*What about?* TJ could list a hundred reasons off the top of his head. *About how I'm so damn hot for you I can't even see straight. About how you take hundred-dollar pens off my desk right under my nose because you know I can't deny you anything. About the way you come to work and talk about getting laid the night before. About how I think maybe you do it to make me crazy jealous. And it works. Every. Single. Time.*

Instead he just said, "Please."

Jen stared back at him, and TJ heard Charlotte suck in a tiny gasp. It was possible that he was playing this wrong. Maybe when they'd both been drinking wasn't the ideal time to make a move. But then when would be? Because he'd been around Jen in all kinds of scenarios. At work, in class, at parties, even in a hospital emergency room. But it was this moment—while he was witnessing another man touch her—that he'd found his nerve. God, she would call him a misogynistic asshole for this and he couldn't even argue. But never before had she felt so much like his, and this was unacceptable. If he didn't stop what was happening, she and Bodisto might end up together tonight. She may not have sex with the guy, but it was a possibility. One that TJ couldn't stomach.

"Fine," Jen replied, shocking him. She grabbed her purse off the table. "But only since you said 'please.'"

His shoulders relaxed instantly.

She turned around and looked at Bodisto, giving him a pouty face. "I'm so sorry, but I may not be back. I know what he needed to tell me. I forgot I have to go home and check on my mom tonight. She's sick." The lie fell out of her mouth so easily, TJ wasn't sure if he should worry or love her a little more.

Jordan, no dummy, realized he was being given the slip, but stayed cool. "No problem. I'm sorry to hear about your mom," he said. TJ wanted to punch the fake sincerity off his face. There was no mistaking the fact he was peeved. Anyone would be able to see it in his eyes and his body language, but like a gentleman, he doubled-down on the kindness. "I'm glad you came. Maybe I'll come by and see you this week."

TJ was tempted to yell out a definitive negative, but kept his mouth shut.

"Maybe you will," Jen said, smiling. Then she wobbled on her feet a bit.

Making his way around the table, TJ grabbed her hand, then gave a quick wave to the table. No one had officially said they wouldn't come back in after this "talk" he'd suggested, but he knew everyone understood.

"Be safe, slick," Jake called out, his voice full of humor. "And I don't want you back."

# Eight

Jen tried to focus on staying upright as she rushed through the crowd at Shakers, but most of her brain was trying to decipher what had just happened. She'd just sung onstage, for the first time in over a year. And now her hand was in TJ Laughlin's. TJ was leading her out of the bar, because the minute he'd said the words *Can I talk to you outside a minute?* she'd somehow known he only wanted her away from Jordan Bodisto as soon as humanly possible. It had taken her about zero seconds to work out the irritation in his eyes, but she still hadn't quite decided what his motive was. Part of her didn't even care.

Jen's weaknesses and insecurities were deep and wide, but she always counted on her premeditated hubris to throw everyone off. It was a well-honed craft of hers. But when it came to TJ—especially lately—she was finding her chutzpah difficult to muster. She wanted him, and the idea he might want her back, even for a minute, was too powerful a weakness to fight.

"Where are we going?" she asked as they crossed the street toward the square.

"I don't know," TJ said, clasping her hand harder as they hit the grass.

He finally slowed so they could walk side by side. Jen glanced over at him, feeling a little dizzy. She'd drunk a little too much and this quick walking was making it very apparent. "I thought you needed to *talk*," she teased. They both knew that had been a ruse.

"Needed to get you out of there." His words were clipped, his jaw hard.

"I was having fun."

"I could tell."

They were silent for a moment as they passed a group of people talking and laughing. They appeared to have just left the wedding at the Stag. Jen glanced up at the building to see the lights still on and the music just barely audible through the brick-and-glass walls.

TJ stopped once more when they made it to the street on the opposite side of the square, looking left then right before pulling Jen onto the concrete and into the road.

Jen glanced at his hard profile again, which was currently lit up by a streetlight. "Are we leaving?"

His eyes shot to her quickly, then ahead once again. He was leading her to the side of the Stag now, toward where they'd both parked in the alley.

"We are, yes."

She relaxed, because she'd wanted—needed—him to take control here. If it was up to her, she'd lose her nerve, because this wasn't just any guy, this was him.

TJ. The guy she'd crushed on for many years. But he was also the teenager who she'd overheard badmouthing her to his friends in high school, making her feel so beneath him, that for a while she didn't think she'd recover. But she had, and in the end, TJ's disdain and rejection of her had been another stepping stone in becoming the hard-hearted woman she was today. Or that she was *trying* to be. The fact that she was letting him lead her toward his fancy car in a dark alley was just proof that even the mighty could fall. Maybe she could relate to her mother's man weakness after all.

"Are you good to drive?" she asked as they stepped up to the Camaro. "Because I'm a little tipsy."

"I switched to water almost an hour ago, and I only had two beers all night," he said. "Do you trust me? I would never put you in danger."

They were now standing face-to-face beside the car, staring at each other. That was the moment she decided. It was bad enough that her ridiculous obsession with this man wouldn't wane, but if she was going to let him take another piece of her soul, she would do it on her terms.

"I trust you."

"Good."

She stepped forward slowly, and even in the dim light of the streetlight twenty feet away, she could see those sunrays staring back at her. He swallowed audibly, and that was when she felt his hand on her hip, gently tugging. Instantly she slapped it away.

"*I'm* making the first move," she snapped in a quiet voice before getting a handful of his shirt.

"Then make it." His voice was nearly a growl, low and clipped.

Her brow creased in irritation. "You *would* make this diffic—"

She was shut up by his lips smashing into hers. *Oh God.* No problem, because whatever she'd been about to say had evacuated her mind the minute he kissed her. She was now too busy feeling, responding, tasting. His mouth, soft and firm at the same time. Jaw, roughened steel underneath her fingers as she cupped his face. How many times had she imagined this moment?

Enough to realize that even her fantasies had been inadequate. She hadn't known how gentle yet insistent his tongue would be as it enticed her mouth open. Who would have thought that sliding her fingers through the fine hairs at the nape of his neck would turn her—and him—on?

She knew because he groaned, his hands once again on her hips, pulling her against him with no plan of stopping this time. He was hard, gloriously so, and it was obvious that he wanted her to feel it. She let out a soft whimper at the pressure, acknowledging that she'd received the message. *I want you too. Can't you tell? Haven't you always been able to tell?*

The kiss went on and on right there in the alley. Sometimes ebbing with moments of such frantic passion that she was ready to rip his clothes off, and then flowing into soft languid swipes of his tongue that had her body shivering with need. She was hot, wet, and ready in every way necessary to take this to completion.

Pulling back, she ran a nail along the tendon in his neck. "Is this what you meant by talking?"

He grinned. "It's exactly what I meant."

"I'm sort of drunk, TJ."

He huffed out a laugh. "I know. Which is why I'm going to drive you home."

Jen fell asleep in the front seat of his car as he drove to her apartment. As much as his body was begging him to get her home and finish what they'd started, he didn't want Jen to make this decision under any influence. He'd waited this long. Shit, he'd never even expected to kiss her, so theoretically he should be satisfied. But he wasn't. He wanted more, but not like this.

He pulled into her apartment complex and took the first parking spot. As soon as he killed the engine, she woke up with a giant yawn.

"Stay there, I'm coming around to help you," he said. But before he could get out and around to the passenger side, she was already shutting her car door. She wobbled on her feet, and he instantly put out a hand to keep her upright.

"I've got you," he said, leading her through the lot toward the row of buildings.

As soon as they started up the steps she leaned on him. "No judging my shitty apartment, rich boy."

He almost laughed, but her words had him glancing around. The apartment complex left a lot to be desired. From the road, it didn't draw your attention, but up close it was obvious that detailed maintenance was not a priority to the management. The sidewalks were cracked and crumbling, the handrails to the second floor wobbly. TJ was no expert on municipal code and ordinances, but he'd bet money that some of what he was seeing was illegal.

"Where're your keys?" he asked when they got to her door.

She shuffled through her purse for so long he finally just grabbed it from her. Pulling them out immediately, he noticed she'd leaned against the wall.

He led her inside, and Jen flipped on a lamp. The night he'd dropped her off from the ER her place had been dark, so he hadn't seen anything. But now, he smiled. The apartment was small, but it wasn't at all shitty. It was totally Jen. Eccentric, bright, and bold, and it smelled like the vanilla tangerine lotion she kept next to her computer at work.

There was one small sofa littered with mismatched pillows and a small chair that she'd tried to slipcover with what appeared to be a giant plaid flannel sheet, but the best part was all the plants. Every surface was covered with them. Big, tall, short, flowering, and spiky.

His eyes glanced around the room until they landed on her. She was standing near the short hallway, watching him. Waiting for his reaction.

"I love all the plants."

The corner of her mouth lifted. "So do I. They're like my children."

He watched as she tried in vain to toe off her heels, which were strapped to her ankles. Walking up to her, he kneeled down at her feet. "Lift," he instructed, gently grabbing the back of her shoe.

She did as instructed, placing a foot on his thigh as her hands settled on his shoulders. It was all he could do to not run his hands up her long legs. Or press her against the wall, shove up her dress, and press his face against her softest parts.

Shaking that thought off, he motioned for her other foot and removed that shoe before standing up. "Where's your bedroom?"

She smiled up at him. "Not wasting any time. I like it."

He laughed, amused by her playful voice. "No, Jen, I'm going to help you to bed. You're wasted."

"It hit me hard when we left," she muttered. "I never drink that much."

"Happens that way sometimes." TJ began to guide her down the hall, and since the place was tiny as hell he could see that one door was to the bathroom and the other to her room. Although it was dark, intoxicated Jen seemed to sense her bed nearby and walked right over and lay down.

TJ flipped on the bedside lamp just in time to see her pulling her dress over her head. *Oh shit*. All of Jen's beautiful skin—some creamy, some colorful— was exposed for his viewing as she tossed her dress to the floor and flopped back on the bed. She wore a lacy black bra, but her panties were cotton with yellow and white stripes. The contrast made him smile, as did her tattoos. Finally he knew how much of her they covered. The first fairy was small, hovering just above her left breast. Above it a green vine covered with exotic-looking flowers twisted up and over her shoulder and down to her elbow. There were four fairies total. From the front view, anyway. It was beautiful, and he didn't have to ask to know that she'd drawn all of it. How many talents could one woman possess?

Placing his hands under her knees, he lifted and pivoted her body so she lay lengthwise in bed. It occurred to him this could be another vulnerable moment she may not appreciate tomorrow, but he sure would. He'd take whatever moments he could with her, and accept the responsibility of making sure she didn't regret it.

"God you're strong," she said. "Shit, why am I so tired?"

Pulling the sheet up over her, TJ frowned down at her face. Surely Bodisto wasn't the type to slip her anything.

"I'll be right back," he said. He went into her tiny kitchen and opened the fridge. Inside he grabbed a bottle of water and then spotted a small thing of acetaminophen on the counter. Shaking out two, he headed back to the bedroom. Jen's breathing was already steady, her eyes closed. He laid the pills on her bedside table and then looked down at her. Damn she was beautiful.

"Jen," he said quietly.

"Mm-hmm," she muttered, her eyes fluttering. When she saw that he had water, she angled her body up on the bed and took the bottle before downing several mouthfuls. With a satisfied gasp, she handed him the bottle and flopped back down on the sheets. The small bit of hydration brought a bit of alertness, and she stared up at him.

"When you wake up tomorrow, give me a call. I'll come back and drive you to your car."

Her eyes went wide. "You're leaving?"

"Well, I just—"

"I thought you'd stay. Can you?"

The sweet sound of her request nearly undid him. Could he stay? Absolutely. But it was the "should" that he was getting hung up on.

"Please."

Glancing down into her eyes, he knew there was no denying that request. "Okay. Scoot over."

"Take all that off so you're comfortable," she said, wagging a finger at his body.

He nearly groaned. "Killing me," he muttered.

She smiled up at him as she rolled onto her side, giving him way too amazing of a view of her backside and another fairy on her shoulder blade. "The sheets feel so good and cold. Do you like cold sheets?"

"I guess so." He did, although it was something he didn't often think about. Right now all of his focus was on her yellow-and-white striped ass. He made quick work of putting his keys, watch, and wallet on the bedside table before shucking his pants, shirt, and undershirt. The bed dipped as he slowly lay down beside her.

As he considered the best way to position himself, she reached back, grabbed his arm, and pulled it across her body. And now he was spooning her, that striped ass nestled right up against his dick. *Oh God, give me strength.*

"Thank you for taking care of me again," she whispered.

Yep, she was going to look back on this night and either not remember it, or remember it and cringe. But he would enjoy this moment anyway. With that, he let his body relax against her. This felt so right, it was nearly terrifying. "Always, Jen."

# Nine

Jen's arm was numb, tucked up under her pillow. She tugged at the material with her right hand and a thud, then a groan sounded behind her. Stunned, she jerked up and looked behind her.

"Holy shit. I forgot you were here," she said in a scratchy voice.

TJ's head was lying flat on the mattress. He cracked open an eye and glanced up at her. "Just what I like to hear when I wake up in a woman's bed."

Suddenly a pain shot through her head. Lifting her hand to her temple, she moaned. "Oh God. I feel like I was on a weekend-long bender. Now I know why Glenlivet is so expensive."

"Here," he shifted on the bed. "I brought some medicine in last night."

She opened her eyes and held out her hand to take the pills. He then reached over and grabbed the water bottle and passed it to her.

"Thanks." Jen swallowed the two pills as she suddenly realized that underneath the sheets she was only in her bra and panties. Good lord. She knew better than to drink too much with the antidepressant she'd started taking last year, but clearly her good sense had taken a leave of absence last night. "Did we have sex last night?"

His eyes bulged. "Jesus, of course not."

"Okay, okay. Sorry the idea is so repulsive," she said, sitting up and crossing her legs, careful to keep her chest covered.

He slammed his hands down to his sides, hard enough to hold the covers down tight so that she could see the bulge below his waist. "This is the result of waking up next to you. Obviously, there is nothing repulsive about that idea."

"A boner in the morning. How unoriginal and tragically scientific. I can't take credit."

"Holy shit," he groaned. "You are such a pain in the ass. You know damn well this is all you, and you also know that I would never have sex with you when you can't even remember it."

"And I do appreciate that. Just ignore my snark. You know by now that self-deprecation is my default."

"Yeah, well, do me a favor and try to rein it in. It's insulting."

She put her hands up in surrender. How weird was it to have this man in her bed while they were both half naked? Pretty weird, but her heart was also pounding with excitement. She needed to keep her cool. "Thanks for the ride home."

He sighed. "You're welcome. Do you remember leaving?"

"Yeah. I even remember coming in here, but the details after that get hazy."

"You asked me to stay," he said.

She just shrugged, staring down at him. The sheets were still pulled tight enough to see his impressive anatomy. "All women have their moments of weakness."

TJ's lips quirked at that. "So, you remember *everything* that happened before we got here?"

Jen bit her bottom lip, trying to decide if she wanted to torture him or not. Maybe sleeping in a bed with a half-naked woman and not getting laid was torture enough. "If you're asking do I remember your tongue down my throat, then yes. Thank you for that also."

"You make it sound so memorable."

"Oh it was. Don't mistake my flippancy for disinterest or dissatisfaction. That's just another personality flaw of mine."

"Wish I'd known that a long time ago," he said. "It's another one you can let go of. With me, at least."

She smiled, suddenly feeling vulnerable. Something she really should get used to with this man, apparently. Trying to lean into the emotion—something else she needed to work on, according to her mother—she decided to say what she felt. Even if she had to pick at the blanket while she said it. "The kiss was . . . really good."

Her gaze flickered to his quickly. His sunray hazel eyes were staring back at her, his expression warm, and she could tell that *those* words had pleased him. "I agree. Watching you sing last night was also amazing."

A laugh escaped her at the memory. "I can't believe Ant did that. I guess in that regard it was damn good thing I was intoxicated. Although I probably sounded like shit."

"You sounded perfect."

Their eyes met again and he looked absolutely sincere, staring up at her with his hair sticking strait up on top. Unable to resist, she leaned over and mussed it before trying to tamp it down with her hand. She liked that he just patiently let her have her way with him in any regard. Giving up on his hair, she sat up straight.

"You miss it?" he finally asked.

"Performing? Of course I do. It's the only thing I'm good at."

"You've got to be kidding," he said, angling his head to look at her better. "You're good at so many things."

Her head lolled to the side. "Thanks, boss. But convincing an indecisive bride that she should spend three grand on a rustic but elegant wedding venue does not count."

"First of all, your job at the Stag was not what I was referring to. You're kind of creatively gifted, Jen. In many ways, and you know it. But just so we're clear, what you do at work *does* count. And coercing people out of their money is *not* what you do."

"No? Then what do I do? Because I clearly recall booking a shit ton of weddings for you lately."

"You have. Because you're amazing. But booking weddings is not what you're good at. You're good at *people*. I've listened to you on the phone. You make those brides feel understood. Important. You listen and make them believe that the Stag will make their concerns our concerns also. They are getting married, so they're going to spend that money somewhere. And there are a lot of great venues in KC, and yes, we've become very popular, but you've booked double what we did this month last year. And I know it's because you make them see beyond the antler chandeliers, the included table linens, and the amazing whiskey. They're booking because you make them feel special. You make your bar customers feel special, too, and the people in that crowd last night. The way you engaged that audience . . . it blew my mind."

She stared down at him, eyes wide. "Can you type that up in a beautiful font so I can tape it to my bathroom mirror for when I'm having a bad day? Or maybe give it to my mother? She's never been *half* that impressed with me."

"I don't believe that for a minute. Diane loves you."

"In her own way, yes, she does. But her style doesn't lead to warm fuzzy feelings."

Scooting up in the bed, TJ leaned against her headboard. The position gave her the most amazing sight of his pecs and abs, which were so flat and muscular that the only thing that rolled was skin. That was not fair at all, but damn she liked looking at him.

His eyes roamed over her arms, and he nodded toward her tattoos. "Why fairies?"

Jen held up her left arm and glanced at the artwork she'd once been so obsessed with. She still loved it. It was a part of her. But in her early twenties she'd spent way too much cash she didn't have on this ink. It took nearly eight sessions, and she'd never even added up the cost, too ashamed to figure out the total. Instead she just considered it another one of those horrible money choices she'd made. But she couldn't regret it too much because she loved it.

"Well, basically, my father was a loser of epic proportions according to my mother. But for the first seven years of my life he would send me a birthday card. It didn't say much. Basically, just 'Happy birthday, Jen. Love, Dad.' But there would always be drawings of fairies. I still have them." She thought wistfully of those drawings in the cards that now sat stashed in the bottom of her chest of drawers. "They were so good. Detailed, colorful. He would always write my name above them, as if it were me. I created this story in my mind of what kind of man he had to be to draw fairies so well. A tortured but brilliant artist." She smiled down at the blanket.

"Have you ever met him?"

"Once that I know of, but I can barely recall it. But I do have one photo of us together. I was about two. He died of a heroin overdose when I was eight."

"I'm sorry," he said, reaching out to touch her blanket-covered knee.

Jen shrugged. "It is what it is. So anyway, I've just always had a fondness for fairies. It's not super deep. I just think they're pretty." That was all a fib. She loved fairies, and getting her father's drawings on her skin had been significant and meaningful at the time.

"They look pretty on you. Are some of the ones on your skin his drawings?"

"Yeah. They are." She scooted closer and then turned, pointing to her shoulder. "This one, this one."

Shifting so her back was to him, she pulled her hair over her shoulder to the front. "And that one on my back. With the blue wings."

She felt him move on the bed, his body close behind hers, and then his finger was tracing her skin. "This one? It reminds me of you," he said quietly.

Jen laughed quietly. "Why is that?"

"It's got dark hair, red lips, and . . . it's just beautiful."

Jen froze as his fingertips outlined the fairy on her back. The tattoo was nearly nine years old. She could barely remember the details of that drawing, but suddenly she wanted to see it more than anything. To have just an idea of how TJ saw her.

A featherlike touch pressed on her shoulder blade.

His lips. Oh God. The sound of a kiss broke the silence in the room. Then another pressed lightly next to it. And another. Then his mouth opened over her skin, his tongue sliding, and every nerve ending on her body exploded in delight. He moved on the bed, his mouth never leaving her back as his hands settled on her shoulders. Suddenly she knew without looking that he had gotten to his knees behind her.

On instinct, Jen's head fell forward, giving him access to more of her, which he acknowledged by sliding his tongue up her spine and sucking hard on the base of her neck.

She gasped, the sensation so acute and wonderful it almost brought tears to her eyes. And still he didn't let up, pressing open-mouthed kisses across her shoulders, biting and sucking at her like she was the most delicious thing he'd ever tasted.

"I want you, Jen," he said, deep and husky near her ear.

On that admission she turned her head, lifted her arm over her shoulder, and locked it around his neck. Pulling him against her, he brought his hands around to her front and ran them up her torso, stopping so just the edges of his fingers gently grazed the underside of her breasts. Leaning in further, his mouth sucked her earlobe into his mouth before he spoke again. "Please let me have you."

This was it. The moment she'd dreamed of. Hoped for. They were both single, ready, and willing. So why, suddenly, was she hesitating?

Jen tasted like heaven. Felt like perfection, and smelled like tangerines from her lotion. He'd never even eaten a tangerine, but it was now his favorite fruit.

"Jen," he whispered once more in her ear. She let her head loll back, but still she didn't answer.

"Tell me what you're thinking," he said.

She sucked in a breath and then turned in his arms. They were now kneeling in front of each other on her bed. The sight of her in nothing but her bra and panties was killing him and there was no hiding his physical reaction in these boxer briefs.

"What are we doing?" she asked.

His heart sunk and he sat back, resting on his feet. "I'll stop," he said, meaning it, but also hating the idea. "Is that what you want?"

"No. But I have a track record of making choices that are very bad for me. And while I don't normally second-guess my desires . . . this is you."

Okay, this he could handle. He smiled, lifting a hand to her cheek. "It is me. Which is why this desire is safe, Jen. I won't be a bad choice."

Her lips twisted, as if she wasn't sure she believed that. "And what about tomorrow? We work together. Is this a one-off?"

"Do you want it to be?" he asked quietly.

The furrow of her brow made him think that may have been the wrong answer.

"Jennifer!" A voice called from the living room, making them both freeze. "Are you asleep?"

"Shit!" Jen scrambled off the bed, grabbing a T-shirt off the floor. "Mom, hold on!" she called out.

She rushed to the bedroom door, which was open, and then turned to TJ. "Quiet," she mouthed before stepping into the hall and heading for the living room. TJ sat motionless on the bed, lips quirked. He should have known nothing about Jen would be easy or normal.

"What are you doing here so early, Mom?" he heard Jen ask.

"Early? It's nearly nine, and I haven't seen you in days. Where have you been?"

"Busy, that's all. Did you need something?" Jen's voice was now coming from the kitchen. The fridge opened and shut. "Do you need a smoothie? I'd be happy to make you one. I'll bring it down to you."

"It's fine, I'll wait for it," Diane said. Sounded as if she'd sat down on the sofa. "You've got enough plants in here, don't you think?"

"Probably, Mom. I like them."

"This many seems a little ridiculous, doesn't it? It's like a damn jungle."

"Apparently not ridiculous to me, since I own them all," Jen said.

TJ's eyes widened at the tone of Diane's voice. Every time he'd ever been around her she'd been so sweet, always smiling. He knew she was going through a horrible health ordeal, but damn, this was her daughter. Jen had made several comments about her mother that were starting to make a little more sense now.

"Where were you last night?" Diane asked.

"Just went out."

"No wonder you look all puffy. You must have drunk too much."

"Happens sometimes."

"Yeah, and then you sleep with random strangers."

TJ stood up from the bed, suddenly ready to give her a piece of his mind, then thought better of it. Jen would not appreciate him going out there half naked and making her mother think her comments were justified. Except he wasn't a stranger. And they didn't have sex.

"I'm so glad you popped in this morning, Mom. It makes me feel loved," Jen said, her voice so full of sarcasm TJ smiled to himself as he very quietly grabbed his jeans off the floor.

The sound of a blender going gave him a bit of a reprieve. He jerked his pants on, zipped them, and then sat down to wait this out. It was quiet again, and then he heard footsteps.

"Here you go. Bon appétit. You can take the glass with you, I was just going to get into the shower."

"It's fine. I'll wait," Diane said. *Great.*

"Um, yeah, you could. But I need to shave and stuff.

Why don't I just come down when I'm done? We can make a Target run or something. You up to that?"

"No. I'm fine."

"Okay," Jen said. TJ could tell that she wasn't sure what to do by the hesitation in her voice.

"This is a little thick. It needs more milk," Diane said. TJ nearly growled. God, could the woman say "please" or "thank you"? She sounded so angry and bitter.

"Mom," Jen sighed. "I'm out of the almond milk. I had to make this with regular. Probably makes it thicker."

"Then add some water, whatever."

He could hear Jen head back to the kitchen. But when there was no sound for a while, he wondered what was going on. A minute went by.

"What's wrong?" Diane called out.

"Nothing," Jen said, then TJ saw her step into the restroom with a glass of pink goop in her hand. Her eyes darted to his briefly before she disappeared. A moment later she stepped out and headed back to the living room. "You'll just have to drink it as it is, Mom."

"What for?"

"I . . . I don't . . ." Her last words were inaudible to him.

Diane scoffed. "What do you mean, no water?"

*What?*

"It's obviously been disconnected," Jen said quietly, and TJ could tell that she was trying to speak low enough that he couldn't hear. The thought gutted him.

"Are you kidding me, Jennifer Mackenzie?" A heavy

sigh came from Diane. "This is so damn typical of you."

"Mom, please," Jen pleaded. "Why don't you take this to your house?"

"You're thirty years old, Jen. When are you going to grow up? Now I have to die knowing you can't even take care of yourself."

That was it, TJ couldn't take any more of what he was hearing. He got to his feet and walked down the short hallway and into the living room.

The minute Diane saw him her eyes went round.

"Good morning, Diane," he said, walking up behind the chair Jen was sitting in. Acting purely on instinct—which he prayed wouldn't backfire—he leaned down and kissed Jen on the head. "Everything okay out here?"

Jen glanced up at him, and for once he couldn't read her expression. Thankfully she didn't look angry. More mystified.

"What's going on here?" Diane asked. Now that TJ took a good look at her, the woman didn't look great. Her face was gaunt, her inch-long hair thin and wispy.

"TJ stayed over last night," Jen said, finding her voice.

"Well, I can see that. I hadn't realized you were sleeping with all of your bosses," Diane said, her voice full of condescension.

TJ stiffened at her comment. Did that mean what it sounded like? Surely not, the woman was just being spiteful.

"That's enough, Mom. I think you should go, now."

"Are the two of you dating?" Diane looked at TJ,

and he had no idea how he should answer her question, but he said the first thing that felt right.

"We are. I'm sorry you had to find out this way. I hope you find it acceptable."

Her head jerked back. "I find it shocking, is how I find it. My daughter has never *dated* a well-off man, and she can't even keep her utilities turned on." She turned back to Jen. "You still waiting for someone to save you, Jen? That's not how the world works."

TJ looked down at Jen, and for the first time since he'd known her, she looked . . . broken. Humiliated. Small. The sight was so foreign, so *wrong*, he felt rage burning inside him. He looked at the woman on the sofa. "Diane, I've always had the utmost respect for you. But right now, I need you to get the hell out of this apartment."

Her eyes flared, her mouth dropped open, then shut. Finally, she stood up, setting her smoothie on the scuffed-up coffee table. "I'll do that. But if you're getting laid, how about you at least pay her water bill."

# Ten

The minute her mother walked out, Jen stood up, went to her bedroom, and shut the door before TJ could follow her in. Never in her life had she been so completely humiliated. She wasn't sure what was worse, that TJ now knew she was not even responsible enough to keep her water turned on, or the fact that he now knew what kind of person her mother had become.

A knock sounded at the door. "Jen, open up."

She hadn't locked the door, but she wasn't going to tell him that. Instead she sat on the bed, her hands resting on the mattress on each side of her.

When the door creaked open, she wasn't surprised. He walked slowly into the room and kneeled in front of her. "I'm sorry that just happened. I'm shocked at how she was behaving. Is that normal?"

Jen sighed. "We've never been . . . loving. But it's been bad lately, and getting worse all the time. She's depressed, bitter, hating her life. Wishing it would end. I don't know."

He grabbed her hand and squeezed. "You don't have to put up with that, Jen."

"She's all I have, TJ. And I'm really all she has. If I don't take care of her, who will?"

"I don't know. I'm sorry."

She gave a little laugh, and nodded back toward her bed. "At least you dodged this bullet. Right?"

He frowned. "What does that mean?"

Was he really going to make her say it? Even after hearing she couldn't even pay her bills. Her mother had been mean just now, but one thing she'd said was accurate. A thirty-year-old woman that couldn't keep her water on had bigger issues than a bitchy mother. "You can't be serious TJ. I'm obviously a mess. You see that now and so you can avoid any entanglement with the trashy girl. You knew it back in high school and as you can see, some things never change."

His head jerked back. "What do you mean, back in high school?"

She just shook her head. "Never mind."

"No way. You can't make a statement like that and then shut down on me. I never did anything to you in high school, Jen."

"You thought I was beneath you, TJ. That was enough."

"Why do you believe that?" He asked, gripping her hand. "I'm tired of you insisting that I see you in a way that I clearly don't."

"You said it."

"I never said any such thing," he said, his voice getting louder.

She met his eyes. "You did. I heard you talking to Evan that day senior year. You told him he shouldn't go with me if I asked him to the Sadie Hawkins dance."

At first he looked confused, but then his mouth dropped open a bit and he shook his head. "*Jen . . .*"

She pulled her hand from his and pushed her hair back off her face. "Damn it. I knew that would sound so ridiculous. God, it was *high school*! But I've never forgotten how that made me feel, TJ. You were popular and I was no one." Looking at him, she went on. "And please, God, don't make fools of us both by trying to deny it. He'd flirted with me in Government. Insinuated I should ask him. And then the next day I heard you in the gym. I was the office aide. Went in to deliver something. You were telling him that his parents would be pissed if we went to the dance together because I was weird, and that I didn't really fit in with your group of friends. And you know the craziest part? I agreed with you."

"No, Jen. Listen to me. You completely misunderstood that." He was shaking his head and trying to grab her hands. Finally, she relaxed and let him get a hold of her fingers. Slowly he linked their hands, touching their palms together.

She watched him open his mouth to speak, hesitate, then finally proceed. "Shit, I'm so sorry, Jen. I'll say that first. And what I said—what I did—was a total dick move. But damn, I was willing to do anything to keep Evan away from you."

"Why? It wasn't as if I wanted to marry him. Honestly, I didn't even like him, but I never had any popular guy make a move like that. Hearing you say those things—"

"I know, Jen. I know. But you have to understand why."

"Because I was the weird—"

"No. Listen to me. It's because . . ." He stopped once more, and Jen just shook her head. He wasn't finished. "Evan was not a good guy. He didn't have honorable intentions toward you, Jen. He'd talked about it with us guys before, how you'd be an easy lay. Had brought it up again in the locker room before we went into the gym. It may have sounded . . . mean, what I said about you. But I was willing to say anything, *anything,* to make him see what a bad idea it was to hook up with you. To convince him not to go out with you."

She stared back at him, stunned. It wasn't hard to believe that about Evan. It was no secret that the guy had been a player, and an asshole to all his exes. But was TJ's motivation all altruistic? Or had part of him really meant it?

"I'm so sorry, Jen. God, if I'd have known you heard . . . I'm just sorry."

She glanced down at their joined hands. "I hear what you're saying. Obviously, I've basically forgiven you. We've worked together for years now."

"But you've not forgotten it, and I don't blame you. I was never proud of those things I said. I never meant them at all. I was just"—he swallowed, his hands giving hers a little squeeze—"I was desperate, Jen. I always liked you. And you were too nice of a girl to go out with Evan. I guess now I know why you never ended up asking him."

"I sure as hell wasn't going to after overhearing that."

He nodded, a small chuckle coming from his lips. "And this must be why you quickly developed that chip on your shoulder when it came to me. Why you're still always accusing me of judging you."

"I hate that I do that all the time, but I can't seem to stop myself. It's an immature defense mechanism." She waggled her eyebrows. "Or possibly a diversion tactic, to keep myself from making out with you."

He grinned. "Feel free to drop that habit anytime."

She laughed quietly, and they stared at each other for a long moment. Her palm shifted in his and she winced a bit when a stich caught. He flipped her hand over and studied the four stitches on her pinky. "I can take these out for you."

She jerked her hand away. "No. I go in Monday to have them removed."

"That's not necessary. You just need some twee-zers."

The thought did not appeal to her. "No way. I don't even have water, TJ. I don't think minor surgery is appropriate."

He frowned. "That is not minor surgery. And I'll take care of the water."

"Absolutely not, TJ." The fact that he'd suggested it was humiliating and reminded her of the insults her mother had hurled her way. Suddenly exhausted and overwhelmed, Jen sighed. "Why don't you just go, okay? I appreciate the fact that we've now aired all our dirty laundry. Maybe we can just . . . I don't know, be normal friends."

A look of confusion crossed over his face as he shook his head. "Why would you say that after what just almost happened?"

"Because it didn't. And maybe for a good reason. The universe was telling us we were being impulsive."

"Jen, I've wanted you for almost *fifteen years*. Having sex with you now would be the most unimpulsive thing I've ever done."

She'd wanted him, too, but now, it all felt wrong. Jinxed. "Still . . . I just . . . can't do this right now."

"I understand if having your mom walk in ruined the mood today. But . . . don't shut me out," he said, looking hurt. Couldn't he consider the fact that this might be best for them both? Maybe this was just a case of pent-up frustration and lust. Giving in to any temptation was usually a horrible idea. Better to end it before anyone got hurt.

"I'm not shutting you out. We still work together. We're friends. But maybe that should be all." And she'd repeat that to herself a thousand times tonight as she lay in bed thinking about what could have happened.

He glanced down at her fingers again, one of his thumbs rubbing absentmindedly over the back of her hand. "For now. If that's what you want. But we're not done here, Jen. And what about your car?"

She shook her head. "I'll worry about that."

"Jen, just let me take you to it."

"I got it, TJ. Please. I really need some time to think."

Finally, he stood up and grabbed his shirt off the

floor. She watched, second-guessing herself, as he covered up his beautiful body. After he collected all of his personal items off her nightstand, she followed him out to her front door. After how she'd just rejected him, she might never again see TJ Laughlin in her space. With his hand on the doorknob, he turned to her. "Why don't you stay the night with me? You can have the guest bedroom. At least until we can get your water turned on?"

"No, TJ. I'm fine."

"Jen, you can't live with no water. The toilet won't even flush."

"I know how it works. Unfortunately, this isn't the first time in my life I've been without running water."

His winced. "Please, Jen. Just until Monday when they can turn it back on."

She shook her head. His words were reminder of how removed from her reality he was, that he hadn't even considered that she still wouldn't have the money on Monday. "Thank you. But no. Despite what my mother says, I'm not waiting for anyone to take care of me."

He stared down at her for a long minute, then finally, he nodded and left. And although that had been exactly what she'd asked him to do, she went into her bedroom, inhaled the scent of him on her pillow, and cried.

# Eleven

Restless, frustrated, and for once in his life feeling grateful that he had a kind mother, TJ picked up the phone and called her. It was something he tried to do once a week, because although he was mostly convinced he had little worry over what his parents thought about his success in life, he still had a ridiculous fear of being labeled the "uncaring child."

His two siblings still spent a lot more time with the family then he did, and while he wasn't envious of them for that, he was a little bitter about being considered the "outcast"—as if it was a choice *he'd* made. At least when he called his mom once a week, his father would know he put in a little effort.

His mother answered with her customary, "Hello, sweetie."

"Hey, Mom. How are you?"

"I'm good. Just sitting here watching your dad clean June bugs out of the pool. You'd think he enjoyed it or something."

TJ could picture the scene perfectly. His mother

was lounging in a long flowy and loud printed cover-up, cocktail in hand. His father was walking around the edge of the pool pretending to listen to her ramble on about whatever drama was going on with the neighborhood, while really just thinking about anything else. Probably planning to leave the house at some point that evening. TJ had no clue what went on in his dad's head most of the time, and he preferred to keep it that way.

"He just has to stay busy," TJ said. His father didn't like to be still, especially around his wife. God forbid they're forced to have a real conversation. He also didn't like to be faithful, but his mother had apparently let that ship sail long ago.

"Hey, we went to a get-together last night at the Coopers', and they were serving your new bourbon. Your father made sure everyone there knew his son made it."

That was a surprise. But also typical that he would make sure everyone else heard his false pride, just not his son. "That's nice. Hope everyone enjoyed it."

"Of course they did. It makes a fantastic mint julep."

"It does, yes. I'm glad you think so."

They chatted about nonsense for a few more minutes. What was going on with his sister and her family, and of course with his brother and his wife. Then his mother went on about the latest medical issue she was concerned with. This time it was a mole she needed to have looked at. Next, she chatted about what some of her friends' kids were up to, as if he cared. He pretended to. It wasn't long until TJ had about as much as he could take.

"Well, Mom. I'd better go."

"Okay, hon. I hope you haven't forgotten about our anniversary party. I know it's weeks away, but be sure to let that sweet Brooke know she's invited."

TJ's least favorite day of the year. The day his parents invited over all their rich friends to celebrate their sham of a marriage. They did it every year without fail.

"Actually, Mom, Brooke and I broke up."

There was an awkward pause before she finally responded. "What? Why in the world would you break up with her?" He liked how she assumed it was his fault. Then again, technically, it was. But they'd only dated for a short time. His mother had only met Brooke by accident on one of their dates when they'd seen her out to dinner with a friend of hers.

"It just wasn't working, Mom. No big deal. But I still plan on being there." Not going would imply he wasn't part of the "team." It was tempting, but so far he'd never had the nerve.

"You know Seth will give you a hard time for showing up single again," she said. TJ could hear the jingle of ice in her glass as she took another drink. She would be passed out within the hour.

"Yeah, you'd think by the age of thirty-four my brother would have moved past giving me shit."

"Oh, TJ. Lighten up. He just teases you. And you can hardly blame him. You're thirty-one. It's time to settle down."

Oh, he could blame his brother for a lot of things. Bullying him through childhood, humiliating him in high school. Basically, being a complete dickhead TJ's entire life. But no, more than anything he blamed his parents for never giving a shit. Ever. Even worse, sometimes he'd felt like not only did they not care, but they thought it was funny, which encouraged Seth even more. Stupidly, TJ almost didn't even blame his brother anymore. He was just as much a product of their upbringing as TJ was, even if he hadn't realized it yet.

"You're right, Mom. I'll keep that in mind." It did no good to argue. "I'll talk to you next Sunday then."

"Sounds good, sweetie."

They disconnected, and TJ dropped his phone on the bed and headed for the master bath. It wasn't unusual for him to have a post-phone-call hangover after talking to his mother, but after his morning with Jen, he was feeling especially messed up and confused.

TJ had a lot to be grateful for. By all standards, he'd lived an ideal life. He knew that, and didn't take it for granted. His parents—for all their faults—had paid for whatever college his scholarships hadn't, but that didn't mean he hadn't worked his ass off. Through high school and college, he'd worked multiple jobs in addition to maintaining a 4.0, mainly out of fear that his father would hold it against him if he let his grades slip. Both of his siblings had gotten scholarships, and TJ would be damned if he gave them another reason to see him as the black sheep. A role he'd never understood. He'd been successful in college, earned a degree in business and finance. By the time he turned twenty-two, he'd purchased and renovated two small rental properties.

And still his father never seemed impressed by his youngest son.

These days TJ owned and managed five residential rental properties in addition to his job as a co-owner and operator of the Stag. He had a lot going for him, and yet on most days he felt like it wasn't enough. But after what he'd just gone through this morning with Jen, a heavy dose of guilt was setting in. He really had absolutely no reason to feel slighted. Not by life, by circumstance, or even by his parents. By most accounts he was one lucky SOB, and clearly that was how Jen had always seen him. No, it didn't paint the whole picture, but was it right of him to complain or feel sorry for himself?

The words he'd spoken to Evan in that gym had come so easily because they'd been true. None of their parents would have been okay with them dating a girl like Jen. She'd worn odd clothes and too much makeup, and at the time her mother had been a waitress at Flaming Ray's, a place his parents considered a dive that catered to truckers and trash. He knew how wrong and stereotypical that was, but it was his reality at that time.

And he had been desperate to keep her and Evan from going to that dance together. Jen would have only ended up hurt, either from Evan himself or his parents, or possibly even from the snobby girls they'd hung around with. Of course, the biggest reason had been his own jealousy. He didn't want anyone to be with Jen but him, and yet not even he'd had the guts to make a move. His parents—and his siblings—would have been relentless.

So, shit. Maybe her point was valid, even if he didn't want to admit it. His judgment of her had been a factor in everything. He'd wanted her, but part of him had always been frustrated that he wanted her.

Not anymore.

He knew better now. As a man, he only wanted to be there for her. He knew she and her mother hadn't been well off. Knew that her father hadn't been around. But in the past twenty-four hours he had earned a fresh new perspective on Jennifer Mackenzie. The entire thing left him pissed and feeling helpless.

Jen was proud as hell. Always had been. But damn, the thought of her at home with no running water made him feel crazed. If it was a weekday he'd have already been to the city utilities office and paid the balance, to hell with her pride.

Problem was, as much as he wanted to fix her situation, he also couldn't help wondering how she'd allowed things to get so bad. Were there other bills unpaid? There was no doubt that if he inquired, she would freak out. Trying to fix anything for her would be the final nail in the coffin of any chance that something might ever happen between them. Of that, he was certain.

He stepped into the shower and let the hot water beat on his back. Thoughts of her made him imagine her in bed this morning, so warm and sweet. Those few moments of kissing her back and neck were some of the best—and most peaceful—of his adult life. The feel of her pressed against him, the way her arm had locked around his neck, pulling him close. He'd wanted her more than ever, felt so close to finally having her. Just imagining it was enough to make him hard.

How many times had he fantasized about bringing

her home? Taking her on a trip? Buying her things? And that was before he knew how much she really needed help. When she'd announced the community theater she'd worked for shut down due to a lack of funding a month or so ago, he'd looked into buying it. But as well as he did for himself, he'd quickly realized it was out of the question. It would have required moving it out of the city building, paying salaries, and more. But he'd considered it, for her.

His obsession with Jen Mackenzie was years and years old. There was just something about Jen that he craved like a drug. Now he knew it was partly because he saw some of himself in Jen. That brokenness he'd seen on her face had felt like a glance into a corner of his own soul. Their wounds weren't the same, but pain was pain, and rejection was rejection.

Grabbing a towel, he stepped out of the shower.

He could tell himself he wouldn't, but TJ knew himself well enough. Tomorrow morning he'd be downtown at the Maple Springs City Hall the minute it opened. She could scream and yell at him if she wanted, but there was no way he could live knowing she was struggling. Maybe she needed to know that someone was willing to take care of her. Him.

Monday mornings were always the worst, but after her insane weekend, Jen was exhausted. After TJ left Sunday morning, she'd walked to the Stag to get her car. Not ideal, but it had only taken fifteen minutes. Having no water that whole day had been annoying, but the worst part had been running up and down to use the nasty restroom in the basement laundry facility.

When it came time to shower this morning, she'd had little choice but to go to her mother's and ignore her snide comments about her irresponsibility. Then the woman had the audacity to try and pry info about dating TJ out of her. As if Jen was going to engage in fun girl talk after the way her mom had been acting. Never mind the fact that him saying they were dating was a lie.

After stopping at the hospital this morning to have her stitches removed—which had been much easier than she'd feared—Jen walked into the Stag. Things felt different today, yet familiar. Like her first few days working there all over again. The thought of seeing TJ made her feel queasy. She was torn between wishing the past week hadn't ever happened and excited about this new open attraction between them. But the whole thing left her feeling uncertain, an emotion she was not particularly fond of. Was it too much to hope that he'd taken a personal day? Not possible. The man was a workaholic.

Since the building wasn't open to the public until ten, she locked the door behind her and went straight to the front desk. After locking her purse in the bottom drawer, she got to work checking the main info email. Three wedding reception inquiries. Good, something to keep her busy, checking dates and responding. The first two were out of luck, so she responded with the customary "Sorry your date is already taken, but good luck" email. The third date they had available, which meant she followed up with a phone call. That procedure was one she'd just implemented, and she already knew it was one of the reasons bookings were up.

TJ had been right, she did listen to brides, and she enjoyed doing so. It wasn't just an empty sales tactic. Hearing about their weddings made her smile. She liked to ask questions, get a feel for their vision, and then offer tips on vendors and shops that would help them achieve their goal.

She called the number on the email in front of her and, once again, booked within twenty minutes of chatting with the bride-to-be. A little later she sent an electronic contract for her to sign, and then charged her credit card the thousand-dollar down payment to rent the Stag for her reception for the following October. If only everything in Jen's life could be so easy.

As she clicked open another email, Jen realized she wasn't alone in the front room. She turned to see Jake and TJ talking—no, cracking up—near the office hallway. They were both wearing shorts and T-shirts and were also drenched from head to toe. What had they been doing? And what the hell was so funny? Must be nice that he wasn't feeling nervous about seeing her today.

TJ said something quietly, chuckled again, his eyes cutting to Jen for a moment. Then without saying a word to her, he headed for his office and Jake did the same.

*Seriously?*

She'd been battling the butterflies in her stomach at seeing him again after their intense emotional interlude on Saturday, and the jackass didn't even have the decency to acknowledge her presence? She sat at her desk fuming for a minute. How dare he spend the night in her bed, lick her neck, witness her complete humiliation, and then have the balls to ignore her the next work day.

Screw that.

Getting up from her desk, she strode through the main room and right up to his office door, which he'd shut. Too damn bad. She turned the knob and pushed in only to find him at the side of his desk, shirtless and staring at her wide eyed, hands in the process of undoing his fly.

"Oh—" Flustered, she turned to walk back out.

"Stay where you are," he said. Jen froze, suddenly annoyed all over again. "Come in and shut the door."

She backstepped into the room far enough that she could close the door without turning to face him. "Normal people lock their office doors when they're getting naked," she bit out.

"Normal people also knock before bursting into closed rooms."

"I'm turning around," she warned.

"That's your prerogative, but you may see more than you're ready for."

She heard his wet pants hit the floor. "Fine. I'll wait. What were you guys doing to get all wet?"

"Washing the Stag Wagon in the alley."

Ah. Now *that* made sense. They'd purchased the RV a while back for Jake to take on a marketing tour. It had been renovated inside and the outside repainted. Jen didn't even want to know what might go on in the thing while Jake was trekking across country to concerts and festivals, passing out booze to beautiful women. All she knew was that on its return it would need a deep cleaning. With bleach.

"When does Jake leave? . . . And are you dressed yet? Good grief."

"For the most part," he said. Jen turned around to find him in jeans and nothing else. Gosh darn him. There was that beautifully perfect torso once again. The ideal amount of chest hair, which narrowed and trailed down to hide beneath the denim. "And Jake leaves Wednesday."

Jen took a step further into the small office and sat down in the chair in front of his desk. "You realize he's going to sleep his way across the Midwest in that RV."

"Possibly. But I know Jake, and he won't embarrass us. He'll be discrete."

"Think what you will," Jen said in her best smart-ass, melodic tone. He ignored her comment, but of all people, TJ should know Jake better than that.

She watched him pull a T-shirt over his head and then sit down in his desk chair and began to pull on dry socks. She wondered what his feet looked like, so she tilted forward and looked under the desk.

"What the hell are you doing?"

She sat back up. "Looking at your feet." They were nice feet. Slim and long, and not too hairy.

He shook his head, a grin on his face. "If you'd have turned around a few minutes ago it would have saved you the trouble."

She scoffed. "That is not why I was looking. And you know that's an old wives' tale. There is no correlation between a man's dick size and how big his feet are."

"Think what you will," he said in a sassy high voice that was so clearly meant to imitate her, she nearly laughed. Instead, she sucked both her lips in.

She waited quietly while he put on a pair of athletic shoes that looked like they cost a week's pay for her. "Did you get your stitches out?"

"I did." She held up her hand.

"Good. So, then I assume you have something you want to discuss?" he said, still leaning down to tie his shoes.

"Yes, I do, as a matter of fact."

Finally, he sat up, scooted his chair forward, and linked his fingers together. "Okay, shoot."

"*Shoot?* Look who's cocky now?"

"*Jennifer,*" he said in a low growl.

"*Trevor,*" she reciprocated. When he glared at her, a surprised look on his face, she finally conceded. "Fine. I want to know what the hell we're doing. Did we agree to go back to normal after the travesty that was yesterday morning?"

"The travesty? Not sure I'd call it that. But I only recall agreeing to go back to being friends at your insistence."

"Is it even possible for us to go back? I mean . . . we almost had sex if I'm not mistaken."

He smirked. "Yes, that had been my goal, and I'm still trying to get over that loss. Is that why you're here? To pick up where we left off? Because I'm all for it."

"Nice try. I'm here to remind you, once again, that we're co-workers. And we should probably figure out a way to make this as unawkward as possible."

"And by that I assume you mean no sex?"

"TJ, we went over this yesterday."

"*You* went over it yesterday. I recall asking you to come home with me."

She sucked in a deep breath. He was not going to make this easy, was he? "You offered your guest room."

He grinned. "I'm a stand-up guy, Jen. But we both know that if you'd taken me up on my generous offer, I'd have tried to get you in my bed."

She sucked in a breath. He was right, she absolutely did know that, and worse, she'd have probably gone willingly. "You're not making this any easier. We need to decide right now how we're going to go on from here."

He groaned, leaned his elbow on his desk, and leveled her with the most intense glare. "Jennifer Mackenzie. Are you willfully choosing to ignore the fact that I spilled my guts to you? Admitted that I'd wanted you for over a decade? Because I clearly remember saying it. Do you really think my feelings have changed—or are capable of changing—in the last twenty-four hours?"

"No. And I do remember you saying those things. I just think . . . going back to normal is what's appropriate."

"Appropriate, or safe?"

"Both, I guess."

He nodded. "I've been doing a lot of listening to what you want. How about I tell you what *I* want? Then we can negotiate."

"*Negotiate?*" She rolled her eyes, but she really

hadn't been expecting that, and she supposed it was only fair, so she gave him a "go on" face with a hand flourish.

"I can tell you're struggling with this thing between us. So, I suggest that you allow me to take you out."

She inhaled deeply and then blew it out slowly. Considering.

"You can't deny I'm right, Jen. There is a thing going on here, and you can sit there and tell yourself otherwise, but you know I'm right. This week it's become more apparent than ever. But we've gone about it all wrong so far. We're now both single. There is no reason for us not to explore this. I'm suggesting we get back to the basics."

Ever the businessman, TJ was. Jen sat up tall, still considering this. "Is this . . . 'getting back to the basics' code for 'let's just have sex already'?"

TJ leaned back in his chair, clearly exasperated. "Hell, Jen, what do you want from me? I like you. I want to take you out." He sat up and threw his hands out dramatically. "Do I want to have sex with you? Hell yes. Do I want to take you out even if sex is off the table? Yes, I do."

He ended that sentiment by slapping his hands down on his desk.

"You're really getting worked up about this," she said.

"Because you drive me crazy!" He sighed. "Dealing with you is maddening. But trying to pretend I don't want you is even more difficult because I do. Damn it. I want you bad."

They sat in silence a bit, staring at each other. Quite

honestly, his outburst had her speechless for a second. Finally, she managed a few words. "Fine. We can go out."

He sighed, his shoulders sagging in relief. "It's about time. Why don't I pick you up at six thirty?"

"You want to go out *tonight*? On a *Monday*?"

"Why not?"

"I don't know. I just hadn't considered it. Where are we going?"

"How about you leave something to the imagination, huh? You've already given me hell for this. I'll worry about the details."

"Whatever." She got up and headed for the door. Before she stepped out, she looked over her shoulder. "You know there's a good chance you'll end up regretting this."

"Possibly. Guess I'm willing to take the chance."

Jen shrugged. "Don't say I didn't warn you."

# Twelve

That evening, Jen waited for TJ at the curb, her body primed and ready to give him a dressing down. When she saw his Camaro pull up and park, she headed into the lot. The minute he got out of his car, she was ready.

"Did you pay my water bill?" He hadn't said a thing about it at work, but she knew it had to be him. A city could do a lot of stupid things, but accidently turning on unpaid utilities was unlikely to be one of them. She'd come home today prepared to get ready for their date down at her mom's, but out of curiosity she'd tried the faucet, stunned to see water come out.

He sighed, shutting the door. "Hello to you, too. You look beautiful."

"Answer the question, TJ."

"Of course I paid it."

Her shoulders dropped. "What is wrong with you? How can we possibly go out now that you've done that?"

Putting his hand on his hips, TJ let his head fall back as if dealing with a petulant child. The exact reason she didn't want his help—so he wouldn't have that feeling about her. After taking a deep breath, he brought his head back up and eyed her. "I paid one bill. It was less than a hundred dollars. I would have done it for any person important to me. It was not a power move. It was me doing you a favor. Get over it."

"Get over it? I told you not to do that. I was very clear."

"Jen, for God's sake, you had no *water*. What the hell did you expect me to do?"

"Respect my wishes."

"I respect your wishes, but in this case, I respect you as a human more, so I paid your goddamn water bill because I am incapable of sleeping at night if I know you don't have basic life necessities. Shit, give me a break for once."

That stopped her immediately. She stared at him, trying to decide if she wanted to hug or punch him, because let's face it, nobody *wanted* to have to go to their mother's place just to use the toilet or the shower. But like most people, Jen also tried her best to avoid humiliation. Good grief, wasn't it bad enough that he'd been there when she'd discovered her water disconnected?

To add insult to injury, he stood here in her shitty apartment parking lot looking every bit the part of chivalrous savior. He wore high-dollar jeans and an ironed navy button-up, cuffed on his forearms. He'd applied some gel to his hair, and sported a big chunky silver chronograph watch that probably cost ten times what he'd spent on her this morning to have running water.

But that was not a bad thing, right?

He had money. So what? Why not let the guy help her out? It was nothing to him. And yet, Jen knew that help usually required one of two things: strings or trust. Experience had taught her that both were riddled with land mines, so she usually just opted out of help altogether. It was safer that way.

"I'm sorry for freaking out just now," she said quietly. "And . . . thank you. But don't do it again. Okay?" she pleaded.

"I hear you," he finally said. But she didn't miss the fact that it wasn't a concession. He was placating her. "We still doing this tonight?"

Damn him for looking so earnest. And sexy. She had her pride, yes. But she was also hungry, and he looked good enough to eat. However, the most appealing thing about him right now was the fact that he kept showing up. Taking her shit that he probably didn't deserve. "Yes. We're still doing this."

He visibly relaxed. "Good. Can we take your truck?"

She glanced at his very expensive car as she processed the thought of them getting into her clunker of a vehicle. "Uh, what for?"

"I want to go somewhere specific, where a truck could come in handy."

"Sure, but you could have just asked to borrow my truck if you needed to buy some furniture or something. It didn't require a date."

He chuckled, shaking his head as he held his hand out for her keys. "Hush your mouth. This is our date, and something I want you to do with me."

Curious, Jen followed him through the parking lot.

"You're awfully brave to leave your fancy car parked here for too long. You know these are not luxury apartments."

He shrugged. "It's insured. Besides, it sat out here all Saturday night if you recall."

Good point. But still, why tempt fate a second time? But if he wasn't going to worry, she wasn't either. They got out into her truck, and it suddenly felt way older and nastier than it did the last time she was in it. When he started it up, it made an embarrassing screeching noise.

"Don't even comment," she said, tossing a pile of unopened mail behind the seat.

"Wouldn't dream of it." He backed out of the parking lot, and fifteen minutes later they were pulling into Fine Living Nursery and Greenhouse. Jen's heart began to race with excitement. She'd driven past this place a million times, admiring the trees in the spring, mums and pumpkins in the fall, and even the Christmas trees in the winter. Her limited funds—and her lack of a lovely home to decorate—had always kept her from stopping. Places like this were for grown-up, got-their-shit-together kind of people, and she was far from one of those on her best day. She loved plants, but hers came from Walmart and Home Depot, often from the clearance section, which usually meant they were on their way to the trash bin. Not that she loved them any less because of it. She was no high-class lady either, so she wasn't one to judge, and often all they'd needed was some loving care. Bringing them back was a pleasure.

But this . . . shopping at this nursery would be a

plant nirvana like she'd never experienced, and she couldn't wait to get inside. When he'd mentioned liking her plants, she figured he was just being nice.

Her anticipation reached a frenzied state as he found a parking spot and they both got out. After waiting for his second attempt to get her driver's side door to stay shut, Jen walked over, lifted on the handle, and gave it a hard shove.

Without a word, TJ reached out and grabbed her hand.

"Why are we here?" she asked, trying to pretend she wasn't freaking out inside. Between the hand-holding and the impending plant overload, Jen's body was on the brink of cardiac arrest. "Are you buying me a plant to apologize for paying my bill?" she asked excitedly.

He leveled her with a glare. "So, let me get this straight. You would let me buy you something you want, to apologize for buying you something you need?"

She lifted a shoulder. "It's hard being a man. I get it. Women can be such trouble."

He laughed, giving her hand a squeeze. "Men would be nothing without women. And I want you to help me pick some plants for my house."

She struggled to maintain step with him as her head jerked to the side. "Really?" She was slightly embarrassed about the slight shrillness in her excited reply. She knew he didn't miss it when he grinned over at her.

"Yes, really. I have never had plants, and I while I'm not interested in having a bunch, I liked how they looked in your place. Makes it seem homier."

"Of course, they do. Good ones can be expensive, you know."

"I don't doubt it, but we'll worry about that when we find something you like."

Jen bit at her bottom lip trying to process his words. *Something you like.* He still had a hold of her hand as they entered the front area of the nursery, which held rows and rows of outdoor plants, flowers, and trees.

It was beautiful, and instantly Jen felt at peace being surrounded by such a vibrant display of life and regeneration. Plants soothed her in a way she couldn't explain, and for some reason being here with TJ wasn't killing her buzz. In fact, it was nice.

They walked each row, and he paused without question or annoyance every time she stopped to feel the texture of a leaf or read a description.

"Someday I hope I have a yard to fill with any plant I want," she said, looking at a row of rose bushes. "With a bench. No, a swing. Yes, I'd have a swing and maybe a fire pit. And a fountain. Hell, I just want a yard," she finally conceded.

"You will," he said.

"Hmm. Maybe. Says the man who just paid my water bill because I suck."

"You don't suck, Jen," he growled. "And you need to let that go. Everybody hits a rough patch at some point."

She wasn't going to mention that her rough patch could be labeled "adulthood." That it was no longer a patch, but a lifestyle. Her financial immaturity was one of the many things about herself that brought her shame. She was much better now, but years of stupidity had caught up with her and she was struggling to get her footing. Losing her job at the community theater had been a major setback in her efforts.

"I should ask if they're hiring. I could take care of plants," she said, thinking out loud.

He angled his body toward her, a concerned look on his face. "Why would you do that? You have a job."

"I do *now*. But Tara will come back from maternity leave this fall. Then what? Bartending at weddings won't cover my living expenses. I might as well start looking for another full-time job. Hell, I'm barely making it as it is, as you now know."

They'd made their way into the evergreen tree area, and as Jen reached out to touch a cluster of tiny frosted berries on a branch, she was pulled to a stop by TJ still clasping her other hand. She turned. "What's wrong?"

"We need to talk about this."

"About what?"

"*You*, needing a job. I'll figure something out at the Stag, Jen. I don't want you worrying about it."

"Well . . . that's been the plan since the beginning. The receptionist job was temporary, that's not your fault."

He stepped closer to her, his brow furrowed in frustration. "Maybe not, but you have to know there's no way I'd just turn you out without enough money to survive on. I know bartending once a week isn't enough to make it on."

"TJ, I'm not looking to you to be my savior. I've lost jobs before, I'll figure it out. Besides, what happens at the Stag is not up to just you. Dean and Jake have a say also."

"They'll agree with me. I know they will."

"And what if I don't want to keep working at the Stag?"

He suddenly looked shocked . . . and more than a little hurt. "Why wouldn't you?"

"I don't know. I guess I stupidly keep thinking I'll find something in theater where I can act, sing, or teach. That's my passion. It's what I've always wanted to do, more than anything else. I miss it like crazy."

"I understand that, Jen. Your talent is . . . incredible." He sucked in a breath and then blew it out. "It's just, I've gotten used to seeing you every day. And you're also good at what you do there. Surely you don't mean you'd give up your bartending gig also?"

She shook her head. "We didn't come here to talk about this." Uncomfortable with the conversation, Jen pulled away. "Let's find the greenhouse."

He shoved his hands into his pockets and followed her. The minute they entered the massive room full of houseplants, Jen grinned from ear to ear. This was her new happy place. "Isn't this beautiful?"

"It's overwhelming. And very green," TJ said. Jen looked over to find his wide eyes roaming over row after row of leaves, from the floor to the ceiling. Hanging baskets, potted plants, even a perfectly styled koi pond in the center.

Jen took off for a nearby cactus display. Walking a little farther she found a row of succulents at least twenty feet long. There were so many varieties, colors, and textures: light, dark, flowering, thorny. TJ was right, but it was "overwhelming" in the best way. It was hard not to want to have them all.

"These are weird," TJ said behind her, glancing down at various plants. "What do you do with little nubby plants like this?"

Jen gasped in mock horror. "They're succulents, and very popular right now. And don't talk negatively about them. You should apologize."

He glanced down, then up at her, brow furrowed. "Apologize? To the *plants*?"

"Of course. I talk to mine daily. I'm convinced they respond to the feelings we project onto them. I mean, how well would you grow if someone called you weird?"

He frowned. "I've had worse."

"And it affected you. Didn't it?" she insisted, charmed by the wary look on his face. When he raised an eyebrow, she doubled down. "Listen, if you're going to become a plant owner, you're going to have to learn how to love them. It's the only way they'll thrive."

He hesitated, angled his head, but then nodded slowly, his mouth parted in surprise. After a moment, he squatted down to a pallet sitting on cinder blocks, rested his elbows on his knees, and quietly muttered. "Sorry, plants—I mean, succulents. You are not weird at all. You're beautiful and rubbery-looking." He glanced down the aisle to see two women staring. "And I hope you appreciate the fact that I just lost a piece of my dignity in order to make you feel loved."

The sexiest laugh escaped Jen's bright red lips as she watched him straighten from talking to the plants. "I can't believe you just did that."

His hand jerked out to grab her, but she yelped and

skittered away. Wobbling as he stood upright, TJ took off after her. It only took two swift, long strides for him to catch up and get ahold of her, yanking her back against his chest. She was still laughing when he leaned down into her neck and inhaled her scent. "I hope you enjoyed that, Jennifer."

She turned into him, their bodies plastered together chest to chest, and when she grinned up at him, his heart squeezed. How would he survive if he never knew what it felt like to have her fully?

"I enjoyed it immensely, Trevor. It was adorable. And I wasn't kidding you completely. I do talk to my plants."

No one called him by his full name anymore, which made it sound even sexier on her lips. It was a reminder of how long they'd known each other. And how many years he'd been attracted to her. He lifted his hand and gently ran the edge of his finger down her cheek. She was so damn pretty, her red lips glistening and her dark hair pulled back, exposing the creamy skin on her neck.

He'd never known another woman like her. She was special, with a wild but endearing personality, colorful tattoos, and more natural talent in her pinky than ten normal people put together had.

"Well then," he said, looking in her eyes, "if you're so good at conversing with the plants, I'm going to need you to talk to them and find out who wants to come home with me."

"Oh, that will be a tough one." Untangling herself from his body, she began to walk backward. He kept hold of her hand, not wanting her to get too far.

"They've seen you walk in, and they're already worried."

"And why is that?"

Jen appeared to consider his question as she looked him up and down. Using her free hand, she pointed at him. "Well dressed, handsome, obviously wealthy." She grinned. "And kind of sexy. That combination is a real cause for concern."

"Oh really?" he asked, genuinely confused, but also a bit excited. "And what do you mean, *kind of* sexy?"

She laughed again. "Don't get paranoid. The plants are already thinking that while you look like a catch, you're only here on a whim. Maybe you're only interested because they look fun and colorful, a novelty. But they fear that once you get them home you'll get bored. Maybe neglect them, or throw them away when you see how difficult they can be to care for."

That statement could not go unchallenged. TJ gripped her hand and tugged her back into his arms. "They should understand that I've always been attracted to plants. This is not a whim. I was just nervous. Afraid I wouldn't know how to give them what they needed. But now that I've made the decision to act, I'm committed. Ready to do whatever I have to do to make them happy."

"That's a lofty goal, TJ. Some plants are incredibly needy. They want it all. Light, water, perfect soil, ideal humidity. They don't just want to stay alive. They want to grow."

He laced his fingers in hers. "Luckily, I have you here, to tell me exactly what she needs."

"'She,' huh?" Jen smiled. "Let's see what we can do."

Breaking the spell, she pulled away and headed down a row full of large potted plants. He watched her backside shift as she walked, her small shorts revealing plenty of leg. This evening she'd worn a red sleeveless top that showed off all her tattoos, something he didn't get to see that often on normal days. It was a reminder of how much he wanted his mouth on her again, to taste her tangerine skin and feel her softness against him. Her hair was pulled into a low wavy ponytail that trailed to the middle of her back.

She stopped in front of a pallet and pointed. "I love these. I've always wanted one myself," she said. "What do you think?"

"It's nice. I like it. Which ones should we get?"

Her eyes widened. "You're easy. How many plants are we getting?"

"I don't know. Three?"

"Three. Nice. What's my budget?"

"I have no idea. How much are we talking for like . . ." He pointed to a large one with full leaves. Almost like a small tree. "One of those."

She checked the price tag and then raised her eyebrows. "You like the pretty, expensive, popular ones. No surprise."

"I recall you liking these first. I just pointed at one. How much is it?"

"Two hundred."

"Oh shit, seriously?" He balked, completely not expecting that price.

"They're not all that expensive. Let's keep looking. How about a rubber plant?" She pointed to one good-sized one with big, thick leaves.

"Yeah, I like that one. How much?"

She leaned over, located the price tag. "This one is ninety-five."

He nodded. "That's a good price. Let's get him." TJ bent over to pick it up off the palate. When he turned around and set the plant down near his feet, he found Jen smiling at him.

"What's so funny?"

"I'm just curious why he's a him?"

TJ shrugged. "I don't know. He's just kind of rugged and strong-looking."

"Of course." She stared down at his new rubber plant. "I see it. His leaves are on the thick side. All girls love a nice, thick, man," she added with grin.

"I'll keep that in mind."

"What next?" Jen looked down the row once more. "He needs a girlfriend."

"If I buy him a girlfriend, does it save me from having to talk to them every day?"

Jen laughed that sexy, throaty laugh again. The one that had the power to make him hard in a second. Thankfully, so far, he'd managed to keep himself under control in the greenhouse.

They found a small flatbed cart and chose two more plants: a calathea that Jen declared was most definitely a girl and was also one of her favorite plants and a large split-leaf philodendron, which TJ had reservations about due to its sheer size and price, but Jen had gotten so excited he couldn't say no.

By the time they chose containers, potting soil, and plant food, he knew their total was going to be outrageous. However, he didn't even hesitate as they made their way to the checkout.

When he realized she'd been quiet for several moments as they waited in line, TJ leaned in to look over her shoulder. She was touching something in a display on the checkout counter.

Stepping around to get a closer look, he realized they were ornamental stakes made from colored glass. Just something pretty and unnecessary you'd put into the dirt in a garden or a pot. There were various designs: mushrooms, dragons, ladybugs . . . and fairies. He watched her finger slide over the shiny yellow glass, obviously admiring it. It was beautiful and looked handmade, with sparkly wings. It was something he never would have noticed himself, but she seemed mesmerized by it.

Before he could mention it, she shoved the stake back into the pot and turned to face him, unaware that he'd been watching her. "I'm excited to get these potted and put in your place."

"Me too."

"I've never seen your house. Is it fancy or frat housey?"

"What does frat housey look like?"

She shrugged. "Kind of like my place, probably. Random. Crowded. I'm sure you don't live like that. You're too mature and well mannered, but I've found that a lot of single guys do."

Was she touching his shirt consciously? Didn't matter to him either way, he loved it. She would never need a reason—or permission—to touch him.

"My house is actually new. But I wouldn't describe it as fancy," he said. She just nodded in response, and then he had an idea. "Hey. What do you think about pulling the truck up when it's our turn? Then I can load everything up?"

"Okay. That's probably a good idea." She looked at their collection of plants and then back at him. "I'll be out front in that circle drive."

The minute she was out the front door and the person in front of him was finished, he grabbed three fairy stakes of various colors and laid them on the counter. Then he proceeded to spend six hundred and ninety-two dollars.

She was worth every penny.

# Thirteen

Jen pulled up to the loading area of the nursery and parked her truck. The past hour had been one of the most fun she'd had in a long time. Still hard to believe it had happened with TJ of all people. Who knew he could be so sweet and so funny, and that they could actually not annoy each other for a while.

When she finally saw him heading her way, pulling the flatbed wagon, she got out of the truck and lowered the tailgate. Together they loaded the three plants and all of the paraphernalia, and then Jen grabbed the handle of the cart and put it away in the cart corral. When she walked back to the truck, TJ was behind the wheel.

Once she was buckled up, they headed to the west side of Maple Springs, somewhat out into the country. Surprised, Jen watched out the window as they headed down a state highway lined with tall, sundried cornstalks. Finally, they turned on a smaller road, and drove for about a mile.

"How far out here do you live?"

"Almost there." Within minutes he was pulling into a driveway.

Jen nearly gasped. "This is your house?"

"Uh-huh. You like it?"

She gave him an annoyed glare as he put the truck in park, smiling at her. "You told me it wasn't fancy, you liar. It's beautiful." She immediately got out to take it all in. The house itself was new, but obviously made to have the charm of a much older farmhouse. It wasn't giant, it was just big enough, with a big wide front porch.

And a swing.

She was nearly in shock at how beautiful the property was. The right side of the lot was lined by a field of corn, the left, nearly a quarter mile away, was a fenced-in area full of cattle. The yard itself was vast and fairly unadorned. She recalled TJ moving over the winter, but never in her wildest dreams had she pictured this.

"Don't tell me you farm in your spare time." She looked back at him. He was leaning against the front of her truck, watching her look around.

"Of course not. I only own ten acres. I lease seven of it to my neighbor for his cattle."

She shook her head and walked back toward him. "Always looking to make a buck. You're good at it. I'm impressed, TJ."

"I'm still getting used to living out here," he said. The sun was low in the sky, and she loved the way the light brought out flecks of color in his hair.

"Don't you get lonely?" she asked.

He turned to look at her. "Yeah. I do. Which is why I'm glad you're here right now."

"Me too."

He pushed off the truck. "Let's get these plants inside."

They walked around to the back and lowered the tailgate. Jen instantly grabbed the calathea, since it was smaller, and TJ got the split-leaf plant, which was about three feet tall.

"Still can't believe you talked me into this monster."

"Hey, language," she scolded.

He rolled his eyes as he made his way to the front door. "Oh yes. I forgot." He leaned closer to the leaves. "I'm so sorry, Mr. Plant. I can't wait to welcome you to your new home."

Jen cracked up, loving that he chuckled also. He had the best laugh, something she'd never really noticed until recently. Even the creases around his eyes were incredibly sexy. He set the pot down and went back for the rubber plant. While she waited, Jen couldn't help trying out the swing.

It was so lovely and peaceful looking out at the corn, the cows, and the field beyond the road. It appeared to have been harvested already, probably wheat. A girl didn't grow up in Kansas without knowing a *little* something about agriculture.

After he stepped back onto the porch and set the rubber plant down, he came over and settled beside her on the swing. The slatted seat wasn't that wide, so they were close, and despite it being hot out, she liked his nearness. Maybe even leaned in his direction a little.

"What made you add a swing?"

"Seemed like the right thing to do with a porch like this."

"I would agree," she replied. "I'll be honest, I never saw you as a country house kind of guy. This really surprises me."

"Yeah, surprised me too, actually. I used to live in town. The first house I lived in was three blocks off the square, an older bungalow that I'd bought intending to flip. Instead I moved in. I liked it okay, but I just wanted . . . space. Something I could see living in forever, maybe have a family in."

They were both silent for a moment, and Jen couldn't help imagining TJ as a father. He'd probably be a really good one.

"But I wanted a place different than where I grew up, which was in a gated subdivision with nosey neighbors and wife-swapping."

"Stop it!" she said, turning to stare at him. "*Wife-swapping*?"

He laughed. "No lie. My mother was always sharing all the neighborhood gossip. I was hearing about the soap opera of my neighborhood my entire childhood it seems."

"Wow. I knew you were a rich kid but I hadn't realized you'd lived in one of *those* neighborhoods."

"There were decent people too, of course. But they didn't get talked about near as much. There was always plenty of crap going on."

"Wow. I knew there was a reason I never liked rich kids." She looked out in time to see a lightning bug fly by. She looked back at him. "That must have really twisted your view of what a healthy relationship is, huh?'

"I suppose. If not that, my parents did a pretty good job of messing me up."

"Tell me your dad didn't swap your mom." She said, mouth dangling open as she awaited his response.

"God, I hope not. Don't even make me think about that." He chuckled and then sobered. "They just don't really love each other. That's all. It's sad, and I feel bad for my mother. I think she tried for a long time."

"How do you know? Maybe they've just lost touch. People get comfortable. Doesn't mean there's no love. Or so I'm guessing. Trust me, I know nothing about healthy relationships either."

"Nah. I'm certain of it. There's not only no love, there's not even much like. My father is not really a good guy. I wish I could understand why he is who he is, but I don't, and it looks like I never will."

"I'm sorry to hear that." Jen looked over at him. "I always assumed you and your dad were like two peas in a pod."

"Why would you think that?"

"In my eyes you were always the perfect student, handsome, well liked, and popular. Why wouldn't a father eat that up?"

TJ sighed. "It's a question I've been asking my entire life. But I've sort of come to terms with the fact that my success has to be for me. No one else."

"I admire your success. I always have. You're a hard worker."

TJ smiled over at her. She liked that his long legs were keeping the rhythm of the swing, allowing her legs to just glide back and forth against the wood. It was relaxing.

"If I had known how messed up you were, I might have liked you sooner," she said.

TJ watched Jen arrange the calathea on a table near the window in his living room.

"Notice how the leaves are starting to look higher?"

He analyzed the plant. "Maybe. Why is that?"

"I honestly don't know why it does it, but it's the reason these are my favorite. This variety is called a peacock plant. The leaves move all day. At night, they will be straight up in the air. Then in the morning they'll be down again. It's so amazing."

"Wow. That's really bizarre. But cool."

Even besides the moving leaves, he could see why she liked it so much. The leaves were an incredibly vibrant green with purple undersides, and the bold pattern made the entire thing striking.

"So do I need to write down all the instructions for you?" she asked, moving the soil around once more before stepping back to admire her work.

"That would be nice. I sure as hell won't remember it."

"Okay, I will, but keep in mind, every plant is different and so is every situation. You'll have to get to know them. Sometimes you just have to go with your gut."

*Great.* "I'll get the hang of it I'm sure." *Or I'll just have to find a way to convince her to be here more often.*

When they'd first gotten inside, they'd had some

sandwiches and fruit salad he'd picked up at a deli after work. Then he'd given her a tour of the first floor. Or rather, she'd begun to give herself one so he followed along. But he'd loved sharing his home with her, telling her about the building process and why he'd chosen the finishings he had.

Now that they were done with the major task of the evening—the plants—he felt a little panicky. He didn't want her to leave. In fact, had he known that finally giving into his craving for her would be so good, he might have given in years ago. All he wanted was more. More time, more kissing, and definitely more touching.

"I have a homecoming present for the plants," TJ announced, grabbing the last bag from the nursery that he'd left near the entry. Jen's eyes narrowed as she watched him walk it over. He smiled tentatively as he pulled out one of the fairy garden stakes.

Her mouth dropped open, eyes wide. "You bought one?" she asked in a whisper.

"I actually bought three. One for each plant." He held out the pink one for her to take and then retrieved the other two. Yellow and blue. "Now they can think about you even when you're not here."

His comment implied that sometimes she *would* be there, and he so wanted that to be true. He watched her turn the metal stake over in her hand, admiring the fairy again.

"I know they seem kind of silly. I just thought they were so pretty." Her words were quiet.

"If I thought they were that silly, I wouldn't have bought them." It still shocked him a bit that he did, honestly. Buying plants and garden stakes were not par for the course in his world.

"So, you're going to let me put *fairies* in your plants?"

*When she put it that way.* Her crooked smirk was his undoing. "Yeah. I am. If you want to, that is."

"Even the man plant?"

He smiled. "Even the man plant."

She turned and went back to the window, turning the pot this way and that, searching for the perfect spot. The entire time she was humming to herself. After a short pause, she pushed the metal into the soil. It gave the effect that the fairy was flying around the leaves.

Turning back to him, Jen grabbed the other two and walked into the entryway to put one in the rubber plant, and then the breakfast room for the philodendron.

And just like that, she was part of this home.

# Fourteen

Thursday morning, TJ was late to work. His morning had consisted of errands to the bank and the post office. Things he hated doing on a normal day, but were made even worse because he'd gotten a late start from oversleeping. Something he rarely did. But this entire week he'd felt off his game.

He knew exactly why, and he was dying to see her.

After parking in the alley behind the Stag, TJ came in the back door and immediately ran into John, their newest employee and Dean's distilling apprentice.

"Hey, man," TJ said, shutting the supply room door. "How's it going?"

"I'm good. Busy morning."

"Yeah? What batch are you guys doing today?"

"Vodka."

TJ nodded. "You still enjoying this?" John hadn't been there long, just a couple of months. They'd hired him after he'd gotten laid off from his finance job in Chicago and had to move back home. It was an extreme change of career, and TJ had worried that John might not stick around. So far, so good, but he didn't consider them out of the woods just yet.

"Yeah, absolutely. I enjoy it a lot. Feel like I'm learning something new every day, and Dean's a good teacher."

"I bet he is." And TJ meant it. It took a special kind of man to hire his girl's ex-fiancé and work with him day in and day out. TJ sure as hell couldn't do it.

"Anyway"—John nodded toward the distilling room—"Dean told me if I saw you out here, to tell you he needed a minute before you go anywhere else."

TJ frowned. "Okay. Everything alright?"

"Yeah, yeah. I think, uh . . . well, he just seemed to want to tell you something about Jen."

His heart suddenly skipping a beat, TJ stepped around John and headed for the long distilling room that ran most of the length of the building, separating the front room and offices from the back work space where they bottled, stored supplies, and did any other messy work that needed to be done.

Opening the door, he stepped inside and found Dean moving a hose into one of the fermenting vessels, ready to fill it with mash. "What's going on?" TJ said in greeting.

Dean looked over and gave him a tilt of his chin. "Hey, man. Not much. Turn this hose off will ya?"

A bit relieved that Dean didn't seem overly concerned, TJ reached over and turned a nob on the wall. The room quieted significantly. He glanced through the display glass out into the main room, but while he could see the front desk, he couldn't see Jen.

"What's wrong?" TJ asked, wanting to cut straight to the chase.

"Nothing is *wrong*," Dean said, stepping closer. He lowered his voice. "But I did want to inform you that Jordan Bodisto stopped by this morning. About an hour ago."

"What the hell for?" TJ asked, jealousy and anger suddenly rushing through his body.

Dean tilted his head to the side. "What do you think? It sure as hell wasn't to put in an order."

TJ ran a hand through his hair. "What a dick. He doesn't take a hint, does he?"

"Well, it's not you he needed the hint from. It was her."

TJ glanced through the glass again. Still no sign of *her*. Had she stepped away? "So what happened?"

"Nothing, really. They talked a few minutes, but I didn't go eavesdrop on their conversation. Not my style. But it seemed low-key."

"Low-key my ass," TJ said, heading for the door.

"Hey, man, wait," Dean called to him. When TJ turned back to his friend, Dean sighed. "I told you because you're my friend. But so is Jen, and she didn't do anything wrong."

TJ frowned. "Jesus, man. What'd you think I was about to do? Yell at her?"

"I have no idea, but you're about to storm out of here like you have a right to demand answers. And while I'm not up in your everyday business, I'm guessing you don't have that right. So just think about cooling off before you say anything."

"You have no idea what's going on between us."

"No, I don't. But the more important thing is, do *you* know what's going on between you two?"

TJ considered that. "Truth? No. But I'm starting to feel the need to put a label on it."

Dean nodded. "Good luck with that."

"Thanks. I'm probably gonna need it." TJ headed out of the distilling room, into the back, and then down the hallway toward the front. She'd asked him to drive her home the other night after they'd wrapped up with the plants, but she had kissed him good night in her truck when they'd parked in her lot, then again when he'd walked her to the door, which had been amazing. He hadn't pushed for more, remembering her suggestion that they take things slow. But if she was entertaining the thought of flirting with Jordan, he was going to have to call bullshit.

Just as he made his way to the desk, she stepped in the front door, which made him feel panicked. What had she been doing out there?

The minute she saw him she smiled, which eased his mind a bit.

"Hi," she said, swiping a windblown hair from her face. She was wearing a black-and-white striped skirt—one his favorites because of the way it hugged her backside—a white sleeveless top, and strappy little black shoes.

"Hey." Shoving his hands in his pockets while she walked around the desk and sat down, he tried to play it cool. "What were you doing out there?"

"Nothing. Just fixing the rug," she said coyly.

He sucked in a breath quietly, held it for a moment,

then blew it out. "Sorry I was late this morning. Had to run some errands."

She shrugged. "No problem."

He walked around the L-shaped desk and counter to the entrance. "Anything happen while I was gone?"

No dummy, Jen turned in her chair, crossed her legs, and stared up at him. "I know there are a lot of eyes in this place. Do you have something to ask me?"

"I guess maybe I do."

She put out a hand. "Please proceed."

"Did you tell that asshole to stop coming around?"

Staring at him for a long moment, she finally held up a finger. "One," was all she said.

He frowned. "What does that mean?"

"'One' is the number of times you and I have been out together."

Turning back to her desk, she wiggled her mouse to bring her computer back to life. She was dismissing him, and that was not going to sit well. He still needed answers.

Standing quietly, he tried to decide what to do next. Then it hit him. He glanced at the door, then the main room, and then reached down and spun her chair to face him. She let out little yip, her eyes wide.

He held up a finger, inches from her face. "One," he said, before resting his hands on the arms of her chair. Their faces were now a foot apart.

She narrowed her eyes, then crossed her arms over her chest. "Go on."

"'One' is the number of times I'm going to kiss you. Right now. To remind you that something is going on here between us."

Her eyes widened the slightest bit, and he watched her lips began to part, the full lower one so plump and perfect he could stare at it all day.

"I'm waiting," she whispered.

Leaning down, his mouth met hers softly, with a gentle press. She didn't kiss him back, yet, but she would. He wouldn't stop until she did—and this was his bull-headed Jen, so he could be here awhile.

Reaching a hand up to her neck, he caressed her skin as he continued to place soft kisses on her mouth. Her lips relaxed the slightest bit further, allowing him to penetrate her with his tongue.

And that did it—she let out the faintest moan, her head angling to take him in deeper. Their tongues met, her lips now fully engaged as she began to take over. Her hand settled on his jaw, the feel of her skin on his like a balm to all his frustration and doubt, and with that release of tension, his body felt the pull of gravity. He lowered to his knees in front of her, grateful for the mat on the wood floor.

She responded by parting her legs to make room for him, and then scooted to the edge of the chair. TJ's hands went to her back, pulling at her, wanting them close as their mouths and tongues explored each other.

The sound of a delicate cough pulled them apart. Looking up, they saw the FedEx lady standing at the counter. TJ jumped to his feet as Jen scooted back to her computer.

"Sorry to break that up," she said quickly. "But I need a signature."

TJ cleared his throat. "No, I apologize. That was"—he grabbed her device and electronic pen—"inappropriate."

"No problem with me. At least someone's getting some action," she said with a wink as she walked out the door. "Feel free to resume."

TJ glanced down at Jen, who was leaning her face on her hand, staring up at him with a grin on her face. "You got dirt on your knees," she said, nodding to his pants. Sure enough, there were light-black smudges on each of his knees.

"How dirty is this floor?" he asked, wiping at his pants.

"Nobody cleans the mat I'm guessing. But you look cute like that. Looks like you've been up to no good."

"Uh-huh, which I have. Because this"—he waved a finger between them—"this is a thing."

"Okay, but honestly, we didn't even do traditional date stuff yet."

His brow furrowed. "What we did was better."

She smiled. "I enjoyed it, yes. I'm just saying, letting me decorate your fancy house with plants does not make us a *thing*. That makes us friends. So what are we doing next?"

He considered that.

"Where did you take tiny cheerleader on your first date?"

"You can't be serious. I'm not answering that."

She twisted her lips. "That good, huh?"

"Wha—"

"She was new. You wanted to impress her."

"That is an entirely different scenario. I *know* you."

"Exactly. That's why you could get away with taking me to your house. A new woman would have been freaked out."

"Oh for God's sake." He walked around the front of her desk, talking as he went. "You can keep trying to mess with me. Playing your mind tricks to convince me this is never gonna work. But you're wrong. It only makes me more determined." He pointed at her. "I'll take you on a traditional date. Tomorrow night."

"Are you asking me, or telling me?"

"No way," he said. "I said no more of those mind tricks."

"Okay. Tomorrow it is. And just so you know . . . 'one' is the number of men I'll give my attention to at any time. So no need to get jealous again. I made it clear to him that it wasn't going to happen."

He looked at her, relief flooding his body. She'd known that was exactly what he'd needed to hear, but she'd just needed to be stubborn and make him work for it. She was maddening. "Thank you."

Jen put her hand out and shooed him away. "Get to work. I'm busy today."

Damn, she was a pain in the ass. But he was still intent on making her *his* pain in the ass.

After work that day, Jen paused near the mailboxes and stared at her mother's front door. She'd started stopping in to check on her less and less, hoping maybe it would prompt a little gratitude. For over a year now she'd been regularly bringing smoothies, checking in, making sure everything was okay. And rarely was any of that met with a thank-you, let alone kindness.

Jen could understand the bitterness that might come with battling cancer—and giving up addictions—but didn't it get exhausting being so crotchety? If anything,

Jen had hoped that giving up those unhealthy vices would eventually help Diane feel better, and hopefully improve her outlook on life. But that hadn't seemed to have happened. It was hard to understand someone choosing to live that way.

Then again, she almost understood the looking at life through a glass-half-empty lens. Didn't she constantly do the same thing? Jen lived on the defensive, always had. Maybe she was no better.

With a sigh, she headed to the sun-faded door and knocked. There was no response. She knocked again. When still no one called out or opened up, she dug through her purse and found the spare key.

Inside, the apartment was dark, with the blinds closed and the curtains drawn. Not unusual, but the fact that there was no sign of her mother *was*.

"Mom?" Jen called out.

"In here," a voice answered. Jen's entire body exhaled with relief, but then quickly returned to concern. Why hadn't she gotten out of bed?

After setting down her purse on the chair, she walked down the tiny hall and stepped into the bedroom. Her mother lay on her side, hands pressed under the pillow almost like a child. Her eyes were closed, but her breath appeared steady. She almost looked . . . peaceful. Maybe she was just napping.

Jen walked closer to the bed, noticing a scent of staleness in the room. The entire apartment needed a good cleaning, and that meant she'd need to do that this weekend if it was going to be done anytime soon.

"Mom, you okay?" she asked quietly.

"Mm-hmm," the woman muttered.

"You just napping? Or are you feeling bad?"

"I've got cancer, Jennifer. Of course I'm feeling bad," she said without opening her eyes.

Okay, understanding was one thing. But Jen was also over this poor me act. "You sure do have cancer. And you'll never not have it if you don't change your attitude."

That got her mother's attention, but only an opening of her eyes. "What the hell is that supposed to mean?"

"Just like it sounds. Your outlook on life is not inviting any health to the table."

Jen had made sure to keep her tone light, but her mother managed to jerk her head back while resting it on a pillow. "Do you really think I want to hear nonsense like that?"

So much for light. "Obviously not. But it's the truth. You think your thoughts don't affect your health? Then you're crazy."

"You should start taking your own advice," Diane said, then rolled over and faced the other way. Jen looked at the ceiling in frustration. Half of her wanted to tell the bitter woman in the bed to go straight to hell, but the other half was afraid that if she did, then that's exactly what her mother would do. And then not only would Jen have no family left, but she'd feel enough guilt to last a lifetime.

"Well. I'm going upstairs. Call if you need anything. Or . . . if you're lonely," she added, once again taking the high road.

There was no response, so she walked out of the bedroom. Before leaving she checked her mother's fridge to make sure she had something to eat. Applesauce, some frozen dinners, and several ripe bananas. Good enough.

Once upstairs, Jen took a hot shower—*thank you, TJ*—then lounged in bed eating a can of heated-up chicken noodle soup and watching *The Sound of Music*, her comfort movie. What she always popped in when she was sick, depressed, or tired but couldn't sleep.

She wasn't necessarily any of those right now, but the past week had been bizarre. Times were always tough—throughout her life there'd been little reason for optimism, and this past year was no different. But tonight, something was . . . off. She was restless. Still thinking about all the kisses she'd been having with TJ, trying to decide when it would be okay to take it further. Would it ever be okay? What was with this sudden desire to help her? It was still hard for her to believe that he was interested in her and supposedly had been for some time.

She couldn't make sense of that without resorting to seeing herself as a charity case for him. Or a tempting walk on the wild side. She wasn't stupid, and couldn't deny the fact that she got a lot of male attention, although it wasn't always the kind she desired. Or at the very least, the kind that involved commitment. Which was fine, she'd never been looking for that. But sometimes a woman wanted to know that she was worth more than a good time if she *did* want that.

When it came to TJ, she wondered if he saw her as the girl who represented everything he wasn't. A tattooed, damaged, fallen angel that he could come along and save to stroke his ego. Now that she knew he felt like the outcast of his pretentious family, that possibility seemed even more likely. Maybe he wanted to rub her in their face.

She could still recall Mrs. Laughlin when they'd done a *Grease* teaser for the PTO. She'd worn a fitted navy blazer, a white blouse underneath with the white collar *flipped up*. Who wore their shirt collar flipped up? But that woman had pulled it off with a chunky beaded necklace. Like she'd just stepped out of the fall fashion issue of *Vogue*. Even her jeans had looked expensive, and pressed.

Quite a contrast from Diane's ancient Lee's and GAP-logo tee that had probably been purchased at a yard sale.

She and TJ were from different planets when it came to how they were raised, but Jen still couldn't help feeling like they'd started to connect on another level. She'd enjoyed being in his house, and hadn't felt out of place. That was because of him, shockingly. He made her feel welcome.

Hard to believe that for so long she'd felt like he was judging her, and according to him, he was instead . . . *wanting* her. Maybe her own insecurities had blinded her. But it was beginning to feel like there was no holding back. Whatever their reasons then *and* now, there was no denying the chemistry between them. She wanted him, too. Always had.

Her mother was right, she did need to start taking her own advice. The story she kept telling herself, that she wasn't good enough, that TJ looked down on her, was toxic to her own happiness. She knew down deep that he wasn't a jerk. He was a good man, and it was terrifying. Still, it was time to stop assuming what his intentions were and give in to her own desire. She deserved that, and if she didn't change her attitude, she would push away a good thing. Just like she always did.

# Fifteen

Jen jerked awake. Lights flickered in her bedroom, but she looked down to see that her movie was repeating the menu screen, with the music playing softly. Pulling her hand out from under the covers, she ran it over the blanket searching for the remote. Locating it, she turned off the DVD player and then the TV.

Laying her head back down, she closed her eyes and snuggled back into her sheets. Then the sound of someone yelling caught her attention and she listened for a moment without opening her eyes or getting up.

It was not unusual to hear random noises at night in the Shady Meadow complex. Sometimes there were sirens, even though that was rarer. But it had happened.

She was just settling back into sleep when there was a bang on her front door. Cursing under her breath, she sat up in bed, her heart pounding. Her immediate thought was that going out there and opening it was a terrible idea. If there was some sort of commotion or scuffle between tenants, she wanted no part of it. But what if someone needed help?

The pounding came again, this time harder and frantic, followed by someone yelling what sounded like *"Fire!"* Jen jumped out of bed and raced to the bedroom window. Nothing.

Pulling on a pair of yoga pants, she ran out of her bedroom and headed for her front door. She looked out the peephole but saw no one. Then someone yelled again from somewhere else in the building.

"Everybody get out! There's a fire."

"Oh God." Jen quickly glanced around the room, no idea what she should do next.

Rushing back to her room, she grabbed her phone and then opened the bottom drawer of her dresser to grab the small box that contained her father's letters. After slipping into flip-flops, she ran back to the living room, grabbed her purse, and opened the front door.

She smelled smoke. *Mom!*

Up until that point, waking up to the yelling and banging had felt oddly like a dream. Despite the calls of "fire," her apartment had seemed fine. Safe as on any other night. But now, with the stench of smoke and the faint sound of flames, she knew it was real.

The woman who lived across the breezeway from Jen came out of her apartment with a baby on her hip and holding the hand of her toddler, eyes wide with panic.

"Where's it at?" Jen asked her.

"First floor," she said without stopping. "North side I think."

*First floor.* Shady Meadows was made up several buildings, each with eight apartments, four on top, four on bottom. Many of the buildings were connected by concrete breezeway-type porches, which would make it easy for a fire to spread through the wood roofing and stairs that ran between them.

Jen followed her neighbor down the stairs, suddenly worried that the little boy was having trouble navigating the steps. She leaned down. "I've got him," Jen said as she scooped him into her arms. "Go."

She followed the mother down the steps and into the yard, past the mailboxes, and near the parking lot. Setting the boy down beside her mother, she looked up. "I've got to get my mom."

As she turned back toward the building she saw flames coming out of the apartment next to her mother's. *Oh God.*

Without hesitation, Jen ran through the yard in that direction. As soon as she reached the mailboxes she heard a familiar voice screaming.

"Jen! Jen, open up!"

She stopped in her tracks and glanced up at the second-floor breezeway where her front door was located. And there was her mother, banging on her apartment door. Diane was throwing her arms against the metal door like she could break it down, and the look of anguish on her face made Jen's heartbreak.

"Mom!" She screamed. But the sound of the quickly growing fire and the bustling of hysteric people had become a buzz of noise around them. Jen began to take the stairs two at a time. "Mom, I'm down here!"

Hitting the second floor, Jen pivoted and headed toward her apartment. Her mom was still standing there, now beginning to become frantic. "Jennifer! My daughter's in here." She yelled over her shoulder to the ground below.

"Mom! I'm here!" Jen yelled.

Diane turned, and her face took on a look of such intense relief it made Jen gasp.

"Jen!" Her mother burst into tears. "Oh, Jen!'

"Mom, it's okay. Come on."

Grabbing her hand, Jen begin to lead her down the steps, through the smoke now wafting up from the first floor. Her mother continued to sob, and Jen squeezed her hand as they rushed down the sidewalk and onto the grass on the far side of the parking lot.

There were now at least fifty people watching the flames travel quickly through the buildings, and that's when they heard the sirens. Jen turned to her crying mother, opened her arms, and they embraced.

They were both alive. They still had each other.


The sound of his phone vibrating on the nightstand roused TJ from his sleep. Reaching out, he grabbed it and turned it over. Dean. Weird. It was a little after three in the morning.

"Hello?" TJ said, after clearing his throat.

"Hey, man, sorry to wake you up."

TJ rolled over and ran a hand down his face. "No problem. Something wrong?"

A heavy sigh on the other end of the line got his attention.

"Dean? What's going on?" TJ asked, suddenly feeling uneasy.

"Everyone is fine. I probably should have waited till morning, but I knew you'd want to know right away."

TJ sat up in bed as Dean continued. "Jen's apartment building caught fire."

TJ's heart crashed into his stomach. "What?" He instantly threw back the sheet and got out of bed. "Where is she? Her mother? Are they okay?"

"Yes, yes. Relax. They're both fine. Actually, they're both asleep in Charlotte's guest room.

TJ grabbed a pair of jeans. "I'm coming over."

"No, listen, man. Don't do that. Everyone is fine. Wait until morning."

"You're kidding, right?" TJ asked, walking over to his dresser for a clean shirt. "There's no way I'm going back to sleep now."

"I get that," Dean said. "But they were exhausted. They're asleep now. And we're going back to sleep, too. There's nothing for you to do here. But she'll need you tomorrow."

Unsure what do to with himself, TJ walked into the bathroom and sat down on the edge of the tub. "How did it happen?"

"No idea yet. Hopefully they'll know more in a day or so."

"Did . . . anyone die?"

"No. When we left, only one man wasn't accounted for, but they think he might be at work or at a girl-friend's. A few people were taken to the hospital to be checked out, but I don't think anyone was seriously injured."

That was good news, but he was still shaking with emotion. "I can't fucking believe this. That place is a pit. What I'd like to do right now is go strangle who-ever runs the place."

"I understand how you feel," Dean said quietly.

TJ sat up straight and rubbed at his chest, which was feeling tight. He'd never experienced the sensation before. "Why didn't she call *me*?"

"I don't know. Didn't want to bother you, maybe?"

"That's bullshit, Dean. How could she be okay bothering *you*?" TJ was suddenly furious at that thought.

"She didn't call me. She called Charlotte."

TJ sighed, feeling a little better with that, but still not satisfied. They were now a thing—they'd just discussed it that day. And he'd kissed her not even twelve hours ago. He should have been her first call. No hesitation. But she didn't choose him, and he wasn't sure if that made him furious or hurt. He was angling toward both.

*Oh God*, if anything had happened to her. That burning in his chest started up again. He stood up. "Shit, I feel like I'm gonna have a goddamn heart attack," he muttered.

"Take a deep breath," Dean said. "It's anxiety. I've felt it, trust me."

He walked back through his room and headed for the hallway. "I need to see her, Dean. I've got to come over."

"You'll be no help here, TJ. What you can do is start thinking of what we can all do to help. We're too exhausted after this, but you can start making a list. Do some research."

That all made sense, but TJ was hung up on one thought. As he made his way down the stairs, he asked, "What time did Charlotte hear from her?"

Dean hesitated. "About twelve thirty."

"And you're *just now* calling me?" He stepped into his kitchen and flipped on the light.

"She asked me not to," Dean said. "I'm sorry. Truly. But Jen asked that of me, and I couldn't blatantly disrespect her trust like that. Even though I'm doing it now, but because you're my friend and I'd want you to do the same for me."

TJ cursed under his breath, nearly bruising his fist on the quartz counter of his kitchen island. How could she do that to him? Especially after this morning's conversation.

"Hold on, I hear something," Dean said. The phone muffled and then Dean was back. "Sorry, somebody just went into the bathroom."

"Was it her?"

"Might have been. Charlotte was falling asleep when I came out to call you."

TJ's phone alerted him of another call. Pulling it away from his ear, he saw her name. "Dean, I gotta go. It's her."

Without giving his friend a chance to reply, he hit the SWAP button. "Jen?"

"Hi," she said in a voice so quiet and vulnerable he might not have recognized it to be hers had he not known. "I'm sorry to wake—"

"Babe, I know. I already know. I'm so sorry."

As if relieved from the need to explain, she began to cry. The sound—her quiet gasps and sobs—nearly ripped his heart out.

This . . . this was different. The sounds traveling through the phone were of her completely breaking down. Tears of pain and despair. And it was killing him.

Bending over, he laid a hand on the counter, as if it could hold him up. "Jen. Tell me what to do. I want to come over."

"No," she cried. "We're fine." She sniffled, and then the crying resumed. "I'm sorry. I just . . . I can't stop."

"Baby, it's okay. I know," he said. "Are you sure you're not hurt?"

"Yes. I'm sure."

"What about your mom?"

"She's fine."

"And you don't know how bad the damage is yet?"

"I'm pretty sure my mom's unit was destroyed. It was hard to tell how bad it had gotten from all the smoke. But it was just so terrible," she cried, fresh tears starting up again. "One woman—my mom's neighbor—has three kids. She's a single mom. And she stood there bawling as she watched her apartment burn up. What if she hadn't gotten all those kids out, TJ?"

"But she did, Jen. It sounds as if everyone is safe."

"What will we do now?" she asked quietly.

"Don't worry about that right now, Jen. We'll figure it out. You're not alone."

When she didn't respond right away, he spoke again. "Jen, did you hear me?"

She cleared her throat and said, "Yes," her voice a little stronger.

"I want to come over there with you."

"No. That's not necessary. I just . . . I guess I just wanted to call you."

"I'm glad you did. I really wish you'd have called me right away. You have to know that."

"I hate needing anything, you have to know *that*."

He threw his head back and sighed. "Jennifer Mackenzie, I *want* you to need me. Can you please get that through your thick skull? I want to be the person you call. Always."

The line went silent.

"Jen?" he prodded.

"I heard you. It's just difficult for me."

"I understand, but you need to realize that needing help is not a character flaw. Or a sign of weakness."

"I'm trying, TJ."

"I know." The damaged sound to her was so unfamiliar, he was struggling not to get in his car, to hell with her wishes. But he also knew that this was exactly the kind of emotion Jen probably avoided at all costs. She hadn't called him—or wanted Dean to call—for a reason. She had too much pride for her own good. But she'd finally called him anyway, and he had to see that for the gift it was. If he pushed too hard right now, he'd end up regretting it.

"I'm going to go back to bed," she said.

Panic seized him again, but he pushed it down. He understood she was tired. "Okay. I understand. I'll be there in a few hours. Okay?"

"You don't hav—"

"Jen. Stop. I will be there in a few hours."

"Okay," she finally said.

"Okay."

"Good night," she said quietly.

There felt like more he needed to say and promise. But instead he just replied in kind.

"Good night, Jen."

# Sixteen

Jen opened her eyes when she felt a tap on her back.

"Are you awake?" her mother asked.

"I am now," she answered, rolling over in the bed. Thank goodness Charlotte had a guest room with a queen-size bed for them to use. After getting off the phone with TJ, Jen had slept like the dead.

Now, facing her mother, she gave a tentative smile. "You sleep good?"

"Had a lot of nightmares."

Jen frowned. "I'm sorry. What about?" Although she could guess. She'd had a few herself.

Diane sighed and rolled on her back. "Variations of last night."

After the fire trucks had shown up, they'd watched them work, completely in shock, for about twenty minutes. Everyone had wanted answers, but they just kept saying it would take a few days to know.

Along with the fire department, three ambulances had come to check everyone out. That was when Jen had called Charlotte, after debating who to call for a while. She'd wanted to call TJ, and almost had, but it had seemed so presumptuous. And it was late. They'd just started to be more than friends.

She'd had a million excuses.

But she didn't regret calling Charlotte, who had come with Dean immediately and insisted they come home with her. After hot showers and some tea, Jen and her mother had gone to bed. It was then—after Diane had begun to snore—that the despair and trauma of the night had set in. That was when she'd suddenly needed to speak to TJ so bad that she felt like she'd burst apart if she didn't. And she hadn't been surprised that Dean had already called and filled him in. She'd almost expected it.

"We're safe. That's all that matters," Jen said to her mother.

Her mom was still staring up at the ceiling, and a tear ran down her face, trailing into her wispy hairline.

"I was so afraid, Jen."

As she watched her mother's lips tremble, Jen felt her own begin to do the same. "I know."

Diane shook her head back and forth. "You don't understand. I smelled the smoke, heard someone bang on my door, and I debated just not doing anything about it."

"*Mom.*"

"The only thing that finally got me out of the bed was realizing that if my apartment was in peril, then yours was, too. And then—" She broke at that point, and let out a quiet sob.

"It's okay, Mom." Jen patted her mother's arm. They'd hadn't been affectionate in what felt like a

lifetime. As a little girl Jen would be the one to initiate it, and her mother would reciprocate to a point, but
it had never been enough. Eventually, she'd sort of just
stopped trying. Right now, touching her on the arm
felt like an intimate gesture. "We're both okay."

"If anything had happened to you, Jen . . ."

"I know," Jen said, wanting to take her pain away.
It was hard to process the fact that this was her
mother—Diane Mackenzie—lying here and exposing
herself in such a raw and emotional way. When Jen
imagined the sight of her mother pounding on the door
like a madwoman, it was like she was witnessing an
alternate reality, and although it was only hours before,
it felt like days had passed.

Diane used her hands to wipe under both eyes.
"Goddamn it." She slapped her arms down on the bed.
"I've never wanted a smoke so bad in my life."

Jen winced. It was almost tempting to get up and
go get her some after what they'd just been through.
"You've come so far, Mom. I'm really proud of you."

Her mother turned and looked at Jen, a partial smile
playing at her lips. "Didn't think I had it in me."

"You're strong," Jen said, realizing she meant it. Her
mother was—and was not—many things. But she was
always strong as hell.

Diane groaned quietly, staring up at the ceiling once
more. "What the hell are we going to do now? No
home. No belongings. Not even a clean pair of underwear."

Jen almost laughed at the change in tone. But it
wasn't that surprising. It wasn't as if she thought they
were going to hug and start making up for lost time.

"I don't know. I guess we go see if we can salvage anything. I heard someone say all the sprinklers in each unit came on, so I'm guessing a lot is ruined."

"The smoke damage alone will have destroyed everything in the building, I bet," Diane said. "And we know those flames reached mine."

"Yes." The image of what was once her mom's front door engulfed by fire was imprinted on Jen's brain.

"You have renter's insurance, don't you?" her mom asked suddenly.

"I had to, but I know I got the cheapest option available."

"Better than nothing," Diane replied.

The sound of voices beyond the door caught Jen's attention. "What time is it?" Jen asked. She knew it had to be late because, although the blinds on the window were pulled, the sun penetrating the cracks was bright.

Her mother turned to look at a clock on the bedside table. "Nine forty-eight."

"Holy shit." Jen sat up and rubbed at her face. "We're being rude."

"Jennifer, we were up all night watching our apartments burn down. I'm sure they understand us sleeping in."

"I know, but still." Plus, she wondered where TJ was. She should check her phone. Standing up, she walked over to the chair where she'd left her clothes, to find that Charlotte had washed and folded them. Yoga pants and a tank top. Now possibly the only clothes Jen owned in the whole world. She didn't even have a bra, because she hadn't been wearing one when she left her apartment.

Thankfully when Charlotte and Dean had arrived, Charlotte had gone to grab a jacket she'd had in her car for Jen to wear so she could stop crossing her arms over her chest in embarrassment. It hadn't even occurred to her to grab a bra when she'd left.

What a harrowing thought, to realize you may not even own one single bra. Jen glanced down at what she'd slept in. A pair of sweats and a T-shirt that Charlotte had given her. Diane had received the same thing. They really owed her for coming to their rescue.

Deciding it was better to wear this out into the kitchen to say good morning, she turned to her mom. "I'm going to go out. You coming?"

"Maybe in a little bit."

Jen nodded, and then opened the door. Before she headed to the kitchen, she made a quick detour to the restroom and took in her appearance. *Ugh.*

Red eyes stared back at her from the mirror. She looked like she'd just been through hell. Which, she figured, was a fair statement, all things considered. Her hair was clean, but she'd slept on it damp, so it was crazy. But there was nothing to be done. She had no brush. No makeup. That thought alone almost made her weep.

Thankfully Charlotte had given her an extra toothbrush, so she quickly brushed her teeth. That would have to be enough.

When she opened the bathroom door, she immediately recognized TJ's voice coming from the kitchen, which gave her a sudden feeling of excitement, but also panic. She stepped down the hall, through the living room, crossing her arms over her chest to conceal her lack of an undergarment.

TJ was sitting at Charlotte's small island on a stool. They were all drinking coffee. It smelled like heaven.

Dean saw her first. "Morning, sleepyhead. How you feeling?"

TJ jerked around and was off the stool, wrapping his arms around her before she could even take a breath. And then she actually couldn't breathe, because he had her in a vice grip, with her arms at her sides, and his strong arms around her entire body. If she was going to pass out from asphyxiation, this would be the only way to do it.

"It was killing me to let you sleep. I was dying to see you," he said against her hair.

Angling her hand, Jen tapped him on the hip.

"TJ . . . I think you're hurting her," Charlotte said from the kitchen.

He immediately let go and stepped back. "I'm sorry."

"It's okay." She smiled, a little embarrassed at his display of affection. But when she glanced back to the kitchen, Dean and Charlotte had left them alone. Glancing back at him, she saw he was staring down at her with an odd look on his face.

"What is it?" she asked, suddenly feeling self-conscious.

His lips quirked. "I've never seen you with no makeup on." Before she could reply with some self-deprecating retort, he went on. "I've never seen you look more beautiful."

She was speechless.

TJ put his hands on her face, leaned down, and kissed her softly. "Is this okay?" he whispered against her lips.

"Yes." It was more than okay.

She could feel his grin, before he kissed her again. Wrapping her arms around his waist, she kissed him back, finally feeling something beyond despair and sadness. This was what she wanted.

His tongue twisting with hers. His lips on her face, jaw, and neck.

Once he'd kissed her thoroughly, and for long enough to make her warm and melty, he pulled back. "I've been up since we talked."

"You're kidding. I'm sorry." Jen gently pulled from his embrace and walked into the kitchen. A mug sat beside the coffee maker, so she used it. "I should have waited to call you."

"Jen, no. I already made it clear how I felt about that." He followed her into the kitchen, leaning a hip on the counter as she filled her mug. "What I was going to say is that I've had all morning to think about what we should do."

She opened the refrigerator to look for some sort of milk or creamer. "TJ, I don't need you to worry about this. My mom and I have each other. We'll figure something out." How or what, she had no idea, but him feeling responsible for helping her was one of the reasons she'd hesitated to contact him last night.

"I know I don't have to worry about this. But I want to. And my thought was that . . . you and Diane should stay with me for the weekend."

She looked up at him. "Are you serious?"

He pushed off the counter "Yes. It makes perfect sense. Where else would you go?"

"I actually hadn't thought that far ahead yet. But I honestly don't know." She bought herself some time to think by taking a sip of her coffee. He took the opportunity to step closer and touched her elbow.

"I have two extra bedrooms at my house. You have nowhere to go, and it's already Friday. Stay the weekend."

"I'll talk to my mom. See what she wants to do."

He nodded. "Okay, good.

A laugh escaped her lips. "Not even an official date and we're talking about me staying the weekend. With my mother."

He grinned. "I can't think of anything more official than that."


The first thing Jen and Diane did was call their insurance companies, at TJ's insistence. "It's Friday. Let them hear from you as soon as possible so you can get this going."

That was the kind of thing she normally might have procrastinated on, but she was glad he'd made a fuss, because at least now she knew what she was dealing with. And as it turned out, Jen *had* gotten the cheapest insurance. No surprise. They informed her that she would receive replacement value on her possessions up to twenty thousand dollars, but they would need documentation, and pictures would be even better. Her policy had covered no interim housing. Basically, she was homeless, but she'd kind of already deduced that when her apartment caught on fire.

Her mom on the other hand, had been a little wiser. Her policy not only covered housing in a temporary apartment unit for six months, and replacement value, but also for her salvageable things to be professionally cleaned.

"Not fair. How much were you paying for that?" Jen asked after they'd both finished.

Diane shrugged. "Fifty bucks a month."

"Damn. Mine was thirty. If I'd have known . . ."

"No big deal," TJ said. "At least you get the replacement value. And you have a place to stay. We can go in there as soon as they give you the all-clear and take some photos."

She didn't push him on the place-to-stay comment. After the insurance phone calls, they'd driven back to the complex in daylight. Jen and her mom had both agreed that they needed to see what had happened. It was a harrowing site. Diane's building was gutted, since that was where the fire had apparently started. Jen's side wasn't nearly as bad, since the two were separated by open breezeways, but the flames had traveled through one unit on that end to the north side of Jen's place, destroying it, and effectively turning on all the sprinkler systems in the building just as Jen had heard from another tenant the night before. According to the fire chief they spoke to, the smoke and water damage was bound to be extensive throughout the entire structure. It was likely that almost all of Jen's possessions would be in need of cleaning, or beyond repair.

The man had also mentioned that they believed there was asbestos in the ceiling, so there was a chance they wouldn't be able to go in for even longer than first thought. Maybe not even for a week.

Even though they'd expected the visit to be difficult, all of that had been hard to hear. And even harder to see, although her mother seemed to handle it better than one would have expected. Jen assumed it had a lot to do with the fact that for most of her life, Diane had been a wanderer. They'd had so many temporary homes, and they'd always traveled light. There probably weren't a lot of sentimental possessions, but they had both lived at Shady Meadows for about six years, so it was difficult with or without the loss of stuff. It had been their home.

As Jen kept randomly thinking of something she'd lost, her sadness would renew all over again. Her signed copy of *Outlander*, the pictures and playbill of *Grease* from high school, and her favorite pair of boots. That one alone had nearly made her cry.

But she was also secretly grateful that she'd had a moment to retrieve her special box. It contained what mattered most. The things that could truly never ever be replaced. Her father's letters and their one photo. The only piece of him she'd ever had. She hadn't shared that with her mother, since it was uncertain how she would react.

The day didn't seem to get any better until she and her mother had gone to Target to get some of the bare necessities. Toothbrushes, makeup, underwear, bras, and a few articles of clothing for each of them. Because her mother hadn't even made it out with her purse, Jen had opened a new store credit card before they started shopping, just so they could get what they needed. She knew her mother would pay her back when she got her insurance money, but the whole thing still made her feel a little nervous. Those were the kind of decisions that had gotten her into the bind she was in today. She'd been surprised they'd even issued her a credit card.

Thank goodness they had, though, because by far the best part of the day was the shopping. They'd truly seemed to enjoy each other's company, something that Jen had never experienced. Her mom had even laughed a couple of times as they'd tried on clothes, then quietly allowed Jen to help her choose a pair of shoes. Even suggested a few things for Jen, which she'd actually liked. As great as it was, it almost made Jen sad, because now she knew what she'd been missing. What she would lose, if her mother didn't beat this cancer. For the first time in a long time, they'd felt like a true mother and daughter, not just two women tolerating each other.

On the way out to TJ's, Jen picked up some pizza. It was the least she could do, besides, she and Diane hadn't really eaten all day and they were starving. As soon as they pulled into the driveway, TJ came out the front door. The sight of him had Jen holding back a smile as she got out of the car.

"Need help?" he asked, heading for the bed of her truck.

"We do, actually. We had to buy quite a bit."

"I bet." He instantly grabbed a half dozen plastic bags in his big hands. "Diane, you go on in. I'll take care of all this."

"Thank you, TJ. And I'm very grateful to you for

letting us stay the weekend." Jen watched her mom squeeze TJ's arm as she walked around the truck. Diane's insurance agent had guesstimated that he'd have living arrangements for her by Monday, so the weekend idea had worked out perfectly. Her mom had casually mentioned that Jen could stay with her in whatever place the insurance company provided, but as great of a day as they were having, the thought of living with her mother for any extended amount of time sounded kind of awful. She had, however, appreciated the offer. Then again, there was a chance Jen wouldn't have a choice but to accept it.

"You go in, too," TJ said to Jen. "I can come back and get the rest."

"That's ridiculous, I'm right here." She scooped up the final three bags and they walked up to the house.

"This is just beautiful." Diane was sitting on the porch swing waiting for them.

"Thank you," TJ said. "I just had it built last year." He went to the front door and opened it for them, letting Diane and Jen go in first.

The rubber plant was still in its spot, with its little fairy, which made Jen smile. In general the home was pretty gender neutral, with earth colors like white, gray, and hints of blue. But that fairy was decidedly feminine. It wasn't ostentatious so if you didn't know it was there, you may not notice it, but Jen knew. And she loved it.

"You want all this on the table so you can go through it?" TJ asked.

"Uh, sure. I guess so," Jen said.

Diane interjected. "Why don't we take it to where

you want us to sleep? I'd hate to make a mess in your kitchen."

"Whatever you want," he said. "Won't bother me either way." He looked at Jen and gave her a subtle wink. "I guess it might be easier to take it up in bags, though."

It was decided, so they both followed TJ up the stairs. Jen hadn't been up here yet, and to say she was curious was an understatement. At the landing, he took a right, but Jen's eyes went left, into what had to be the master bedroom. The bed was unmade, bright white sheets and a gray blanket tossed back. That surprised her. TJ seemed like a make-your-bed every morning kind of guy. Of course she and Dean had woken him up in the wee hours of the morning.

"Here's one bedroom," he said. It was plain, with light-gray walls, a queen-size bed with side table, and a small dresser, and that was about it. "Sorry they aren't fancy. Thankfully, I got some basic furniture when I moved in, but I just today took the mattresses out of the plastic and made the beds. These rooms have never been used."

Jen couldn't help imagining him rushing home to make up beds for her and her mom. It was possibly the sweetest thing she'd ever heard of. "Thank you. This is just fine," Diane spoke up, sitting down on the bed. "It feels better than my own." Nobody mentioned that she no longer owned a bed.

TJ set all the bags on the mattress beside Diane and then turned to Jen. "Okay, other room." He nodded toward the door and she followed him.

"This is the bathroom." He pointed to a room at

the end of the hall, and then pivoted to the room closer to the master bedroom. He flipped on the light and stepped in. "And this is the other room."

It was slightly smaller than the first one, but still nice. It had the same dresser and side table as the first room. The only difference was a plant sitting on the dresser. The calathea and its fairy. The sight of it made her eyes begin to burn a bit.

She felt TJ step up beside her, his chest touching her shoulder as his hands settled on her arms, then his nose brushing the curve of her ear. "I'm glad you're here," he whispered.

Turning her head, she glanced up at him, and his mouth settled on her forehead. Closing her eyes, Jen relished this moment. The feeling of being cared for. Even though he'd made her feel that way before, it still felt foreign. But it was beginning to be a little less terrifying since he insisted on making a habit of it.

Trust was something Jen was unfamiliar with, but she was starting to see what it might feel like. Vulnerable and uncertain, yes. But with TJ, also a sense of relief. Comfort. Optimism. Things she'd almost never felt before with any sort of consistency.

"I'm glad too," she said. "And I love the plant in here."

He touched her face. "I wanted you to feel at home."

"I do. I'm just . . . still not used to this. You helping me. Touching me . . . like this," she whispered, glancing at the door.

Never missing even her most subtle cue, TJ reached back and pushed the door shut so they'd have privacy. Then he looked down at her and responded. "Well, you need to get used to it, Jen. Because I'm happy to do it. You have no idea."

She sucked in a breath. "I hate that it's because my life has been such a mess lately."

He shook his head. "Jen, everyone has times like this. And I don't care what the reason is. I'll take any opportunity to be what you need."

Her stomach growled and they laughed silently, foreheads close to touching. "Right now, I need some pizza. I brought some. It's on the seat of my truck."

"You didn't need to do that. But I'll go get it. Grab your mom and meet me in the kitchen."

She nodded as he stepped toward the door. Before he left, he looked back at her. "Just so you know"—he glanced at the bed—"I'd be just fine if you chose not to sleep in here."

And then he was gone.

There was only one way to interpret that.

# Seventeen

Later that evening, after they'd eaten and sorted out all their things, and Jen had done a load of laundry, she said good night to her mother.

"I'll see you in the morning, Mom. Do you want your door shut or open?"

"Shut. In case I snore."

Jen smiled, still amused by the sight of her mother in her new cat pajamas. Seeing her in such a flimsy top reminded Jen of something. "Mom, you need to call the doctor and let him know you don't have access to your medicine. They will definitely want to get you some right away."

"Oh, yes. I already did that," Diane said.

Jen tilted her head. "When?"

"Earlier today. I'll ask Terri if she can run me over tomorrow to pick it up."

"I can take you."

"Oh, okay. We can talk about it tomorrow."

Jen nodded. "Night, Mom."

"Hey," her mother said. Jen turned back. "Why aren't

you sleeping in his room, if you guys are seeing each other?"

Jen hesitated, then sighed. If she wanted a close relationship, she'd have to be honest. "That wasn't true, Mom. TJ was kind of protecting me from your judgment. He and I . . . this is all sort of new."

Diane stared at her from her seat on the bed. "He likes you a lot."

Jen shrugged. "Maybe."

"Maybe my ass. He does, and it doesn't surprise me one bit. Any man would be lucky to have you, Jen, and TJ is obviously a good one. You should give him a chance."

Considering that, Jen smiled and nodded, then pulled the door shut. She turned to head to her own room, then stopped at the doorway and listened. She could hear water running from the master bedroom as if TJ was brushing his teeth or washing his face. It was easy to picture him standing at the sink, bare chested, sexy as hell.

Without thinking, she walked to his door, gently pushed it open, and stepped quietly into his room before shutting the door behind her. The bed was still unmade, a soft lamp lit on his nightstand. The room smelled spicy, like his cologne, and she was tempted to just lie down in that big bed and wait for him. Instead, she peeked in through the bathroom door.

Sure enough she'd imagined correctly. There he stood in front of a beautiful double-sink vanity, in low-hung jeans and no shirt. *Thank you, Universe.* What struck her the most was that he was . . . flossing. She grinned, watching the flex of his biceps and shoulders as he worked. How could a human look hot flossing? Somehow he pulled it off.

"As if you weren't perfect enough," she said. He jerked a little at her voice, but his face was full of amusement. "You're also a flosser."

He dropped the string in a small trash can and then stalked slowly toward her. "Isn't everyone?"

"Pshh." She pointed at him. "Only the sexy people, apparently."

Now toe to toe, he looked down at her. "That theory doesn't hold up unless you floss, because you are definitely one of the sexy people."

Sometimes she felt pretty, and she liked her looks. But often she just felt like that weird girl back in high school. Just trying not to make a fool of herself. Or at the very least, make it look like she was weird on purpose. But right now, she wanted more. Wanted to feel beautiful and sexy. And she wanted it from him.

"Then make me feel like one," she whispered.

His hands instantly came up to cup her jaw on both sides, tilting her lips up to his. And he leaned down, his mouth pressing into hers so lovingly she wanted to cry. But tonight she needed something different, so she pushed back with a little more aggression, letting him know exactly what she wanted. Instantly he received the message and began to devour her, his mouth attacking hers with so much force she had to step back, her hands going to his waistband to hold on.

Finding her footing, she kissed him back, and it was like a match sparked between them. Their lips fusing, tongues clashing, each seeking dominance over the other. His kisses trailed down her neck, up to her ear, sending all the heat in her body to one place.

"I need this," she said against his mouth. "I need you."

"I'm right here. Whatever you need," he muttered, his teeth nipping at her lips one last time before he stepped away far enough to get a hold of her pajama top and pull it over her head in one quick motion.

Jen had always had mixed feelings about her somewhat large breasts. They caused backaches, kept her from wearing cute bras, and made certain tops out of the question. But as TJ looked at her bare chest, all she could think was, *Yes, look at me like that forever.* She had heard his intake of breath, watched his throat as he swallowed. As he reached one hand up to gently run a finger along the underside of her left breast, his lips quirked. "This might be the best night of my life."

"Make sure it's mine, too," she responded with a smile.

"It will be my pleasure." He grabbed her hand and walked backward toward his bed. The minute he sat down, his hands grasped her torso and he yanked gently, insinuating her between his legs as his mouth instantly closed on her nipple. Jen's head fell back as he slid his large hands over her ribs, under each breast, plumping them up toward his mouth as he sucked and licked.

"Oh my God," she said quietly, her hands threading into his hair. "Don't stop."

"Never," he muttered, moving to the other nipple. And he didn't for several moments, as if he could die making love to her breasts.

Jen had finally had enough. She wanted more.

She shoved his shoulders, and he fell back onto the bed. Her eyes took in his beautiful chest, covered lightly with hair that led down his abdomen and then grew sparser as it disappeared under his jeans. And that was exactly where her hands went, to the fly on his pants.

TJ angled up, leaning on his elbows and watching as she undid the button and zipper, and then gently pulled down on his underwear. She just wanted to see him, couldn't wait any longer.

He lifted his hips off the bed so she could get a hold of his jeans, and she tugged gently, her breathing growing shallower as dark pubic hair came into view. Pulling again, she got the pants halfway down his butt, far enough the see the very base of his shaft, and the outline of what lay beneath his light-blue underwear.

Before she could take what she wanted, he rolled onto one elbow, reached into his underwear, and pulled out his erection for her.

"Impatient?" she asked, amused.

"You have no fucking idea."

Oh she had an idea alright, because her mouth was already watering at the sight of him. Just watching him grab a hold of himself like that was a turn-on. She needed it in a GIF on her phone, so she could play it over and over until she was an old woman.

But for now, she would do what came naturally. What she'd only dreamed of. Leaning down, she angled her head just right in order to lick him long and slow from base to tip before sucking him into her mouth.

TJ just barely held in a deep, chest-aching groan, as he watched Jen's mouth engulf the head of his dick.

She gave it a hardy suck, and his ass came off the bed.

"Holy shit," he whispered, suddenly remembering that they weren't alone in the house. She lowered her hot mouth, taking him in as far as she could, and his eyes nearly saw the back of his head.

This was certainly not his first blow job, but this was Jen. And seeing her plump lips wrapped around him was almost more than he could bear. She returned to licking, her tongue running carefully up and down his shaft and then swirling around the top.

"Yes, do that again," he muttered quietly. She did, this time with more pressure, ending with another long slide inside of her mouth. At that moment, he couldn't help pumping once. When she didn't seem to mind, he braced his feet on the bed frame and did it again, slowly but a little deeper this time. Her eyes met his, and the site was pure bliss as her lips met the dark hair at the base of his erection. "You're killing me, Jen."

After a few minutes more, he was so close it was painful. "Get up here, babe."

Releasing him, she stood, her mouth red. TJ nodded toward the little pajama shorts she had on. "Take those off."

"These?" she asked coyly.

He grinned, as he worked his jeans and underwear off the rest of the way. "Yes, those. Please."

When she hesitated, giving him a haughty look, his only thought was, *There's my girl*. He'd loved this new vulnerability to her he'd seen lately, but it was the fierce, sarcastic woman that he'd always been obsessed with. There was no better time to see that side of her than right now, while he was naked and at her mercy.

"Do I need to entice you?" he asked.

"Maybe so," she said, taking a step back.

"I'd be happy to." Sitting up, TJ got off the bed and slowly kneeled in front of her. The first thing he did was run his hands up her legs—so soft, so strong—around to her ass. He cupped it, slipping the tips of his finger under the elastic of her shorts and panties. Her hands went to his head, weaving into his hair, and he tilted his eyes up to meet hers only to find that they were closed, her eyelids fluttering like fairy wings. She still hadn't put any makeup on and it was like looking at a softer, more innocent version of the Jen he adored. No more, or less beautiful, just . . . pure.

This was the Jen that only he could have. That was how he wanted it to be.

Instead of pulling her underwear down over her bottom, he tugged her forward, forcing her front against his chin. Her eyes flew open, meeting his, and he placed a kiss on her mound.

"Take them off," she whispered.

He smirked, slowly pulling the cloth down. First over her backside, exposing her ass. He gave each cheek a firm squeeze and then let his palms slide up to her hips where he finished lowering the pants completely. She parted her thighs a bit so he could get them off fully and toss them to the side. Then he just took her in. Perfectly groomed—not too much, not too little. Running a finger down through her folds, he leaned forward and placed a soft kiss on her skin. Another.

Finally, he pivoted on his knees, turning her body with him until her butt was against the mattress.

He didn't need to tell her what to do, she laid right back on the bed. TJ grabbed her feet, one in each hand and placed them up on the mattress to each side of her. He waited for her to protest—many women would at being so completely exposed—but she said nothing. The site had him hard as steel.

"Jesus, Jen," he said. "You are so beautiful."

This time when he ran his finger down her, it slipped inside, and she moaned.

"Shhh," he said, before leaning in and giving her a long, firm, lick from bottom to top.

It wasn't long before he was all over her. Lips, tongue, nose, pleasuring her however he thought would bring her to climax.

This was the closest to an out-of-body experience TJ would ever come. The sound of her quiet moans and whimpers, the feel of her hands locked down on his hair, and the taste of her in his mouth. It was too good to be true.

"Oh my God, right there, TJ. Please." Her whispers were so quiet he almost didn't hear her. But he stiffened his tongue, pushed her thighs back, and licked at her until she finally broke, her legs vibrating against his palms, her head jerking off the bed. He lifted his gaze to see her eyes pinched shut, front teeth biting down on her lower lip, and oh shit, it was so good to know that she was coming this hard because of him.

When her head fell back to the bed, he slowed down,

easing her from her orgasm. He placed soft kisses over her wet skin as he listened to her shaky breaths.

"You ready for another one?" he finally asked.

She laughed quietly and then lifted her head to look down at him. "I'm ready for as many as you can give me."

He smiled and then grabbed a condom from the nightstand as he stood up. She waited patiently, watching him, still in that erotic pose on the edge of the bed. Perfect, he would have absolutely love taking her just like that.

She lifted up, leaning on her elbows and watched him roll on the condom. Stepping forward, he rested one hand on her knee, and with the other held his cock right at her entrance.

"Ready?" he asked quietly.

She laughed quietly. "Did you really just ask if I was ready? As if this position implied anything else."

He smiled. "This position"—he stroked the head of his penis through her folds—"is the most perfect sight I've ever seen in my life. It will forever be my go-to mental porn."

She gave a light moan, her eyes fluttering shut for a moment. "Just please put it inside me. Right now."

"Say that again." He slid in just an inch.

They stared at each other, and she whispered. "Fuck me right now, Trevor James."

He shoved in the rest of the way, her slickness sucking him in, her heat enveloping him. She lowered her legs, wrapping them around his waist, pulling him in deeper. That was all it took to know this was what he'd always wanted. This was heaven.

It wasn't long before he was pounding into her as hard as he could while simultaneously trying not to make much noise. When he was close, and her legs began to shake, he leaned down and muted their cries of release by kissing her deep and thoroughly.

His first thought after coming down from the high was that it had been well worth waiting for.

# Eighteen

That Saturday, to TJ's dismay, Jen had to bartend a wedding at the Stag, and unfortunately it wasn't his night. It was Dean's, which meant it was just him and Diane alone in the house. Although she wasn't anywhere as outgoing and funny as Jen, TJ had always liked Jen's mother. He hadn't spent a lot of time around her, but a few times she'd been at the Stag over the years for one reason or another. She was a little sarcastic and salty, but usually in a likable way—if he didn't count that morning at Jen's when he'd overheard her being so awful. From what he could tell, the two seemed to have been getting along, so he hoped things would continue down that course.

As for him spending an entire evening with Diane? That was different. Fine—he didn't mind it—but he had no clue what to say or do. She'd spent the late afternoon taking a nap, and he decided to make them a couple of salads with some chicken on the grill for dinner. He planned to just see how things played out after that. He'd leave her to the TV, or maybe she'd just want to chill in her room. Whatever.

It was a bit awkward that she must know that Jen had spent the previous night in his bed, considering when they'd gotten up that morning, Diane had already been up and made coffee. Jen's bedroom door had been wide open, bed made and tidy. When TJ had pointed it out to Jen, she'd just shrugged it off. She was thirty years old. It wasn't as if she needed permission to sleep with him. But still, it *was* her mother.

It was a beautiful late August evening, so he'd suggested they eat out on the back patio. Things were going well. Diane had praised his cooking skills, which was unnecessary but kind, and now they were sitting outside enjoying the perfect weather.

And then she surprised him with an insane question.

"Do you intend to propose to my daughter?"

TJ nearly choked on a piece of chicken. He took a quick drink of his water to give him a moment to collect his thoughts. "That's quite a question, Diane."

She shrugged and took another bite of her salad. Chewing silently, she looked around his property. "You've got a lot to offer a woman. Seems like you built this house with a family in mind."

He pushed a piece of lettuce with his fork. "It was something I considered. Would have been stupid not to."

"And you like her."

"I do. I have for a long time." No point in lying.

"Do you love her?"

He blew out a breath, took another drink, then turned to the woman clearly waiting for an answer. From what he could tell, Diane was a straight shooter. He didn't see any reason to not be blunt in return.

"I do love her. Of course." And it was true, he hadn't even struggled to say it, which shocked him. "But . . . I'm not sure what kind of love that is right now. I know it's the kind of love that wants to help her through this fire ordeal. It's the kind of love that . . . wants to have a physical relationship with her. But is it forever-and-ever, have-a-family kind of love? I don't know."

He did have a feeling though, but right now it was all one-sided as far as he was concerned, so he wasn't interested in exploring it too deeply. Plus he would never admit that to her mother before sharing his feelings with Jen.

She nodded. "I respect that answer."

He nodded, pleased with himself. "Good. I appreciate that. I'm not sure what she's shared with you, but this relationship between us, it's new."

"She said the same."

They ate in silence for a few moments, enjoying the light breeze, the sounds of birds and frogs, and the rustling of the corn stalks. She cleared her throat. *Great. She wasn't done.* He mentally braced himself.

"I hope you consider it. Asking her."

"Is there a reason you're bringing this up?"

She sighed. "I don't know how much Jen has told you about my health."

"Most of it, I think." But he couldn't be certain.

"That my cancer is back and I haven't received the best prognosis?"

"Basically, yes."

"Well, then it should be obvious why I'm asking. It would ease my mind to know that someone loves her. Wants to be there for her when I'm gone."

That made sense, he supposed. "I think she would be disappointed to know you were planning for the worst." He tried to give her a reassuring smile, but she only rolled her eyes.

"You sound like her. She's always telling me my attitude is affecting my health."

"I think there is evidence to support that. Maybe you should take it into consideration. Besides, this trial medication you're taking could work, Diane. You have no idea what the future holds."

He took another drink and then picked up his fork again. Noticing she'd gone quiet, he leaned forward a bit. "I hope that didn't come off as insincere, I didn't mean it that way."

"No, of course not." She wiped at her eye. Was she crying? Oh God, now he felt like an ass. A few hours alone with Jen's mother and she was crying. Jen was going to kill him.

"I'm sorry. I didn't mean—"

"I'm not doing the clinical trial," she said quietly.

He froze, hating what he thought she might be about to say next. "What do you mean?"

"I didn't qualify for it."

TJ blew out a breath. "Does Jen know that?"

She shook her head. "No, she'd be so upset with me."

"So, what are you saying? You lied to your daughter?"

Diane nodded. "I had to."

"No, no you didn't. You have to tell her."

"I can't!" The pleading in her voice, the panic on her face.

He looked away, fuming inside. Why would she do this to him? Finally, he looked back at her. "Diane, Jen is a strong woman. She can handle it."

"She's the strongest woman I know. That's exactly why I won't do it to her. Right now she feels optimistic, but she knows I could still get worse. I'd prefer to just take this second chance I've received and spend it with her in peace."

"What do you mean second chance?"

"After the fire. TJ, I almost died in there. Almost let myself die. Do you understand what I'm saying?"

This was news to him. He wondered if Jen knew it. Would this be something else he wasn't supposed to share? He shook his head. "You have to be honest."

"I can't. She'll want me to do another round of chemo, and I can't."

"Why? Is it so awful that she wants you to live?"

"Of course not, but my body didn't handle it well. It was like hell on earth, and I refuse to go through it again. Besides, it obviously didn't work because the cancer came back. How do I explain that to her and make her understand?"

He put his hands out. "Like you did just now to me!"

"She won't listen." Diane shook her head frantically. "Jen has spent the past year taking care of a mean and bitter woman. Hell, she's been taking care of me in some respect for almost her entire life. I've been an addict, homeless, and God knows what else. Jen has been the solid person in our relationship. I'm a bitch, and this past year she should have been thinking about herself. Making her own way."

"She does not regret that, Diane. I'm certain of that. Jen is that kind of woman. She takes care of people she loves."

"Exactly, and it's time she and I just enjoy this time. I need to make it up to her for some things. I see that clearly now. During that fire . . . it's like . . . everything came into focus."

TJ leaned back, sucked in a breath, and looked around the yard. "Why are you sharing all this with me?"

"I didn't intend to tell you about the medication. I really just wanted to hear you say you love Jen. I guess the guilt has been eating at me."

"I'll tell you right now. If you want something to happen between her and me, asking me to lie is not the right way to go about it."

Diane nodded, wiping another tear from her cheek. "I understand that. I'll tell her. Just . . . give me some time." She looked at him, her face pleading. "Give me some time with her. Yesterday was so wonderful—it was like we were a real mother and daughter. I want more of that before I get too sick. Then I'll tell her. I promise."

"If it comes up, Diane, I am not lying. I'll give you some time, but you *have* to tell her. By the end of the summer. Or I will."

She nodded. "Okay. I understand."

Monday morning, TJ, Dean, and Jake via Skype— had their monthly financial meeting in the conference room at the Stag. TJ usually led these, sharing all the numbers he could to give everyone a good picture of where the business was at—both the liquor and the wedding aspects. Then they would discuss things they wanted to change or new things they wanted to try. This was also where they'd delegate who would work what wedding weekends the coming month.

So far, every month of this year had been better than the last profit-wise, so everyone was feeling good. As they were wrapping up, TJ asked the guys for another minute.

"What's going on?" Dean asked. "Is it about Jen?"

"Actually, yes." He looked at Dean. "Did you tell Jake about the fire?"

"Fire?" Jake replied, his voice a little tinny from the computer speakers. "Jen had a fire?"

Quickly TJ and Dean explained to Jake what had happened over the weekend at Shady Meadow.

"Damn, that's horrible. I'm glad they're okay."

TJ nodded. "Exactly. Everyone got out safely. But I just wanted you guys to know that Jen is going to be staying with me for a while. And . . . uh, we're kind of seeing each other."

"About damn time is all I can say," Jake said, grinning. "Although the living together thing has shocked me. I'll be honest."

"Yeah, I second that," Dean said. "Are you sure about this? It's awfully fast. Charlotte and I haven't even moved in together yet."

"You plan to though," TJ said, feeling a little defensive. He understood their concerns, but he didn't want to have to explain himself.

"We do, but we also haven't spent the last ten years hating each other."

TJ nodded. "I know it's fast. I agree. The only reason things progressed like that was because of her living circumstances. Her mother's insurance covers temporary housing, but Jen's doesn't. She has nowhere to go." He looked at Dean. "I know you don't want her staying with Charlotte for the next several months."

Dean's head jerked back. "Hell no."

"It feels like the right thing to do. Everything she owned may be lost. We went again this morning on the way in here, and there was a hazmat crew there cleaning up the asbestos. She still hasn't even been able to get in and see what is salvageable"

"Damn," Jake said. "I hope her insurance covers her personal property."

TJ nodded. "It does, but it was a very basic policy. She'll probably only get some money for the few possessions she can prove she lost."

They were all silent for a moment, considering that, so TJ spoke up again. "Listen, I know this is all a little crazy, living together, but it's temporary and . . . so far I have no regrets." The conversation with her mother might be one, but he kept that to himself. "I just wanted to let you all know what was going on."

"Sounds good to me. She's lucky to have you," Jake said. "I hope that's all the bad news you have. It's too early for this kind of stress." He yawned as the RV coffee maker was dripping behind him.

TJ frowned at the screen. "Dude, you're in Nashville. You haven't even left our time zone. And I've been at work for three hours. What do you mean too early?"

"What can I say? Sunday night at Jones's Bar is ladies' night. Our . . . products were very well received." Jake's crooked grin told them all they needed to know about how the previous night had played out for him. Who knew if there was a naked woman on the bed off camera? Actually, TJ didn't want to know.

"I was afraid you were gonna say Sunday night was teen night," Dean said with a laugh.

"Screw you," Jake called out. "That's *you* with the younger women, old man. How about you remind us how old Charlotte was the year you graduated high school?"

Dean held his middle finger up to the screen, but they were all laughing. Teasing one another was part of their dynamic, and while it was no secret that Dean had struggled a bit with the fact that he was twelve years older than Charlotte, he seemed to be over it. Or was trying to be.

When they finally finished up and disconnected from Skype, Dean and TJ left the conference room and headed down the hallway. Before TJ could walk into his office, Dean stopped him.

"Hey, man. You really sure you know what you're doing?"

TJ appreciated his friend's concern. But he was certain that letting Jen stay with him was the right thing. "I am. Jen needs to be taken care of for once."

Dean considered his words and then nodded. "I agree. I hope this ends up being what you want it to be. I care about you both and want you to be happy."

"Thank you. I really appreciate that."

Without another word Dean headed for the distilling room, leaving TJ alone in his office doorway. From here he could hear Jen tapping away on her computer and talking on the phone.

He'd liked her riding into town with him. Liked that they'd be driving home together. He knew his friends were right to be hesitant. But right now, he felt good about it. He'd feel even better after they dropped Diane off at her new temporary, furnished apartment this evening.

# Nineteen

Jen still wasn't used to sleeping in a comfortable bed, even though she'd been doing it for a week. She didn't know how badly she'd been sleeping until now. At TJ's she was up with the sunrise most mornings, even on this beautiful Sunday.

Sitting up, she glanced over at him. Out cold, an arm thrown over his head. She smiled, remembering the previous night as he'd entered her body slowly, making love to her like he wanted to do it forever, and then holding her as she fell asleep.

She'd made a vow to herself not to become too used to this. They hadn't made promises or talked about the future. If she was wise, she would start making a backup plan. Tara would come back to work, TJ would eventually get tired of her mooching off him, and then where would she be? This was a temporary fantasy, but that was okay. She'd enjoy it while it was good, but she'd do well to start thinking about the next step.

Quietly she left the bedroom and headed downstairs to the kitchen, her favorite part of the house. Jen had always considered herself a fairly utilitarian girl. When it came to hair, makeup, and such, she loved to be a little crazy. But only the basics were necessary for her living conditions.

Or so she thought.

It was becoming obvious that her belief had been born of necessity, or to save herself from disappointment, because spending the past week living with TJ's kitchen had taught her something: She liked nice things.

TJ had mentioned to her that he'd had help from an interior designer on the house, and whoever that genius was, they'd obviously put much of their effort into the kitchen. Quartz-counter island, glass-tile backsplash, and custom white cabinets, which even had tiny lights underneath. It was so lovely, she almost couldn't believe the house belonged to a man. She wondered what all he'd had a hand in choosing. She needed to ask him.

Was the big porcelain farmhouse-style sink something he'd always wanted? Or was it like the claw-foot tub in his master bath, a suggestion by the designer to favor the style of home? Jen would never have guessed this very traditional house was her style, but man how she loved it. It was homey and warm, and it made her wish some grandmotherly figure would come around the corner and start making her pancakes.

But since dreams were only dreams, Jen decided to make breakfast herself. This was their first lazy morning since she'd moved in, so she thought it would be a nice gesture to show her thanks.

She located all the ingredients, surprised to find

TJ kept a decently stocked pantry and fridge. The basics anyway. Made her wonder if that was a byproduct of him recently having been in a relationship, but she pushed those thoughts aside and got busy making coffee.

It wasn't long before she was sipping French vanilla brew out of a Stag mug, waiting for the griddle to heat up on the stove, and scrolling through Facebook on her phone. She snarled at a photo of *another* high school friend's new baby, but still responded by liking it with a heart, because that's what you do on social media. Seemed like everyone she knew was married, having babies, or going on luxury vacations. She was 0 for 3 these days, and would be for the foreseeable future.

It was tempting to take a selfie in this beautiful kitchen. Pass it off as hers. Why shouldn't she? She sighed, imagining what the real caption might read: "Shitty-ass apartment burned down, so I'm screwing my boss and cooking in his awesome kitchen! #winning"

The thought made her laugh as she loaded the griddle with batter, held up her Stag mug in front of it, and took a shot of her provisional awesome life. She uploaded the photo and captioned it "Domestic AF." Post. It got three likes within seconds. She grinned. Maybe she could manifest this life into existence.

Footsteps on the stairs got her attention, so she put her phone down and braced herself for TJ's reaction to her making herself comfortable in his kitchen. She flipped one pancake, then the other, when she felt his arms go around her waist and his face nuzzle into her neck. He really liked doing that, and she really didn't mind one bit. She smiled as he kissed her cheek. Maybe this manifesting shit worked.

"This is a nice surprise."

He let go and stepped over to the coffeepot.

"Hope you like pancakes," she said, plating up the first stack.

"Doesn't everyone?"

"They should." She turned, holding out the plate, just as he walked back up to her. "Here you go. Hope they're good."

"I'm sure they are. They smell great."

She frowned. "Shoot, I didn't check for syrup. You may not have any."

He walked over to the pantry, stepped inside, and came out holding some up. She sighed in relief and poured some more batter. Once the next couple were done, she plated them up, grabbed her plate, coffee, and phone, and joined TJ at the breakfast table.

"These are really good," he said, already two-thirds of the way finished.

"Thank you. It's the least I could do for a place to stay."

He turned to her. "You don't owe me anything for this, Jen. Remember that."

She nodded. "I was just thinking this morning about what I'm going to do next."

He sat up straighter, his brow furrowed. "What do you mean?"

"Exactly what it sounds like. I have a temporary full-time job, a temporary living arrangement. Possibly even a temporary mother. I need to stop shitting around waiting for life to happen and figure some things out."

He stared at her for a moment and then finally went back to his breakfast. "Well, don't think you need to hurry. Wait for the right thing to come along."

Jen wasn't sure why his response left her feeling . . . unsettled. It was a fair and kind thing to say. She wasn't even sure what she'd hoped his response would be.

Her phone rang, surprising them both for so early on a Sunday morning. She read the caller ID. "Chicago. That's odd."

"Do you know someone in Chicago?"

"Not that I can think of." She let it continue to ring.

"You're not gonna answer it?" he asked, bite halfway to his mouth.

"Eh, nah. Probably a telemarketer." More like a bill-collector was her worry, but she wasn't going to say that. Broke-ass people did not answer phone numbers they didn't recognize. "If it's someone important they'll leave a voicemail." A moment later, her voicemail dinged.

TJ, now finished with his breakfast, raised an eyebrow at her. The last thing Jen wanted was to listen to a voicemail tell her how behind she was on her credit card, so she just turned her phone over and went back to her pancakes. She could feel TJ looking at her, so she decided this was a good time to ask him about how this kitchen was designed.

Turns out he had a lot to say on the subject, and they talked about it for over an hour. Jen was fascinated by the process, and loved hearing how he'd made the decisions he did about the counter, the sink, and even the location of the electrical outlets.

"I would have never even thought to consider where I would plug in my toaster," she said.

"Neither would I. Luckily I had help."

"Did your mom come over and give you any advice?" she asked, somewhat teasing him.

He shook his head. "Not really. My parents have only been here once. Right after I moved in."

*"Once?"*

He took a sip of his coffee, which they'd now re-filled twice as they talked. "We're not that close, really."

"Well, yeah. You mentioned that before. But . . . that surprises me."

He shrugged. "Yeah, I honestly don't know where things went wrong with my parents. It's like they hit their capacity for love and attention with kid two. I get the leftovers. Especially my father. Mainly, my father. I'm not giving my mother enough credit, she's loving most of the time. But with him, nothing I did was ever good enough. He's just a cold, selfish, prick who treats my mother like an afterthought. My siblings are self-absorbed and self-righteous, and my poor mom copes with it all by drinking too much and pretending none of it's happening."

Jen stared at him with her mouth open for a long moment, and then an awkward laugh escaped her lips. "Good lord, Trevor James. That was some messed-up after-school-special shit right there."

He laughed. "It was. You're right. I'm not usually much of a sharer."

"You've shared some with me. But not much. And I usually over-share."

"Sometimes. But not usually when it comes to your family life. But I'm glad you've been sharing it with me." He reached out and grabbed her hand. She let him.

"We're hopeless," she said, smiling.

He returned it, giving her fingers a squeeze. "No. Not hopeless. We have each other."

That afternoon, TJ shocked Jen by going outside to mow the yard. She teased him about not having a landscaper, but he replied that he enjoyed using the riding mower, which she had to admit, was a lot different than a push mower. She was also enjoying her frequent peeks out the window to see him riding around shirtless, sweaty, and so damn sexy.

She'd cleaned up their breakfast dishes, made the bed, and taken a shower while he did his yard work. Sitting down to look at nonsense on her phone, she remembered the voicemail from earlier and decided to listen to it.

Her stomach always bunched into knots when she had messages from callers she didn't recognize, but she braced herself and hit PLAY.

"Hey, Jen, my name is Erin Kingman. I'm a friend of Anthony's. We went to college together. I happened to see the video he posted on Facebook of the two of you singing a few weeks ago. It was . . . quite amazing. I reached out to him and he told me you've taught voice and drama. It kind of seemed like fate, so he gave me your contact info. I'm in Chicago and I work at the Uccello Canoro Academy. We specialize in drama and voice for children three to eighteen, and we're looking for a voice teacher. I know it would be a big move, but Chicago is amazing, so I couldn't help reaching out to you. You never know, right? Anyway, I'd love to chat if you have a few minutes."

Jen listened in shock as Erin recited her phone number and urged once more for Jen to call. Her heart skipped in her chest as she listened to the message one more time to be sure she hadn't imagined it.

It was out of the question. Her mother was sick, she had no money, and Chicago was . . . so far.

But oh God. The thought of being asked to do such a thing was exhilarating. Teaching voice again to children would be everything to her. She'd loved her job at Maple Springs Community Theater so much. She would love nothing more than to do something similar again.

The sound of the mower shutting off caught her attention, and she walked over to the window to see TJ walking toward the house. Jen looked down at her phone and closed the voicemail screen.

When things seemed too good to be true, they usually were.

TJ pushed the cart down the dairy aisle of the supermarket, unable to take his eyes off Jen. Something was bothering her, no mistaking that. He'd spent enough of his life trying to analyze this woman, so he knew when her mind was on something. Trouble was, he was almost afraid to ask her what it was.

There was a good chance he wouldn't like the

response. Or he'd feel like he needed to share what he knew, which he did not want to do. Several times he'd considered showing up at Diane's new apartment and insisting she put an end to her charade, but then Jen would go over and spend some time with her mom. She'd come back happy, talking about Diane's change in attitude. How they'd gone to dinner. Talked. Basically, she was acting like this fire had given her the mother she'd never had, and he couldn't bring himself to ruin that. Not yet, anyway.

"Do you like Greek yogurt or normal?" Jen asked.

"I'll eat any kind without chunks of fruit," he answered.

She laughed. "A picky eater, are you?"

"Not usually. I like fruit. Just not little mushy surprise pieces of it."

She shook her head, shoulders shaking with laughter as she picked out a few containers and placed them in the cart.

He liked this. Them being domestic. They'd left work together and came to the store, like a newlywed couple. Having her in his home had been a bit of an adjustment, but not in bad way. It was nice. He kissed her when he wanted to, sought her out in the middle of the night when he wanted to, showered with her. It was like his life had done a one-eighty, and he had no desire to go back to the way things were before.

And as happy as she seemed most of the time—all things in her life considered—something was off. It could be the fact that her world had also done a complete turnaround. Things had happened fast. They'd finally received the all clear to enter her apartment, but they hadn't gone yet. He knew she was nervous, and there was no telling what kind of settlement she'd get. Insurance wasn't known for its generosity.

TJ wasn't worried about the money situation, but he knew she was. He hadn't forgotten about the unpaid water bill, and he couldn't help wondering how bad her finances might be. It was a subject he wasn't ready to broach with her. As much as he wanted it to be, right now, it was none of his business, and he knew bringing it up would only make her mad and feel defensive. But he was a facts and numbers kind of guy, so it was killing him not to know exactly what they were dealing with. What *she* was dealing with.

He continued to follow her with the cart, answering her questions, throwing a few things in he usually bought for himself.

"Miss Mackenzie!" A child at the end of the aisle screeched.

Jen's head jerked over, and TJ watched her face light up. "Jade, hi!"

The little girl ran toward Jen, who knelt down just in time to practically be tackle hugged. She laughed, grabbing onto the edge of the cart. "My goodness, what a greeting."

TJ looked up to see a woman pushing a cart toward them, a smile on her face. Jen looked up at the woman. "Hi, Stacy."

"Jen, we've missed you so much. As you can see." She nodded toward her daughter.

Jen stood up. "I've missed you guys, too."

The little girl looked up at Jen with such admiration in her eyes. "I start fourth grade pretty soon and my mom said I can try out this year for the kid parts in the high school plays. Will you come and see it if I'm cast?"

"Of course I will," Jen said, ruffling the girl's hair. "Have you been practicing?"

TJ figured this little girl must have been one of Jen's students at the community theater that had closed a couple of months ago.

"She does scales every morning and night. And talks about you constantly." The woman frowned. "Do you have any word on if they plan to ever start anything new in Maple Springs? We had such an interest and such a good group. Hard to believe something else won't start up."

"I know. Hard for me to believe, too. A couple of people discussed starting a nonprofit, but it's a real time commitment. No one seemed to be willing to step up."

"I understand that. I wish I could do more, but it just isn't feasible with my work schedule."

"I understand, Stacy. I think that's where most of the parents are at, and lord knows if I had the money I'd do it . . . but I don't." Jen smiled and then seemed to remember TJ standing there. "I'm sorry, this is TJ, my . . . boyfriend," she said. Her eyes darted to his as if asking if her answer was acceptable. He just gave her a wink, actually loving that she'd said it.

"It's so nice to meet you." Stacy put out her hand. "I'm Stacy Sanchez. You are very lucky. We adore Jen, as do a lot of families in the community that she taught."

TJ smiled. "She is pretty amazing. I was sorry to

hear about the program closing. I know Jen was really disappointed."

"We all are. I just hope they figure out something else. There are too many talented children in Maple Springs not to have some kind of theater program."

They finally said their good-byes, and TJ and Jen headed further down the aisle. "You really miss teaching, don't you?" he asked. Is that what had been bothering her? He knew she'd been sad about the community theater program shutting down, but he'd stupidly thought it was about losing a job. About losing income. But it was obviously about a lot more than that.

She smiled at him. "I do, yeah. I loved it. The pay was shit, obviously. But that wasn't why I did it. All through school I was so insecure. At some point, I learned that drama and singing were my way of not only expressing myself, but gaining confidence. I like nurturing that in other children. It's incredibly rewarding."

God, could she be any more amazing? "I bet you're good at it."

She gave him a side-eye. "Was there any doubt?"

TJ chuckled. "My bad. Of course not."

He watched her choose a loaf of bread from the bakery section. Then a package of cookies. And another package of cookies. He smiled. "So, can't you find a similar job somewhere else? We're so near all the other towns in the metro. Surely there's another group like it."

"There are others, but . . . I don't know. I've been kind of looking, at jobs." She glanced at him and he suddenly felt a pit in his stomach.

"Oh yeah?"

"Well, I mean, I can't wait till the last second. You know?"

"There's no rush, Jen. You have a home. I told you I wouldn't let you go without a job."

"I can't accept your charity forever, TJ. And bartending alone won't pay my bills."

TJ stopped in the middle of the grocery aisle and grabbed her. With a hand on each arm, he looked into her eyes. "This is not charity, Jen. Why can't you see that?"

"I live with you for one reason. Because my place burned down."

"But we are seeing each other. You just said it to that woman. I loved hearing you say it."

She stared up at him. "You'll get sick of me if I'm always needing to be helped. It's one-sided and unfair."

"How can you say that? Do you think I don't get anything out of having you in my house?" He gripped her arms harder. "You know better than that."

She huffed out a laugh. "On-call BJ's for room and board? There's a name for that, TJ." She whispered the last part.

His eyes went wide. "What the hell are you talking about? You know damn well I don't think any such thing. I can't even believe you just said that."

She looked down at his hands still gripping her arms and then over his shoulder, down the aisle. "Dude, this is the cell phone age. You're gonna be on the news tonight for a domestic dispute in the bakery aisle."

Damn. TJ dropped his arms instantly. "Was I hurting you?"

"Of course not." She turned away.

No, she'd been changing the subject. Deflecting. "Listen, I don't want you to move out. I don't want you to worry about a job. I want you with me. I know that's selfish, but I think you want it, too."

She turned on him. "What are you saying, TJ? That we should get married? Or just shack up until it's not fun anymore?" She laughed. "This was all kind of an accident. I mean, obviously I'm not moving out next week. But let's not make each other promises we may not be able to keep. Okay?"

He blew out a breath. This conversation was far from over, but this wasn't the place to continue it. "Fine." He grabbed onto the shopping cart again. "Let's get out of here. What else do we need?"

"Condoms." When he glanced at her she just held up her hands. "*What?* I said let's not make promises, not let's stop having sex. That would be stupid."

TJ just shook his head. This woman. What was he going to do with her? Or worse, what would he do without her?

# Twenty

"This time, I'm treating," Jen said as she and Charlotte looked over the specials at Sylvia's Café.

Charlotte gave her a long look over her menu. "Jen, you just survived a fire. Don't even start with me."

"Fine. We'll split it."

With a deep sigh, Charlotte shook her head.

They ordered the Chicken Avocado Club again. Jen had been craving it since the last time they'd come. When Charlotte came into the Stag today to see Dean and then suggested lunch to Jen, she'd jumped at the idea.

"So how is it going, living with TJ?" Charlotte asked before taking a sip of her lemonade.

"It's good. Hard to believe, isn't it?"

Charlotte shrugged. "Not really. He's been into you a long time I guess. So it doesn't surprise me that he stepped up when you needed it."

"Yeah, he's a good guy. Funny it took me so long to realize it. Or maybe I knew and was just scared to see it."

"Relationships are scary as hell. I get it." Charlotte shifted in her seat. "Learning how to navigate each other's insecurities and inner demons is serious work. But I think that's what makes it all worth it when it's the right person."

Jen considered that. "I can see that. I just feel like I'm going in blind. I didn't know any healthy couples growing up."

"I don't think it matters," Charlotte said. "My parents are great. I mean, they're not perfect. My mom's a drama queen sometimes and my dad likes to tune her out. But they love each other. Maybe those are their ways of navigating. Point is, having loving parents has not made my relationships easier."

"But at least you know it's possible."

Charlotte nodded. "Okay, that's fair. But we all know it's possible, because we want it. We see it in strangers and in movies. And even if we don't know that it will last forever, I still think it's worth it. Why not be happy for now? You never know what's going to happen to you tomorrow."

Jen sighed. "That's pretty deep for lunch, Charlotte."

They laughed, and it felt really good to have another woman to talk with. "I guess I'm just trying to decide if this is the right time to commit to someone. Maybe I should use this opportunity to make some serious changes in my life."

Charlotte's eyes narrowed. "Like what?"

Jen proceeded to tell her friend about the voicemail she'd received.

"Wow." Charlotte blew out a breath. Shook her head. "That's a tough one. What does TJ say?"

"I haven't told him."

"Oh, you should definitely tell him. He might have some good insight." Charlotte leaned forward and whispered, "Maybe he'll go with you."

Jen's eyes went wide. "No way. I wouldn't even let him consider that. He loves the Stag."

Charlotte just shrugged. "He might love you more, Jen. One thing Dean and I have been realizing is how what you think you want may not be what's going to make you happy. Your path might look different than the one you'd had in your head. Do you know what I mean?"

"Of course, yes. But . . ." Jen shook her head. "There is no way I would let TJ leave the Stag."

"And maybe there'd be no way he'd allow you to turn this offer down," Charlotte said, her voice full of conviction. "Just tell him. See what he says. Maybe it will lead to a conversation that needs to be had. It might put some things in perspective. Help you see things clearer. Relationships are all give and take, and TJ's not an unreasonable guy. Don't assume what he may or may not do."

"You're good. Real good." Jen smiled. "You should be a therapist."

Charlotte laughed. "I'm just your friend. It's always easier to tell a friend what they should do from the outside looking in. Next time Dean and I have a problem and I tell you about it, you can have your turn to be a know-it-all."

Jen laughed. This, this was the kind of conversation she'd been missing by having no close friends. "I won't forget you said that."

"Just think about telling him," Charlotte finally said.

"I will," Jen said as their food was set down in front of them. Maybe she would, maybe she wouldn't. Right now, she was just going to enjoy Charlotte's company. And sneakily pay the bill.

That Friday they left work early and drove straight to Shady Meadows. TJ could tell that Jen was nervous by how quiet she'd been on the short drive over. He was nervous for her, and ready to help her however he could once they got inside.

He really had no clue what to expect when they entered, but he decided to prepare for the worst as he sought a parking spot. They'd taken her truck today in case there was anything to load up.

"Ready?"

She turned to him. "I feel sick to my stomach."

He grabbed her hand. "I know. But it's going to be okay. These are just things, Jen. You told me you saved the most important keepsakes, so let's just go in and not worry about what we'll find. Okay?"

She nodded. "Okay."

They held hands as they made their way up to the building. The entire property had been roped off and a man was there checking identification to be sure anyone who entered had the right to be there.

TJ stood and waited while Jen gave her name and then they were both given a face mask to cover their noses and mouths.

"This isn't a good sign," Jen said as she pulled her mask on.

"Don't worry. Just a precaution." But secretly he was not feeling optimistic.

They proceeded up the newly rebuilt stairs to her unit. The minute they hit the second floor she let out a tiny gasp. The apartment was wide open, the door stripped off the hinges and sitting against the outer wall.

"Wasn't expecting that," she said, stopping on the landing.

"Come on." TJ put a hand on her lower back and led her to the door. He let her step in first.

"Oh my goodness," she whispered. Jen had stopped dead in her tracks in the doorway, so TJ gently pushed her forward and took in the room for himself.

Holy. Shit.

It was bad. Every surface was covered with soot, the ceiling had been ripped out, revealing the ducting and rafters, and the stench was enough to make you nauseous. He had no idea what to say so he stepped into the room and grabbed her hand.

"I knew it would be bad," she said. "But this . . ."

"I know. Take your time," TJ said. He took in her face, her eyes darting around the room, taking it all in. It was overwhelming, even for him who usually liked to get right to a task without hesitating. But it was hard to know where to start. The carpet and all the furniture had been drenched, and even had it been savable at one time it no longer was. Pieces of the textured ceiling had fallen on it and the soot and smell would never come clean. The place was a wreck.

"Should I start taking some photos for you?" he asked, pulling out his phone.

She could only nod.

Jen's feet were frozen to the floor in her apartment, and she felt so close to having a panic attack it was dizzying. For the past week she'd tried not to think about everything she'd lost, or if the fire crossed her mind, she tried to remind herself that it was still possible her things weren't ruined.

Wrong. This was a nightmare.

Everything was filthy, water-damaged, and smelly. Her eyes continued to touch on every item that she'd forgotten she owned. Books, her favorite fluffy blanket, the vintage side table she'd picked up on someone's curb one day. And then there were her plants. Every single one looked like it was damaged beyond repair, their leaves crispy and lying limp.

The urge to move came over her and she headed into the kitchen. If she didn't, she'd go crazy. The kitchen was even worse. She pulled open a lower cabinet, surprised to find everything looking fairly normal. Too bad it was nothing she cared about, just dish soap, trash bags, and such. But it was a sign that maybe not everything was hopeless.

She headed back to the living room to find TJ still taking pictures with his phone. She was so glad he was with her, because alone, she might have just sat down and cried. Or hyperventilated.

Heading down the hall, she pushed open the bedroom door. Okay, so much for not crying. The bed was almost completely black, as was everything else. The clothes, shoes, dresser, walls. It was clear that none of this would be leaving with her.

Jen's lip wobbled and a shiver ran through her body as the reality of the devastation consumed her. But she would not cry. Not again. There had been too many tears lately and she was trying desperately to be optimistic.

She heard TJ come up behind her. Touch her back. "Jen," he said quietly. "You okay?"

Turning, she forced the tears back. "Yes. I think so."

He stared at her a moment, probably trying to decipher if she was really okay. "I'll get photos in here, but I'll need your help. I don't want to rifle through your things."

She nodded. "Okay, let's start in the closet. I want to leave as soon as possible."

That evening TJ watched television while he waited for Jen to come home. After they'd left her apartment she'd mentioned wanting to go visit her mother, so she'd left almost as soon as they'd gotten home.

He'd hated that because he had a feeling she'd been trying to avoid letting go of her emotions in front of him. She'd handled the apartment visit almost too well, even for her. Hell, it hadn't even been his place and he'd wanted to break down.

Glancing at his watch, he sighed. He wanted her home. Missed her.

He heard her truck on the gravel drive and felt an instant mix of relief and then dread. Every time she went to see Diane he prepared himself for her to find out about her mother's betrayal. It was hard to know how she would react to the news, but he assumed it would not be good. He would know the minute she came in if tonight Diane had come clean. Jen wasn't the best at concealing her emotions.

He walked to the front door, opened it, and called out to her. "Need help with anything?"

She smiled brightly. "Nope. I'm good. But I love the front door greeting."

She didn't know. And he had to admit it was sort of a relief. Today had already been rough with the apartment visit. And they'd been busy the past few days at work bottling a new set of barrels, meaning he hadn't been able to talk with her as much as he liked to. At home they'd both been exhausted, falling asleep while watching the news. He was ready to hold her.

He closed the front door behind her, then waited for her to set down her purse and toe off her shoes. The minute she turned back to him, he got ahold of her.

"Oh my," she said, grinning up at him. "What's this about?"

"Just missed you. That's all."

"I've been gone three hours," she said, amusement in her voice.

He squeezed her tighter. "Three *long* hours."

The feel of her arms pulling him closer made him smile. They stood like that a long moment, just soaking each other in. Then he heard it. A sniffle.

Angling his head, he tried to see her face, but she just shoved it deeper into his chest. "Jen, babe, what is it?"

"I don't know," she whispered.

TJ pressed his lips against her temple. "It's been a hell of a day."

Her head nodded in agreement and he stroked her hair, pulling it away from her face. Slowly, she looked up at him, her eyes shiny and red. "I need you," she said.

He smiled down at her. "And I need you," he replied, before pressing a kiss to her nose. Then her lips. She didn't hesitate to kiss him back and he threaded his fingers into her hair to hold her close.

Finally she broke away, her breath labored. "Right here in the entryway?" she asked quietly.

"Wherever I can have you."

Her eyes were wide now, sparkling in the light of the chandelier above their head. He watched as her fingers began to undo the buttons on her shirt. Within seconds, the material was falling open, exposing her beautiful body.

TJ licked his lips, wanting to get his mouth on the plump swells of her breasts. Her bra was black lace, and he could see her hard nipples straining against the flimsy fabric. Lifting his hand, he ran a thumb over one, watching it pucker even tighter.

Her shirt fell to the floor as she reached behind her to undo the bra. As it sagged forward, he pulled the straps down her arms and dropped it at their feet.

"I'm pretty sure your body was made for me, Jen." He placed a hand on each breast, once again running his thumbs over her nipples as her hands went to his fly. If she was ready to get right to it, he had no problem with that.

Pulling his shirt over his head, he watched as she reached for his pants.

"Hold on," he said, before going for the emergency condom in his wallet. After retrieving it he dropped the wallet on the floor. "Okay."

She smiled and then pushed his pants down his legs. Impatient, he finished the job, chucking his underwear along with it. When he was finished, he noticed she'd removed her own shorts and underwear. She stood there in front of him, fully naked. He wished he could take a picture of her like this. In his home.

Just . . . his. All his.

"The lights are on." She nodded toward the sidelight window next to the door.

After rolling on the condom, he stepped closer, his fingertips trailing up her arm. "Only things out there to see us are some cows."

"What if someone drives by?"

TJ leaned down and gripped her butt before pulling her up against his body. Then he took a few steps and rested her back on the wall. Instantly she wrapped her legs around him, pressing her heat against his lower abdomen, and he swore he could feel her wetness.

"If someone is lucky enough to drive by, then they'll see me fucking you against the wall."

Grinning, she leaned forward and kissed him, her heat consuming him, her tongue filling his mouth. He kissed her back, loving the feel of her breasts smashed against his chest. With her legs locking them in place, he brought his left hand between them and gently pinched her nipple. She gasped.

"Did that hurt?"

"A little," she said, breathless. "Do it again."

He did and she cried out, a sound so sweet he almost came from the sound of it. This time he lifted her breast up and attached his mouth to it. He wanted to get inside of her, wanted to suck on her nipples, and hold her up. As if she could read his mind, she put her hand under her breast so he could continue lapping at it.

His now free hand went right to his dick. Adjusting his stance, he sought her warmth, and pressed up inside her.

"Oh yes," Jen said. TJ sucked harder on her nipple and then felt her other breast brushing his cheek. He pulled back to see her pressing them together.

"Shit, that's hot, Jen. Give them to me." She arched her back harder, her shoulders pressing into the wall, and he leaned down again to suck her into his mouth.

He was doing his best to stroke in and out, hoping it felt good to her. But when he glanced up at her face, her eyes were pinched shut, a tear rolling out of one eye. He froze.

"Jen, babe, what's wrong?" he asked, suddenly panicked. Stepping forward, he flattened her back and ran a hand over her forehead to push her hair from her face.

She shook her head. "Nothing's wrong," she said, looking at him.

"Then why are you crying?" He'd hoped this was making her feel better, not worse.

Biting at her lower lip, she touched his jaw with her

hand. "This just feels so good," she whispered. "You feel so good."

The tightness in TJ's chest almost felt fatal. This woman. He wasn't sure if he could feel any stronger for her. The intensity of it was going to kill him if he didn't get it out.

Grabbing ahold of her, he pulled them away from the wall and very carefully took them down to the rug. She stared up at him, her knees falling open, and he angled his body down onto hers.

She lowered her hand and he felt her grip him, and then guide him to her entrance. The achingly slow slide into her body had them both moaning. There had never been anything so good, so hot, and so beautifully tight as Jen gripping his cock.

He touched her face once more and leaned his forehead on hers. There were so many things he wanted to say, but he settled for one. "When I'm inside you . . . that's when I know you're meant to be mine."

When she made no sound, he went still and looked down at her. Their eyes locked. "I've wanted you for so long, Jen. Waited. Watched other men come on to you, and it killed me. Tell me," he said. "Please, this time . . . tell me you're mine."

She lifted her hand to cup his face. "I'm yours."

# Twenty-One

TJ glanced at his watch. His parents' party had started an hour ago, and while he didn't mind being late, it had been quite a while since Jen had gone upstairs to get ready.

He switched off the Royals game he was watching on TV and headed up the stairs. He heard the water shut off and then the sound of her shoes on the bathroom tile. He still loved the sounds of her moving around in his house. Finding her in the kitchen, doing laundry. It all made him happy.

Walking into the master bath, he saw her and froze.

"How do I look?"

This was a loaded question, so he gave himself a minute. But not too long, or she'd worry. "You look beautiful."

"You sure?" Her eyes got a little squinty, and he tried to figure out the best way to say what needed to be said.

"Jen, you always look beautiful, but I need to say something. So don't be mad."

"I know, I know. This is not me."

He sagged in relief. "No, it's not you. At all. I didn't even know you owned a sweater like that. It has pearl buttons."

"I know that. I borrowed it from Charlotte." She glanced down at the little yellow cardigan she'd put on over her white lace sundress—which was one of his favorites. It was sleeveless and a little snug on her breasts. It fit her body like it was custom-made. He wanted her to wear it alone. "I just . . . thought it was better if my tattoos were covered."

TJ's eyes went wide. "What the hell for? And you curled your hair. You never do it like that." Instead of wavy like usual, it was more round and bouncy. Even her eye makeup was different. Softer. Lighter.

She sighed as he continued to assess her. "Well, do I look ridiculous? I was doing it for you."

"Jen, no." He stepped up to her and grabbed her shoulders. "Don't you change a single thing about yourself for me. Or because of my family. I mean it when I say you look beautiful right now. But I want you to look like you do every other day. That's the you I love."

Her eyes darted up to his, and he processed what he'd just said. Her only reply was to nod her head and turn back to the mirror.

"Did I just hurt your feelings, because that is not what I wanted to do."

"No," she snapped. "But if your mom hates me, I'll blame you."

He walked up to her side, cradled her chin in his hand, and tilted her eyes up to him. "That's not going to happen. But even if it did, I don't care. Your happiness is the only thing that matters. Got it?"

She nodded.

"So, you do what makes you feel comfortable. If you want to wear this sweater, you'll look perfect, but I love seeing your tattoos. Just something to consider."

He left the bathroom and went to sit on the bed and wait for her. It wasn't long before she came out. She'd ditched the cardigan, but everything else—makeup and hair—looked exactly the same.

"This is how I will feel comfortable being there. Please understand that."

He nodded. "Okay. You look wonderful."

Fifteen minutes later they were pulling up at his parents' house, the one where he'd grown up. It was large, but not ridiculously so. But the property was rather vast, with a pool, a pool house, and a basketball court. He was sure it looked incredibly ostentatious to Jen. And maybe it was, with its colonial columns and overly manicured landscaping.

"They have valet parking?" she asked.

"Just for this event. It's an annual tradition. A lot of people come for food, booze, and gossip. All under the guise of celebrating the love of my parents."

"Hmm. Sounds like rich people stuff."

TJ just smiled as he pulled up to the valet line. After they got out, he took Jen's hand. They walked up the sidewalk and around to the backyard. The sounds of laughter, voices, and presumably a DJ met them before they made it back to the party where about a hundred people milled around. Kids played in the pool and ran around the yard, while the adults sipped beer and cocktails and talked about mindless bullshit. TJ was already itching to leave.

"I can't believe you grew up here," she said, leaning into him. "I knew you were wealthy. If I'd have had any idea this was what you went home to, I might have been even more annoyed with you."

TJ leaned down to kiss her head. "Not sure it would have been possible for you to be more annoyed with me back then."

"You'd be surprised." They walked a little further through the guests. "This is so different than where you live now."

"That's the whole point," he said, loving that she'd said that.

"Trevor," a voice called out. TJ turned and forced a smile for his sister.

"Hey, Elizabeth," he said, leaning in to hug her. His relationship with his older sister wasn't so much bad as nonexistent. Elizabeth liked to talk about herself and didn't see much need to keep up with TJ's life beyond what was shared by their mother.

"I haven't seen you since Christmas," she said. Liz was an attorney and always "busy." Her eyes darted to Jen. "Is this why?" She stuck out her hand to Jen. "Hi, I'm Elizabeth. Trevor's sister."

Jen took her hand and shook it. "I'm Jen."

"Nice to meet you. How long have you two been dating?" Liz asked. "I thought Mom mentioned you'd broken up with someone recently."

TJ didn't miss the way his sister's eyes looked Jen

up and down, so he knew Jen hadn't missed it either. Thankfully, there didn't seem to be judgment in Liz's appraisal. More curiosity.

"I don't fill Mom in on everything." He'd even missed a couple of his weekly calls this month, and she hadn't even reached out to check on him. Go figure. "And Jen and I actually live together."

TJ felt Jen stiffen beside him. They hadn't decided what they were going to share or how he was going to introduce her, but he saw no reason to be anything but honest. He rested his hand on her lower back and rubbed.

Liz's mouth dropped open. "Wow! Moving fast. Congratulations."

"I'd appreciate it if you'd let me spread that news."

"Of course. I understand," Liz said. "I still need to get over and see your new house."

"It's very nice," Jen interjected.

"I bet. TJ always had good taste," she said, turning to Jen. "Well then, maybe we'll all see one another at Christmas next time. Sorry to rush away, but I've got to find my kids. I'm sure my husband is not looking after them. It was nice to meet you."

"You too," Jen said.

TJ decided that could have gone a lot worse, as he watched his sister walk across the patio to yell at one of her girls in the pool. The sight of his nieces shocked him. They were so grown up, and suddenly TJ hated that he wasn't very close to them. He sent Liz's daughters cards on their birthdays and gave them presents for Christmas, but that was about it. They didn't rush over to see Uncle TJ at get-togethers like this.

Then again, they didn't do it to Uncle Seth, his brother, either. Whose fault was it that none of Laughlins were that close to one another? Maybe it was everyone's. Himself included.

"She seemed nice enough," Jen said quietly.

"Yeah, I guess. We're just not close. Never have been. Let's keep moving. It's dangerous to stay still too long."

He grabbed her hand and they headed for the bar set up by the pool. TJ knew if he wanted to introduce Jen to his parents, that would be the place to find them. Sure enough, his mother was within six feet, nursing a martini and chatting with two women.

"Mom," he said, lightly touching her arm. She turned.

"TJ, oh you're here." She reached out and hugged him with her drinkless hand, a halfway enthusiastic effort. Literally. "I was starting to wonder where you were."

Was she really? He had a hard time believing she would have even noticed if he hadn't showed. He pulled Jen closer to him. "Mom, this is my girlfriend, Jen. Jen, my mother, Ellen."

"Jen! Oh . . . how lovely," Ellen said, her smile actually sincere. "Aren't you beautiful?" She looked at TJ. "She's so beautiful and colorful. You're like looking at a garden. Ohhh . . ." TJ watched in shock as his mother—overcome with some sort of emotion—put her glass down on a nearby table and pulled Jen in for a two-armed hug. He couldn't believe his eyes, but he couldn't deny the feeling of pride he felt at watching his mom's reaction to Jen. He'd been prepared to not care what she thought. Prepared to explain to Jen how his parents were. But the deep-down truth was that he did care. He'd wanted his mother to see what he saw when he looked at Jen. But never in a million years had he expected her to. Hopefully it wasn't because she was drunk.

"It's so nice to meet you, Mrs. Laughlin," Jen said.

When they pulled back from the hug, TJ's mother was still beaming. "Call me Ellen." She glanced at TJ again. "TJ . . . I'm just so thrilled. She's the most precious thing I've ever seen."

Jen's wary eyes darted to his and he grinned at her. "That she is. I agree."

"Have you two gotten some food? Come on, I'll show you." After leaving her drink where it was, he watched his mom grab Jen's hand and lead her through the mass of guests. A couple of times she stopped to introduce Jen to someone, repeating the same phrase. "Isn't she lovely? This is my son TJ's girlfriend, Jen." And often added something along the lines of "the one who owns the Stag in Maple Springs."

Several people said hello to him and congratulated him on the success of the Stag. Eventually they made their way up by the house, and Jen and TJ both made a plate from the catered barbecue buffet line.

"Don't you leave before I get a chance to chat with you again, promise?" his mother asked them.

"Okay, Mom," he said.

"This is so nice," Jen whispered. "I grew up eating greasy barbecue out of a paper sack from the gas station."

"Don't they say the best barbecue comes from the dives?" he teased.

"Maybe, but this looks pretty tasty." She held out her plate and glanced down at her dress. "Although I'll admit that I'm a bit nervous about eating ribs in white."

"You want to go eat in the house?"

"Can we?"

"Of course. I grew up here." He led her into the kitchen where a few caterers bustled around. "It's busy in here," she whispered.

"Don't worry about it. Come over here." They found an open spot at the breakfast table and sat down.

"Can I get you something to drink?" a young woman in a uniform asked them, setting down some napkins.

"No, thank you. We're just fine." TJ offered the woman a smile and then turned to Jen. "I'm going to grab a couple of waters. Is that okay?"

"Sure. Thanks. Better hurry or I'll eat your food, too."

He placed a quick kiss on her head and then walked over to the refrigerator. When he opened it, there wasn't a water bottle in sight. He glanced at Jen. "Be right back."

Heading through the house, he made his way to the garage, noticing that his mother had redecorated a bit since Christmas when he'd been here last. Not a big surprise. Besides the layout, nothing was the way it was when he left for college many years ago.

After grabbing two bottles of water out of the garage fridge, he walked back inside and met up with his father in the hallway.

"Dad, hey."

"TJ. Good to see you."

"Yeah. You too. I never got to thank you properly for coming out to the party at the Stag last month."

"Of course. We wouldn't have missed it. Seems like you had a good turnout."

TJ couldn't help but notice how glassy his father's eyes were, or how badly he stunk of vodka. The party hadn't even been going on that long, but intoxication was obviously his father's way of dealing with the crowd.

"Yeah, we did. I was pleased with how everything turned out." Except for how the evening had ended. Jen injuring herself had not been ideal. "Dad, that reminds me, I've been meaning to ask you something. Do you have any idea why Neil Bodisto refuses to do business with us? His son came that night, but we still can't seem to get a contract with them."

His father stepped back, his face clearly pondering that. "My only guess is because Neil hasn't gotten over me sleeping with his wife."

TJ stared up at the man he'd always tried so hard to make proud. And for what reason? None came to mind. His dad was a horrible piece of shit. "I see. Well, that does make a lot of sense. Doesn't it?"

TJ started to step around his father, but the man put a hand on TJ's chest, stopping him. "It was years ago, TJ. Don't you walk away from here thinking you know me."

Removing the hand from his shirt, TJ glared up at the weathered face hovering in front of him. "That's the thing, Dad. I don't know you at all. But from what I can tell, you're not a nice guy, and you treat our mother terribly. Now, if you'll excuse me, I need to get back to my girlfriend."

He began to walk down the hall but froze when his father spoke again.

"Girlfriend?" The word was followed by a bitter laugh. His father was definitely trashed. But that didn't excuse this behavior. "Do you mean the young lady in the kitchen? I thought I saw her tending bar at your party."

TJ turned, anger simmering in his gut. "You did, Dad. Jen also works the front desk."

"Fraternizing is never a good idea, Trevor."

"We're not only fraternizing, we're living together. And I think I can handle myself just fine."

The older man shook his head. "Why have her move in if you don't intend to marry her?"

TJ's head jerked back, his anger rising. "Who says I don't?"

His father chuckled again. "You marry the good girls, TJ. You know that. The rest are just for fun."

A quiet gasp caught TJ's attention and he turned to see his mother standing at the end of the hallway with a look of pain and horror on her face. As if that didn't break TJ's heart enough, next to her stood Jen.

Her expression was blank, her eyes meeting his.

"Ellen." His father shook his head. "You know I'm kidding. I've had too many cocktails." He glanced at Jen. "My apologies, miss."

"You're damn right," TJ said quietly, rage suddenly

overflowing. "You owe a lot of people apologies, but right now the only person I care about is Jen. And I'll tell you what, she is exactly the kind of woman I want to live with. *And* marry. Because she's smart and beautiful and loving. And I'll learn from your mistakes and be sure to let her know daily how much I love her so that she doesn't have to cover up her pain with vodka every night."

TJ walked down the hall to Jen, whose eyes had gone wide. He leaned over and kissed his mother's cheek. "Mom, I love you, but we're leaving."

She grabbed his face roughly. "I love you, TJ."

He nodded, pulled away, and reached for Jen. But she stepped around him, her mouth severe. Oh shit.

"Just so you know, your son is the best person I know, and you don't deserve him," she said, pointing a finger at his father. TJ's heart pounded as she turned and took a hold of his outstretched hand. She was shaking. With fury, fear, or both?

He led her through the house and out the front door. Then he pulled up short, pressed a firm kiss onto her lips, and then they proceeded to valet station in silence. When the young kid located TJ's keys he just took them from his hand and slipped him a few bucks. "I see the car. We'll walk."

Halfway across the massive yard across the street, Jen stopped, this time halting TJ with her. He turned to her. She looked so damn beautiful in the fading sunlight. Deep red and gold highlights revealing themselves in her jet hair. And after what she'd just done, he was never letting her go.

"Are you okay?" she asked.

He stepped closer to her and looked in her eyes. "Yes. I'm more than okay. Are you?"

She laughed, glancing down. "Don't worry about me. I'm used to judgment. And being bitchy."

TJ pulled her against him, a chuckle escaping his lips. "God, you were so fucking amazing in there." He thought of the other part of her comment and pulled back to look into her eyes. "But I'm not okay with you used to being judged, Jen. If I'd have known what just happened was a possibility, we never would have come."

"Maybe it's good we did. I'm not upset about what happened."

He shook his head. "No. It will never be okay that my father is that way, and treats my mother like shit."

"You're right. I felt so sorry for her."

"Don't. She's known who he is for most of her life, and she has convinced herself that being rich and ignorant is better than being happy."

"It's all she's ever known, TJ. You need to consider that there's more to it for your mom."

He took her hand and continued to lead them to the car. "I suppose you're right. I guess I'm still seeing it from the perspective of her very angry son."

Opening the passenger door, he waited for Jen to sit down. When she did, he squatted down beside her. "I hope you know I meant every word I said in there. Every word I've ever said. I've been in love with you since . . . since forever. I don't think I knew it back then, but I do now."

Her eyes widened, going glassy. "Forever as in . . ."

He smiled, recalling how long he'd known that she

was special. "I bet you don't know that I showed up for every performance of *Grease*. Just so I could watch you. Listen to you sing."

Her lips quirked to the side and she looked away, swiping at her cheek. "Goddamn you, Trevor James. I was such a strong woman until you decided to be my hero."

He smiled and leaned forward to press his lips into her cheek. "You're still a strong woman. That's why I love you, and why I want to keep being your hero."

More than anything, he wanted her to say it back. Instead she turned to face him, placing a hand on his jaw.

"As my hero, will you stop and pick us up some gas station barbecue on the way home?"

He couldn't help grinning. "Whatever you want."

# Twenty-Two

The following Saturday, Jen was working a wedding for the first time as a pseudo-coordinator, and not a bartender. She'd presented the idea to the guys a couple of weeks ago, only because she'd worked so closely with this particular bride over the past eight weeks. Elaine, the bride, had requested Jen be there if possible, which had made her feel good.

The guys had been happy to agree, although Dean had suggested he still come, since it had originally been his night, and Jen had never been solely in charge of the building before. Once all the vendors started to show up, asking where things were located, where they should park and unload, she was grateful he was there.

Once the band had set up, the caterer had arrived, and all the lights were set just so, Jen glanced at her phone. It was five. The ceremony had just started over at the church, so guests would start arriving for cocktail time in about an hour. She had a minute to grab a drink and a snack, and collect her thoughts.

She went down the elevator and headed for the front

desk where she had some trail mix and water bottles stashed in her drawer. Sitting down, she took a drink and on instinct clicked onto the computer and began to scroll through social media.

After a minute, an alert popped up that she had a direct message. She opened it.

> *Hi Jen-This is Erin Kingman. I hope I'm not harassing you, but I left you a voicemail several weeks ago and realized that some people don't listen to them. Just wanted to try one more time to contact you.*

Jen continued reading. Erin basically spelled out the same thing she had last time. The only difference this time was the last line.

> *If you're hesitant, you might consider just coming up for a couple of weeks and giving it a try. You could stay with me. Let me know if you have any questions.*

Sucking in a deep breath, Jen's eyes darted back over the message again. She'd been trying to put this out of her mind, but it hadn't necessarily been working.

Clicking open a new browser, she did a quick Google search for the name of the school. The minute the page loaded, Jen wanted to weep. It appeared to be a very nice school. The photos showed productions with incredibly high-quality sets and costumes. The kind that any performer would love to be a part of.

She went back to the message and let her fingers

hover over the keyboard. Blowing out a shaky breath, she began to type.

> *Hi Erin. I did get your voicemail and I'll be honest, the idea is intriguing. This sounds like the exact kind of job I would love. However, there has been some hesitancy, the reason I didn't respond. Part of the problem is my mother is currently battling breast cancer and I'm not sure I'm willing to leave her. Would you mind giving me some time to think about it? I'm so grateful you considered me.*

To Jen's surprise, the message showed that Erin had read it almost immediately. She waited to see if a reply would come back. Standing up, Jen glanced around the main room to see if anyone was milling around looking for her. When she didn't see anyone she sat back down.

And why did she feel so damn guilty?

When she glanced to the computer, Erin had replied.

> *I'm so sorry to hear about your mother! I completely understand wanting to be there with her. If it has any sway, I don't need anyone officially until December 1st. We currently make do with interns from the arts college for voice lessons, but recently a benefactor surprised us with a budget increase so I'd like to hire someone full-time.*

*Again, it would be great to have you visit to see what you think. Might help make your decision. Let me know and I could arrange a flight for you. I just need a definitive answer on the position by Thanksgiving so I can start planning for our spring musical, so anytime before then I'd love to have you for a visit.*

*Oh my God.* How could she turn down an offer like that? Without further thought, she replied instantly.

*I may take you up on that offer to visit. Will let you know within the month.*

Jen looked at the calendar on her phone. It was almost October, and she honestly had no idea what she would do. In her head she kept hearing TJ's words. *I love you. Tell me you're mine.* But they were still in the honeymoon phase. That could all fade away. And then what would she do? Be homeless like she had been so often as a child?

Live with her mother? As good as things had been lately, they still weren't great. The last thing she wanted to do was be a thirty-year-old living with a parent. A parent who could potentially die soon.

She knew it was time that she told TJ about Erin's offer. Maybe Charlotte was right. He'd been supportive of everything so far, and maybe he could offer some insight. Plus, she just really wanted to talk to him about it. Tonight when she got home, she would tell him.

The front door opened, startling her. Dean walked up to the counter and leaned his elbows on it, glancing down at her.

"Hey," she said, noticing how shaky her voice was.

"You okay?" he asked.

"Yeah, fine." She held up her trail mix bag. "Just needed some sustenance. Want some?"

He shook his head. "I'm good. Thanks. But I'm glad I caught you here early. I wanted to tell you something. I haven't even had a chance to tell the other guys yet."

"Oh? I hope it's not bad."

"No, nothing like that. Tara and Ben came by yesterday afternoon. You and TJ had already left."

Jen's stomach plummeted. This was it. Tara was ready to come back. This was what she'd been waiting for. Everything would now change. Force her to either get a job or make a decision that would be painful. "And?"

"Well, they're considering having Tara stay home with the baby. They think they can swing it with Ben's income alone, considering how expensive childcare is. And obviously Tara wants that."

Jen was shocked. Of course, she'd known that was a possibility, but she didn't think it would happen. Plus, she figured they'd have heard by now.

"So, what do you think?" Dean asked.

"I don't know what to think."

"Well, I figured I'd hear from you first how you felt about it before I broke the news to TJ and Jake. I wanted to know how I can support you going in. Because I know what TJ will want. But it's not up to him."

"What are you saying, Dean?"

"If Tara decides to be a stay-at-home mom, are you interested in her position?"

Jen's shoulders slumped. *Did* she want that? She'd been enjoying her work at the Stag, but part of her wondered if it had been fun because she'd known it was temporary. It was a far cry from her previous job of teaching kids voice and drama lessons. Taking over Tara's job would feel like . . . giving up. Plus, she'd just replied to Erin Kingman.

"I honestly don't know," Jen said. "I'd have to think about it."

"I understand. Maybe you and TJ can talk it over together. I'll let you tell him."

Well, they'd certainly have a lot to discuss this evening. She looked at Dean. "Okay. Thank you."

Deciding she'd sat down long enough, Jen followed Dean upstairs to the reception room. Things were much busier, with servers setting up tables and musicians tuning their instruments. Jen glanced over to make sure Eric, the bartender, was setting up.

It wasn't long before the wedding guests arrived and began eating hors d'oeuvres and getting cocktails. By the time the bridal party showed up, everything was perfect.

The minute Jen saw the bride, she rushed over. "Elaine, you look beautiful. I'm Jen."

Elaine's eyes went wide and she wrapped Jen in a huge hug. "It's so nice to finally meet you face-to-face. Everything looks so perfect. You have the dance floor right where I wanted. Thank you!"

"It's been my pleasure." Jen smiled at the groom. "Why don't you all go grab a drink from the bar?"

Jen saw Charlotte and her second shooter Lauren lugging their gear to the side room off the bar, where they usually stored their stuff and had dinner. "Looks great in here," Charlotte said to Jen.

"Doesn't it? How has the day gone so far?" Jen asked.

"Really well. We got the most amazing portraits. They're a very photogenic couple."

Jen could imagine that easily, as attractive as they both were. She stood off to the side of the room and let Charlotte and Lauren get to work photographing the bride and groom greeting their guests and giving hugs to family.

She was still people watching when a hand touched her on the arm. A woman stood there, and it took Jen a minute, but she recognized who she was.

"Terri? How are you?" Jen asked, grabbing her hand. "I almost didn't recognize you all dolled up."

The other woman laughed. "I don't do it very often. I haven't seen you in a while."

Jen smiled. "I know, it's so nice to see you. You obviously know Elaine and Brett?"

"I do. I work with Brett's mother at the credit union."

They chatted for a few moments about the couple. "Your mother told me you worked here," Terri said. "What a great way to meet guys, huh?"

Jen laughed. "I don't know about that. But it's fun here."

She had always liked her mother's oldest friend.

"How's your mom doing? I still just can't believe about your building catching fire."

"I know. It was horrible," Jen said.

"Have they figured out how it happened yet?"

"Sounds like it was electrical, down in the laundry room."

Terri's eyes went wide. "So it's the fault of the management?"

Jen nodded. TJ had fumed when he'd heard that news. "Afraid so. I'm just glad no one was hurt."

Terri shook her head. "Well, I'll be. You just never know, do you? I need to get over there and check on your mother. I haven't seen her in a couple of weeks."

Jen's eyes narrowed. "Didn't you just see her a few days ago for her appointment?"

As far as Jen knew, Terri had been driving her mother to all of her checkups required by the trial.

"No, I've been busy. But I am taking her to get her next MRI. That's next Friday. I'm praying for a miracle. I'm sure you are, too." Terri patted Jen's arm.

"Terri, who has been taking her to the weekly appointments?" Jen asked.

A look of confusion passed over Terri's face. "What weekly appointments?"

"For the medical trial," Jen said, worry beginning to buzz in her chest. "She told me you were taking her."

Terri's eyes went wide. "Oh, honey, she didn't qualify for that. She didn't tell—" Terri stopped short. Squeezed Jen's arm. "Oh, Jen. I'm so sorry. I had no idea."

Jen's mouth was hanging open and she vaguely heard Terri mention that "Diane is going to have my head." Barely felt the tug on her arm.

"Jen. Jen?" Terri was saying. Finally, Jen looked at the older woman. "Don't be upset with her. I'm sure she just didn't want you to worry."

Jen patted her hand. "Excuse me, Terri."

She turned and walked across the room, past the bar, and into the side room where she hoped to find Dean or Charlotte. She found both. Charlotte and Lauren were eating dinner and Dean was sitting on the arm of the sofa giving Charlotte a back massage.

The minute Jen opened the door, his eyes narrowed.

"What's wrong?" Charlotte said.

"Can you keep an eye on things for a bit?" Jen asked Dean.

He immediately walked over to her. "Everything okay?"

"No, but . . . yes. I mean, I just need to make a phone call. Please."

"Sure, no problem."

"Jen, what's wrong?" Charlotte asked, standing up. "Is it your mom?"

"Yes, actually. Do you guys mind if I make a call in here?" Jen asked, pulling her phone from her back pocket.

"Of course not. Do you need some privacy?" Lauren asked.

"No, no. You're fine." At this point Jen really didn't even care. When she looked down at her phone she had a message from TJ. It was a selfie of him and the cactus plant they'd bought together a few weeks ago for the patio. He was pointing to a tiny nub on the plant. The woman at the nursery had explained to them how cactuses could sprout babies.

His message said, *We became parents today!*

Jen briefly smiled but then closed out her message app and pulled up her mom's number. The minute it started ringing, Jen felt sick to her stomach.

"Hello," Diane said upon answering.

"Mom, hi." Jen felt flustered and angry, suddenly not sure how she was going to ask this question. Then it just came blurting out. "You didn't qualify for the clinical trial."

There was silence on the other end. Finally, her mother quietly replied, "No. I didn't."

Jen felt like she'd been punched in the gut. "Mom," she cried. "Why didn't you tell me?"

"Because I knew you'd be upset, Jen. You would have and you know it."

"Of course I would have. But I also would have known it wasn't your fault. We'd have just made a new plan. Done chemo."

"And that's exactly what I didn't want. Do you remember what hell that was? Probably not, Jen, because you weren't the one going through it. I was, and it was awful."

"I don't understand how you didn't qualify."

"My prognosis was too advanced."

Jen shook her head. "You're telling me you are too sick with cancer to qualify for a trial that treats cancer."

"Apparently so."

A long silence followed. Jen could hear her mother breathing. Finally, Diane spoke. "I promised him I'd tell you when I was ready. I don't know why he had to do it."

Jen's stomach bottomed out. "What? *Who*?"

"TJ, who else?" Diane cried.

Jen wobbled on her feet. She turned—stunned—to find Charlotte and Lauren watching her. The minute she began to walk, Charlotte got up and took her hand to lead her to the sofa.

She sat down, her thoughts reeling. "When did you tell TJ, Mom?"

"Are you telling me he's not the one who told you?" her mother asked quietly.

"No. Terri did. Now tell me when you told him." Jen knew her voice was beyond stern when Charlotte and Lauren began to look at each other.

Diane sighed. "It was the weekend I stayed there with you guys."

Jen shut her eyes. Weeks ago. Over a month.

"Jen, it's not his fault. I asked him not to say anything," her mother went on quietly.

"Yeah, that was wrong of you. But it was more wrong of him to agree." Jen ended the call, and she felt her body begin to shake.

She wasn't sure what had upset her more. That her mother wasn't being treated in any way. Or that TJ had kept this from her.

"Jen. Talk to me," Charlotte said.

"My mom is getting no treatment for her cancer. And TJ knew it."

Charlotte's brow furrowed. "From what it sounds like, your mom put him into a really tough position."

"But who is he loyal to? Me . . . or my mother?"

She stood up. "Please tell Dean I'm so sorry. But I have to go."

Charlotte nodded. "He'll understand."

Her demeanor and the odd look on her face had Jen turning back to Charlotte. "You knew . . . didn't you?"

Charlotte's lips parted as she stepped forward. "Jen, I'm so sorry. TJ told Dean and obviously Dean told me. If it makes any difference . . . TJ loves you so much. You have to know that. He has for a long time."

"Why didn't you tell me?"

Charlotte sighed. "Because it wasn't my place, Jen. On the flip side I also told Dean about your job offer, and he didn't tell TJ that. Those conversations have to happen between the two of you."

That sort of made sense.

"I'm sorry. I hope you can forgive me," Charlotte said.

Tears suddenly burned Jen's eyes. "Of course I can. You've forgiven me something much worse."

"No," Charlotte shook her head, stepped forward, and wrapped her arms around Jen. The feel of that almost caused Jen to break down fully. "Don't think that way. That had nothing to do with me. I know that."

When they stepped apart, Jen nodded. "I'm gonna go. I'll speak with Elaine on my way out."

# Twenty-Three

TJ looked at the time on the TV. Jen still wouldn't be home for two or three more hours. Which sucked. He hated wedding nights where she worked and he didn't. Now he understood all the times Dean manipulated the schedule so he could be the one on duty when Charlotte was there.

A car coming down the driveway got his attention, and he stood up and walked over to the front window. It was Jen's truck, which had his heart pounding. Walking over to the kitchen, TJ picked up his cell phone off the island and looked at the screen. No calls from her but a text from Dean. *So sorry, man. She knows.*

Shit. What did she know? Then it hit him.

Diane.

He set the phone back down the minute the front door opened, and then she was standing in the kitchen doorway. Her eyes were rimmed red, and she looked furious.

"Why?"

"Jen, listen," TJ said, taking a tentative step toward her.

"Listen?" she cried. Stepping forward, she reached out and shoved him in the chest. "I would have listened to you tell me my mother was choosing to die, if you'd told me a month ago. Now? I'm not sure I want to listen to you."

TJ grabbed a hold of her wrists and held his ground because he'd seen the second push coming. His teeth grit together. "Jen. Stop. Talk to me."

"There is nothing to talk about." She spat out. "Fuck you and your 'I love you.' When people love each other they don't lie."

She pulled away from him and headed for the pantry, where she grabbed a bottle of Stag Forkhorn White Vodka.

"Jen, don't."

"Oh, I'm sorry, is this a trigger for you? Does this make you afraid that I'm going to be an alcoholic like our mothers?" she said in a snotty voice. "Because you know what my trigger is? Looking like an idiot, and that's exactly how I looked tonight when I realized everyone knew about my mom but me. The person who'd been taking care of her for the last year."

TJ sucked in a breath and stared back at her. It felt like there was a vice on his heart, clamping down the blood flow, making his brain foggy. "Jen, please. I told you I love you and I meant it. Even if you never love me back, I still love you."

She stopped pouring her drink and gently set the bottle down on the counter. For a long moment, she stared at him, her eyes watery, her mouth swollen.

Finally, she tilted her head to the side. "I don't know what to do with that."

And then she picked up her drink and left him standing there. He heard her footsteps on the stairs and then the bedroom door slam. He stood there listening to her move around above him. When the bathtub turned on, he waited for a bit, and then went up the stairs.

He was surprised to find the door unlocked and went inside. Slowly he walked toward the master bathroom and leaned against the door frame. Seeing her leaning back in his vintage-style tub, eyes closed, bubbles brushing against her breasts, nearly undid him. It was painful, knowing he may never see her like this again. This was where she belonged. In his house, in his bed, in his life.

"I didn't invite you up here," she said, eyes still closed.

He pushed off the doorframe and walked over to the bathtub. "No, you didn't. Can I sit down anyway?"

Jen shrugged. "Can't stop you, can I? This is your house." She still didn't look at him.

"This is now your house too, Jen."

She opened her eyes just to roll them. "No, it's not. How can you say that?"

"Because it's true."

"We've discussed our issues so many times jokingly, but clearly they're very real," she said quietly. "Maybe this is more trouble than it's worth. We can't even keep from lying to each other."

"There is a difference between withholding information and lying. You know that, Jen."

"Is there? I'm not so sure anymore. These past few weeks have been confusing for me. Amazing, but almost not even real. Like I've been playing house, waiting for this kind of bomb to drop."

"I know what you're doing. You're afraid. Afraid that this is all meant to be. You, here with me. You're afraid that you love me back."

She shook her head. "Don't psychoanalyze me," she said quietly.

He stood up, frustrated by her quiet and apparent acceptance that this was a failed relationship. "Then prove me wrong. You know just as well as I do that sometimes people keep things from their partners to spare them pain. I did it. I'm sorry. I'm sure there were some selfish motives wrapped in there somewhere, but don't tell me you've never done the same thing."

Her lips began to quiver and she sucked in a breath. He kneeled down beside the tub. "Jen, talk to me. Don't let this ruin what we have."

"You're right. I am afraid. And I'm also just as much of an asshole."

His brow furrowed. "What do you mean?"

"I've kept things from you, too. You're right. To protect you. But more . . . to protect myself. I've been offered a job teaching voice in Chicago," she whispered. Every nerve in TJ's body went on alert. He felt dizzy. She swallowed. "And you should also know that I had sex with Dean three years ago."

His mouth dropped open, stomach clenching in pain.

Then he stood up. *"What?"*

"It happened. It was stupid . . . and we were drunk. And . . . it never happened again."

Turning, TJ glanced around the bathroom, his eyes unable to focus on anything. Had he heard her correctly? Job? Sex? Dean? What the hell had just happened?

"TJ," she said behind him. "Look at me."

He heard the water fall from her body as she sat up. But he couldn't look at her. It had been bad enough to know she was sleeping with other men over the years. It had never even occurred to him that one of them was his friend.

He walked out.

TJ had been driving for hours. As soon as he'd left the house, he'd headed toward downtown Kansas City. Just gotten on the highway without a destination in mind. He needed to get away. After driving as far as Preston, twenty minutes north of downtown, he'd turned around and come back.

It was almost eleven. He'd been sitting in his car in the alley behind the Stag for nearly two hours. Waiting. Thinking. Trying not to cry, or vandalize something.

He'd still had enough sense to wait until this evening's wedding had died down. And then he sent a text. *"Can you come outside? In the alley."*

He waited for a reply. After about ten minutes, the back door opened, and Dean stepped out. TJ got out of his Camaro and leaned against the door as Dean walked down the concrete steps next to the loading dock on the back of their building.

"What's going on, man?" Dean's tone was light, but TJ knew the guy well enough to see that he was tense.

"Not much."

The floodlight near the back door gave them plenty of light to see each other.

Dean stopped about six feet away from TJ and put his hands in his pockets. "Everything okay?"

TJ shook his head, trying to decide where to start without losing his shit. "Not really, no."

Dean nodded, glancing at the ground for a minute. "Do I know what this is about?"

TJ inhaled deeply and blew it out. "I'm pretty sure you do."

This time Dean's nod was knowing. He looked at TJ. "I'm sorry. It was a long, long time ago. At that time . . . I had no idea how you felt about her. None."

TJ looked up at the sky, swallowed. "How'd it happen?"

"Come on, man, no. You don't want to do this," Dean said.

"Actually, I do." TJ's voice got a little louder. "How'd it happen?"

"It was after a wedding. One of our early ones, and it was . . . a hell of a night. She'd gotten her ass kicked behind the bar, and shit, we just decided to open a bottle of vodka. We were here alone. That was that."

"That was that? Are you fucking kidding me?"

"What do you want me to say?" Dean said, throwing his hands out to his sides. "We drank. We were grown-ups. It happened. We hadn't flirted our way into that situation. We didn't flirt after that either. Hell, we never even really talked about it again."

They were both silent, long enough for a group of wedding guests to walk through the alley to where they'd parked. Must have been a big one.

Once they were alone again, Dean kicked at the concrete, sending a chunk flying into a fence. "You want to punch me?" he asked, shocking TJ.

"Hell yeah, I want to punch you."

"Then let's get it over with."

TJ shook his head and turned away, hands on his hips. "What fucking kills me is there is nothing I can do to change it. My mind . . . goddamn I can't stop imagining it."

"Don't do that to yourself," Dean said.

"That's easy for you to say!" TJ yelled.

"You're right. I'm sorry, man. You have no idea how sorry. I never wanted to hurt you, and as soon as I started to realize how you felt, it gutted me. I knew finding out would destroy you."

TJ pinched the bridge of his nose, eyes squeezed shut. God, he wanted to beat the shit out of something. Turning back around, he crossed his arms over his chest. "Does Charlotte know?"

"Yes."

"How'd she take it?"

Dean shrugged. "How do you think? But I've gotta give her credit, she didn't confront Jen. Never has."

TJ glared at him. "What the hell does that mean? You think I shouldn't be here right now?"

"No, no. I shouldn't have said that. It's not the same. I expected this if you ever found out." Dean pointed back and forth between the two of them. "The minute I got your text, I knew. Men don't respond to news like this the way women do. I guess I'm just impressed by the fact that it didn't occur to her to stop being friends with Jen because of it. She knew it had nothing to do with her. Just like what happened had nothing to do with you."

TJ inhaled, nodding. "Jen said she got a job offer. In Chicago."

He hadn't intended to share that, but suddenly he needed to get it out. For the past several hours he hadn't wanted to face the reality of what she'd said, so instead he'd poured all of his emotions into his fury at finding out about her and Dean.

"Charlotte told me about that," Dean said.

"God*damn*! You've got to be kidding me," TJ said. "Charlotte knew that, too?"

Dean groaned. "Jen told her. What do you want from me, man? Sounds like the problem is that you two don't talk."

TJ leaned against the car once again. "Apparently not. And here I thought things were going so well. Fuck me."

"You've got to remember, you and Jen, you're still new. This situation you two have found yourselves in—with her moving in and shit—it's a little insane. You need to cut yourselves a break. Both of you. But the communication channels need to open immediately."

TJ knew he was right. They'd gone from zero to sixty in a short amount of time. It wasn't natural. But all he could think was that he'd loved Jen forever, so it felt like an eternity.

"She gonna take it?" Dean asked. "Because earlier

today I told her that Tara and Ben informed me that Tara wants to be a stay-at-home mom."

"Seriously?" he asked, thinking it was the first bit of good news he'd heard all evening.

"Yeah, I told Jen. Told her to tell you. But seeing as you two don't communicate . . ." Dean raised an eyebrow. TJ just shook his head.

"What did she say?"

Dean shrugged. "Not much. She seemed surprised. I told her she needed to consider if taking over Tara's job was something she truly wanted. That was it. Sounds like you need to go home and discuss a few things with her. Or a whole lot of things."

TJ pushed off the car. "I'm not ready to do that. Think I'm gonna sleep in my office."

"Do you really want to do that? You've got a woman at home alone trying to decide if she wants to move away from you." Dean raised both his eyebrows. "If it was me, I'd get my ass back there right now."

# Twenty-Four

For the thousandth time, Jen glanced at her phone. It was midnight. She rolled over and looked at the empty space beside her. She kept freezing, thinking she'd heard something, but it was just her mind playing tricks.

He wasn't going to come home. She could feel it.

Maybe that was for the best, because in the many hours since he'd stormed out, all she'd done was think. About her life. Her passions. The time she'd spent taking care of her mother. Jen loved nothing more than singing and acting, and her previous job had brought her more joy than anything else. She knew in her heart that she owed it to herself to give that a shot. Opportunities like the one Erin had granted her didn't come around every day. If she didn't at least try, she'd regret it for the rest of her life. She knew that in her soul.

But the other half of her was devastated by the look on his face when she'd told him what she'd found out earlier. But the minute he'd turned the tables on her, she'd known he was right. Finding out about her mother from Terri had been heartbreaking. And infuriating. That had been the worst part. Finding out about *TJ* gave her someone to blame, but it wasn't his fault.

Jen considered herself a reasonable person, and that part of her could understand TJ being put in a tough position. She kept thinking about Charlotte, when she'd said, "That was a conversation for the two of you." She was right in many aspects—her mother's health was a conversation for Jen and Diane.

Rolling over, she set her phone on the nightstand, and tried to go to sleep. Just as she was dosing off, she heard the front door creak open downstairs. Stiffening, she waited and listened.

She could hear him go into the kitchen. Then his feet on the steps. In the bedroom. Jen squeezed her eyes shut, facing the opposite wall, as she listened to the rustle of him removing his clothes. When the bed sunk in behind her, she said a silent prayer. *Please touch me. Tell me I'm wrong. Love me anyway.*

And then he did, sliding in behind her, his strong arms slipping under hers, pulling her back against his chest. She closed her eyes, letting her body melt into his.

There were no words between them, instead he leaned down and pressed his mouth against her neck, kissing along her jaw, up to her ear. Jen rolled as much as she could, tilting her head up to look at him.

Their eyes locked in the darkness and held for a long moment.

"I didn't think you'd come back," she whispered.

"No matter how hard I try, I've never been able to stop wanting you."

She could feel her heart break into a thousand pieces as his lips settled onto hers. His mouth plundered, his tongue almost punishing her as he lifted up and rolled her body beneath his.

As he settled on top of her, she dropped her hands down to find his bare ass. She squeezed it hard, and he groaned into her mouth as his tongue danced with hers. As he began to move on top of her, grinding down against her pajama shorts, all she could think about was how bad she needed to be filled by him.

Maybe this was forgiveness. Maybe it was goodbye. Maybe both.

Right now, all she wanted to do was feel.

When he moved to slide her shorts and panties down, she shimmied on the bed to help him. With two quick moves, he was on her once more, shoving her legs apart with his knees. There was anger to his kisses now, as he sucked on her breasts. One, then the other.

Making his way back up her chest, neck, jaw, and finally to her lips, he stared down at her as he slowly slid in deep.

She gasped, her mouth falling open, and his expression almost looked fierce. His brow furrowed, teeth clamped down on his bottom lip. Like an animal. But the minute he began to move inside her, his eyelids fluttered shut. Peace came over his features like she'd never seen before. It was so beautiful she wanted to cry. How would she ever handle being apart from him?

His pace picked up, became frantic, his body slapping against hers. Jen lifted her legs, bringing them back toward her chest, and he didn't hesitate to use the new angle to pound into her even harder.

That was when she felt it, the release she'd been working toward, her body flying apart beneath his. She moaned, squeezing onto his biceps, her lower half vibrating.

TJ knocked her hands away, then took them both into his own, lacing their fingers. He lowered his chest onto hers, forcing her hands above her head as he continued to piston inside of her.

Nothing between them had ever been so good. She wanted to scream, cry, and claw at him. But with her hands and arms locked above her, all she could do was succumb. His thrusts slowed as he came, his face buried in her hair.

When he stilled, she heard him speak. "No matter what you do or where you are, I'll still want you."

She didn't reply. Only the sound of their heavy breathing filled the room. After a moment, he pushed off the bed and left the room.

He didn't come back the rest of the night.

TJ poured Jen a cup of coffee as soon as he heard her walking around upstairs.

He had no idea what things would be like this morning between them, but he owed her an apology after what he'd done last night. Coming into their bed like some kind of angry dog in heat, not even using a condom. The thought still left him cold.

And although he knew she'd have stopped him if she wanted to, he wanted her to know that behavior was not him. He wasn't proud of what he'd done. That was part of the reason he'd left her and retreated to the living room to sleep.

Not that he'd done much sleeping.

Her footsteps on the stairs had him straightening up. When she entered the kitchen, her hair was mussed and her eyes puffy.

"Good morning," he said.

"Good morning."

She immediately saw the coffee on the counter next to him and stepped over to it. He liked that she'd gotten so close, and didn't walk away. Instead she stood near, taking a sip. He turned to face her and set his own mug down.

"Jen, I'm sorry about last night. I acted like a fucking . . . beast and—"

"I loved it," she said, looking up at him.

His eyes went wide.

She shrugged. "Don't apologize again. I wanted it. I loved it." She walked over to the table and sat down with her mug.

*Okay then.*

He followed her and sat down also, deciding to see what she said next, because clearly he was mucking this up. She drank her coffee for a few minutes, holding onto it with both hands. When she finally set it down, he put his elbows on the table, leaned forward, just waiting.

Finally she spoke.

"I'm thinking of going to Chicago."

And now he wanted her to stop talking. *Shit.* His teeth clamped together and his lips pursed. But he held his tongue, before he said the wrong thing. How could she be serious?

"If I don't do it, I will regret it. And then I will resent everything." She met his eyes. "Even you."

He glanced down at the table, trying to decide what to think or say. Nothing came to mind.

"Say something," she said.

He inhaled, trying to catch his breath, and then blew it out. "I'm trying."

"Tell me you understand."

"Uh, okay. If that's what you need. I understand."

She rolled her eyes. "I want *you* to understand. Not just say it."

"Well, forgive me if I'm being a selfish prick, but I *don't* understand." He stared at her, his body vibrating. "You have a home here. With me. A job. Also with me. But it's not enough. I love you, Jen. I've told you several times, and I'm still waiting for you to say it back."

When she glanced down at the table, he cursed under his breath, got up, and left the room.

Monday morning, TJ had a migraine from hell. He had barely spoken to Jen in twenty-four hours. He'd let her sleep in his bed again last night while he'd taken the guest bedroom, and when he'd gotten up she'd already left.

He pulled into the alley behind the Stag, surprised to see her truck already there. How long were they going to avoid each other? When was she leaving? Would they speak again before that happened?

Making his way inside, TJ ran straight into her at the back door. She was wearing tight black jeans with perfect rips in the thigh and knee and a sleeveless red blouse that matched her lips, and she had her hair in a ponytail. His heart nearly broke at how beautiful she looked. He loved her in red. How would he survive not seeing her every day? Every night? A week ago, they'd have spent the morning in bed together. He'd have watched her put on those clothes. Seen her apply her that lipstick. Not anymore, apparently.

"Hi," he said.

"Good morning. I need to speak to you before the meeting I called with the other guys."

He stilled. "About what?"

"Can we just go to your office?"

"Of course." He followed her into the main room, down the hall, and into his office, trying to ignore the tangerine scent of her the entire time. It was destroying him.

He shut the door behind them, but instead of sitting, she got right to it. "Realizing our need to be honest with each other, I wanted to tell you first that I've decided to do a trial run of the job in Chicago."

He stared at her, his heart sinking, although this didn't come as a surprise. "A trial? To see if you can live without me?"

She shook her head. "This is not about you, TJ."

"That's what you say."

"And it's the truth. This is about me. For me. I'd really like you to understand that."

He nodded, thinking of a way to respond that wouldn't be complete assholery. "I've tried to be there for you, Jen. Tried to understand a lot. But I can only handle so much."

"I understand. I'm not asking you to wait for me. Just . . . never mind. I wanted to tell you first. I owe you that."

He had no idea how to reply, so he let her leave without saying a word.

A few minutes later Dean peeked his head in and alerted TJ that Jen had called a meeting in the conference room. TJ felt like skipping it. Let her handle this shit on her own. But he reluctantly got up and made his way into the room and sat down. Jen wasn't there yet, but Dean and John were.

They all sat down and then Jake walked in. He was on a break from his tour, back for a week. "Morning." The guy looked a little rough.

"Groupie life too much for you to handle?" Dean asked.

Jake just smirked and sat down at the table, coffee in hand. "Nothing like life on the road. So what's this about?" Jake asked the room. "Dean said Jen's got something to say. Is this your fault, TJ?"

"Shut up," TJ said, scooting his chair forward.

"You guys should have warned me when I started here how much drama was involved," John said with a smirk.

Dean glared at him. "Seriously, man? You're my girlfriend's ex. You're part of the drama."

"Point taken," John said, putting his hands up.

Then Jen walked in. Even though they'd just spoken, she felt a thousand miles away, and didn't even make eye contact with him when she took her place at the end of the conference table.

"Morning, men," she said.

They all grunted their replies. TJ just stared at her.

"I have some news that might make you panic a bit, but I've spent the morning making a plan. This week I will work my ass off to get things caught up and covered, because next week I'm going to Chicago to do a trial run for a job offer I've received there."

Even though he'd known it was coming, TJ felt the floor drop out beneath him all over again. Dean's head jerked back to look at him, but TJ couldn't take his eyes off of Jen. Finally, her gaze clashed with his. She looked away.

"What kind of job?" Jake asked.

"Teaching voice lessons at a prestigious theater company for children. It's . . . it's something I've always wanted to do and I can't miss out on the opportunity."

"But"—Jake looked back at TJ—"what about TJ?"

Yeah, apparently Jake hadn't been briefed on the drama that had gone down.

Jen cleared her throat. "This isn't going to be easy. But it's something I have to do."

Jake gave TJ a look of pity and then looked down at the table.

"Jen, where will you be staying?" Dean asked. "Have you made arrangements?"

"Yes. The woman offering me the job is a friend of a friend. I'll be staying with her. If I like the job, then I'd have to move there by December first. Hopefully by then I'll have my insurance settlement to tide me over for a while."

TJ could barely breathe. How could she make this

announcement to everyone without talking with him first?

"Well . . . we will support you in this," Dean said. "Even though we don't like it."

TJ nodded subtly at his friend, appreciating his show of support. Finally, he cleared his throat. Every head turned in his direction. "I agree. None of us like it, but we all do support you, Jen. Always."

She stared at him, a bit of shock on her face. But then she gave him a tentative smile. "Thank you."

# Twenty-Five

That Wednesday, Jen insisted on taking her mother to her oncology appointment. Terri had taken her for the MRI the day before, and now they would find out how well her mother's preferred cancer treatment of doing absolutely nothing was working.

Jen glanced around at the light-blue walls of the doctor's office, feeling a little numb. She hadn't spoken to TJ since they'd left that conference room. She'd gone straight back to his place and moved all of her things out, which had been pretty easy considering she didn't own much.

At work, he'd found a million reasons to avoid her and she him. Now she was starting to wonder if they'd really even talk again before she left. Next up on her agenda, telling her mother. No time like the present, since they were on an honesty kick. Or at least she was.

"I'm going to Chicago next week to see if I might want to take a job there," Jen said, breaking the silence in the room.

Diane glanced over at her, stared a moment, and then looked away.

"No comment? Really?" Jen shook her head.

"You're going to do what you think is best," her mom said.

"I do think this is best. I have to see if this opportunity is meant to be. Even if it is a selfish decision for once."

"Oh please," Diane bit back. "You've made a million selfish decisions, Jen. Don't act like your life is one giant martyr-fest."

Jen's head jerked back. "You can't be serious. Do you know all the ways I've been affected by your poor choices in life?"

"I know there have been many, yes, but you're thirty years old, Jennifer Mackenzie. Even I don't have *that* much power."

"You're right. I need to start owning my issues. They're not all your fault. But this . . . choice, is part of me trying to do that. I have to try this, Mom. And I'd really like your support. I need it, actually."

The doctor walked in then, smiling, and greeted them with a hardy hello. Diane turned on her charm, grinning and reciprocating his cheery demeanor, and then shockingly, linked her hand in with Jen's. Jen squeezed.

He sat down hard on his stool and glanced between Jen and her mother. "How is everyone today?"

"Good," the two of them said in unison. When Diane looked over, Jen smiled at her.

"Glad to hear it," he said, laying his laptop on the

counter and then opening it up. Before he took the time
to read anything, he pivoted on his stool and smiled
at them. "I think I might have some news that will
make this good day even better."

Jen's stomach clenched. She glanced at her mother,
who just lifted her eyebrows.

"I looked at your MRI this morning and quite
honestly, I was shocked. That mass is half the size it
was two months ago. And I see no sign of it in that
lymph node. It's quite honestly . . . I don't know. Sometimes things happen that even I can't explain with my
expensive medical degree."

Jen's lips parted as she glanced at her mother, who
looked back at her. Diane gasped, and then laughed.
"I have felt so good the last couple of weeks. I just
thought . . . well, I've just been so happy, and my
daughter had been forcing me to eat all these vegetables and protein shakes in the morning."

The doctor shrugged. "Eating right and being happy
are always a good idea. I can't say what's done this,
Diane. Sometimes . . . miracles just happen."

Diane laughed again, her eyes glassy. Jen felt tears
prickling at her eyes also. The look on her mother's
face was possibly the happiest she'd ever seen. It made
her look twenty years younger, lighter, and freer.

Jen covered her mouth with her hand, feeling a sob
itching to escape. Diane squeezed Jen's hand this time,
and then pulled it up to her lips to kiss it. Sucking in a
deep breath, Jen turned to the doctor, who was smiling at them both. "What do we do now? I mean, it's
not gone, right?"

"No, this isn't a clear bill of health by any stretch.

But I think we should keep doing what we're doing and recheck it in a month."

"So, no chemo?"

The doctor shrugged. "Like I said. Keep being happy and eating your vegetables, and let's see what happens. We can change course at any time, but the improvement on that scan is significant."

Jen was still in shock as she stood there and watched the doctor do some routine checks on her mother. Then he left.

"Can you believe this? I feel like a new person."

"Mom, you heard him. This doesn't mean the cancer is gone."

Diane rolled her eyes. "No, but it's a hell of a lot better than four to six months to live. Now let's go to Target and get you a new outfit for your first day in Chicago."

Jen laughed as they headed out of the building and to her truck. Before they got in, she turned to her mom. "I'm gonna make a call real quick."

Diane nodded as Jen stepped away from the vehicle before pulling up TJ's number. She couldn't help herself. She had to share this news with him, and he answered on the second ring.

"Hey," he said.

"Hi. Sorry to bother you."

"You're never bothering me, Jen."

"Okay, well, I won't keep you, but I wanted to let know we just left Mom's appointment."

"And?" he asked, sounding anxious.

"Her tumor has shrunk," Jen said, with a smile on her face. "By almost half. Can you even believe that?"

She could hear the smile in his voice when he

replied, "I'm so happy to hear that, Jen. That's amazing news."

"I know. We were just so shocked." She wiped a tear from her eye as she turned back to the truck. "I just wanted to tell you."

"I'm glad you did," he said. "Tell Diane I'm really happy for her."

"I will." They were each quiet for a moment, so finally Jen said, "Well, okay. Talk to you later."

"Okay," he said, then just sat there quietly on the other end of the line.

"Bye, TJ."

"Bye, Jen."

She hesitated, but then ended the call.

A week later, Jen watched Erin Kingman as she talked to the parents as they dropped off their kids at Uccello Canoro. The place was so different than the small-town academy she'd taught at. This was the real deal, people paid big bucks, and they had a serious expectation of return on investment. This was training for Broadway, or television. These parents wanted their kids to be stars. And it was stressing Jen out. Big time. Today was parent day, which meant they'd all stay and observe practice. No pressure for her first week.

She'd now been in Chicago for about seventy-two hours and she'd never been more homesick in her life. She kept telling herself to wait it out. What she was feeling was normal, but it didn't seem to help. The first two nights she'd quietly cried herself to sleep on Erin's sofa.

The apartment—if you could call it that—was smaller than Jen's shithole that had burned down. She'd even done a little research and found out that comparable in the same building started renting for twelve hundred a month. For that same price back in Kansas, she could nearly rent a two-story house. It was inconceivable. How did people make a living?

"Hello, Miss Jen," one of the students said. Jen shook off her wayward thoughts and smiled.

"Good morning"—she thought quickly and glanced at Erin who mouthed her the answer—"Kara. Are you ready to sing today?"

Kara nodded. She was five and absolutely adorable. Her singing voice was out of this world, but the kid was wearing a Gucci sweater and jeans. It was a different world.

Once everyone had been dropped off—and the parents were all seated behind the two-way mirror, yikes!—Erin began the class with scales.

The academy had classes Monday through Friday and did three performances a year. Some kids were there for voice, some for acting, and some did it all.

Her first day, Erin had given Jen a nice introduction to every parent that came. Had mentioned her experience and the roles she'd played. A couple of moms had asked where she'd "studied," and the last company she'd taught at. She'd just smiled at said, "I've spent the past five years working in community theater. I have a passion for it."

She'd received a lot of "aw, that's sweet" looks, which had made her feel bad for Erin for bringing her there. Thankfully they'd ended that first day at the local bar where Erin had relayed her own run-ins with parents early on. She'd assured Jen that the parents had no say on the hire, but Jen wasn't so sure. If the school had received money from a wealthy benefactor, someone was pulling strings.

"Jen, why don't you lead the first breathing exercise?" Erin asked.

"Of course." Jen stepped to the front of the group. She let her eyes wander over the dozen or so children in front of her, then the mirror to the far end of the room.

And then she began with a smile. "Posture check," she said in a happy voice. Every little body sat to attention, and then she led them through a breathing and singing exercise.

She felt good about it. The kids had been attentive, she'd felt good about her own voice although she'd been incredibly nervous, and by the end of the day, one of the parents had come up and complimented her. Erin had given her a thumbs-up from across the room.

By Thursday, Jen's head was spinning with excitement. She'd learned so much from Erin and the rest of her staff, but one thing had become incredibly clear.

This place wasn't for her.

Some of the kids were fantastic, and Jen already felt attached. But in general, the parents were too rich and the kids too pedigreed. It made her question what their motives were. Did they truly intend for their child to become famous? That felt like a lot of responsibility. And misguided hope. It all made Jen uncomfortable.

It was an amazing academy, and Erin would be fun to work with, but she was feeling more and more like the job wasn't for her. Jen missed knowing that her work was truly building up a child who needed the extra boost of confidence.

In Maple Springs she'd worked with all kinds of children. Some that were on food stamps, some that were in foster care, and yes, even some with money. But the work had felt *important*. That was the aspect she quickly realized was missing from Uccello Canoro.

However, that didn't keep her from soaking up everything she could, and formulating a plan. She was starting to think this was the reason she'd come.

TJ sat at his desk watching the video of Jen and Ant singing at Shakers posted to her Facebook page. He'd probably watched it six times, and that was just today.

For some reason, this time he decided to click on the comments. There were 132. Wow.

"OMG, Jen, you're amazing."

"Why aren't you famous yet?"

"I was there!!!!! You were so good!!!!"

"You're hot AF."

That one made him growl. He clicked on the profile pic to see a bearded meathead. "You're a dick, Chase Reynolds," TJ muttered to his computer screen. He kept reading.

"I love it when you sing, Jen!!! Hi Ant!! Miss you both."

"Please start teaching again Miss Jen."

"We love you Miss Jen."

"Miss Jen! You're soooooo good. :) :)"

There were several more from what appeared to be her students, which made TJ feel sick to his stomach.

He missed her to the point of tears. Something he might never admit for as long as he lived. And all week he'd been fighting a harsh reality.

He knew she'd made the right decision.

Jen had lived a lot of her life putting herself second, doubting herself, and worrying about how others saw her. She deserved this job. A chance to shine, to do what she loved, and to succeed. She was right, it was an opportunity she couldn't pass up. He hated it, but he knew it.

A knock at the door got his attention. Jake stood there, hands on hips. TJ clicked the browser closed.

"What?"

"Listen. My man. I love you like a brother, and I know you're going through some shit. But if you play that video one more time, we're probably gonna come to blows."

TJ just glared at him.

Jake put his hands up. "Just sayin'."

He walked out and TJ could hear him laughing down the hallway.

TJ looked around as his office. The bottles of Stag Signature Bourbon and Longhorn Whiskey. Their first dollar was hanging on his wall, along with copies of all of their local newspaper and magazine covers. He had so much pride in this work. With what they'd accomplished. The three of them had set out with a goal, and they'd succeeded. He'd achieved what he'd wanted to. Built a beautiful home, learned to have faith in his own abilities.

Another knock sounded on his door and he looked up, shocked to see his father.

Instantly TJ stood. "Dad, what are you doing here?"

His father sauntered in, looking around, casually stuffing his hands in his pockets. "Thought it was about time I came and checked out your office."

TJ slowly sat down. "Of course, have a seat."

The older man did. "Nice chair. I have one similar in my office."

"We both have good taste, I guess." But TJ was just being polite.

His dad just chuckled. "I suppose so. Listen, uh, I actually was in the neighborhood. Just got done talking to Jordan Bodisto across the way."

TJ's brows went up, then he shook his head. "That wasn't necessary, Dad."

"No, it was." The man looked everywhere but at TJ's eyes. "I owed him an apology."

"Sounds like it was his father you owed an apology to."

"Yeah. I'll probably get to that," he said, giving an awkward smile. "But I wanted to encourage him to do business with you. It isn't your fault I'm an idiot."

If TJ had been stunned about his father's appearance at his work, this just about blew him over. "I appreciate that. But you know we'll be fine without a Shakers account."

"Of course you will. This place is very successful. I know that. But . . . it needed to be done anyway. I'd hate to be the thing standing in your way of any business."

TJ nodded. Silently waited to hear what his father said next.

"I'm real proud of what you've done with this place, you know?"

"No, Dad. I didn't know that."

Finally, their eyes met. "Well, you should have. You're my son. I guess I should have told you before now. It's just not always easy for me."

It was hard not to wonder why just the small act of showing your own child your pride or affection could be difficult. TJ really had no idea what kind of childhood his own father had, but it occurred to him then that it must not have been good. And that made him very sad to consider.

"I appreciate you saying so, Dad. Really."

James Laughlin didn't do emotions, as far as TJ knew, but right then, for once, they were evident in his eyes when he nodded. "Well, I guess I'll let you get back to work. And, uh, please give my sincere apologies to your girlfriend about the way I acted the other night. I'd had too much to drink."

"I'll do that."

"She seems to really care for you. I'm glad."

TJ sucked in a breath, holding his emotions in check. Finally, he just nodded. The last thing he could do right now was share what happened between him and Jen with his father.

"Anyway." His father awkwardly looked around and stood up. TJ joined him, following him toward the door. They made their way out into the main room, his dad looking around at the Stag. He glanced over at the distilling room. "I don't have time now, but some-day I'm gonna come in and see how all this works."

TJ smiled. "I'd like that. Anytime."

"Good." He headed for the front door again, but at the last minute he turned back to TJ. "Oh. And don't miss your phone call with your mother this Sunday. She gets sad when you don't keep in touch with her."

TJ's eyes widened. "Okay, I'll make sure I don't. I wasn't aware she even noticed when I missed a week."

John's brow furrowed. "Of course she does. She's your mother."

"She could call me," TJ said matter-of-factly.

His father shook his head. "You know how she is. She doesn't want to bother you." And on that note, he left.

TJ watched his dad walk out to his Mercedes parked on the curb in front of the door. A no-parking zone. The old man didn't care a bit about rules. TJ chuckled to himself.

Walking back to his office, he thought about his mother. What in the world made her think calling him would be a bother? Why did everyone fear imposing on the other? He immediately thought of Jen.

When you loved someone, sometimes you needed to butt into their life and remind them of that. Even if they should already know it. It was necessary.

Sitting down at his desk, he looked around once more. Yes, he'd accomplished a lot. But without that woman, all of it was meaningless. He'd keep telling her that until it sunk in. Opening a new browser on his computer, he started clicking.

# Twenty-Six

The next morning, TJ got off the Metro and walked up the stairs onto State Street. He'd gotten the address of the Uccello Canoro from their website, and John had given him a few hints about navigating the city since he used to live there. This was where he would start. Surely, she was either at the school, or this Erin didn't live too far away.

Taking a deep breath, he pulled out his phone, said a quick prayer to the universe, and called Jen. They'd only spoken briefly in almost two weeks, the day she'd called about her mother's MRI results. It was still hard to believe he'd gone almost that long without touching her.

"TJ?"

His body instantly breathed a sigh of relief that she'd answered. "Jen. Yes. It's me. How are you?"

"Good . . ." She paused, and he realized there was no mistaking the background noise. There was no traffic chaos or car horns in Maple Springs. Not even during rush hour. "Where are you?"

"I'm here, Jen. Where are you?"

"TJ! Where are *you*?" He could tell she'd begun moving. TJ glanced up to the nearest street sign. "I'm on the corner of State and Chicago."

"Oh my God." She gave a nervous laugh. "I'm coming. You're down the street from me."

"Don't let me go," he rushed out.

She laughed. "I'm not, just head . . . uh, north I think. Toward Wabash."

He began walking faster, looking at the sidewalk ahead of him. "Are you at Erin's apartment?"

"No, we were in a restaurant having lunch. Keep heading north."

"I am." And then suddenly, there she was. Standing in the middle of the sidewalk, looking around under a deli awning. People rushed in between them, but he kept his eyes trained on her bright-red lips, dark hair, and beautiful eyes, which he didn't need to see up close to know were sparkly and full of life.

"I see you," he said.

And then she looked right at him. Smiling.

"I see you too," she said, staring at him. The excitement in her voice, and in her eyes, made him feel like he'd just died and gone to heaven. "Oh my gosh, I can't believe you're here."

Neither of them moved. They just stood there, phones to their ears, staring as strangers passed between them, blocking then revealing each other again.

"You're so beautiful, it hurts, Jen," he said into the phone. He could see her roll her eyes.

"Will you stop being so damn creepy and get over here." He watched her end the call and put her phone in her pocket. He shoved his phone down into his own pocket and began making his way toward her. The minute their bodies met, so did their lips, for a long, soft kiss.

When she pulled back, she looked up at him. "What are you *doing* here?"

"Giving you your chance."

"My chance?"

He touched her face. "Your chance to make your dreams come true. I had my chance at success, and I achieved it. Now it's your turn. So here I am."

Her arms looped around his waist. "Are you saying . . . you'd move here for me?"

"If that's what you want. If your dream is here, mine is too." He leaned against her, speaking into her ear so she didn't miss it. "*You're* my dream, Jennifer Mackenzie. I want you for forever. For no other reason but because I'm selfish and I can't live without you."

"But you love the Stag."

"I love you more."

She smiled, then leaned forward to speak into his ear. "Confession. I don't love it here."

TJ laughed and looked down at her. "Seriously?"

"Seriously. I'm so glad I came. It's been a wonderful experience, and I love Erin. But this job is not my dream. Plus . . . I've missed you so much."

TJ kissed her again. When he pulled back, she touched his face. "I love you, Trevor James. I'm pretty sure I've loved you for most of my life."

He leaned his forehead against hers. "I've always loved your voice, but those words . . . that's the most beautiful sound I've ever heard."

# Twenty-Seven

That night they made love in a king-size bed in the Drake Hotel, where TJ had gotten them a last-minute room for the night. She still couldn't believe he was here, in Chicago.

"I don't know what I would have done if you'd turned me away today," he said, playing with her hair.

Jen turned, resting her chin on his chest. "You don't have to worry about that."

They laid there, bodies intertwined, looking out at the city lit up outside their window. "Crazy how you can hear the sounds even way up here, but yet it still feels peaceful," she said. "And that view is crazy."

"It's pretty. But this"—he ran his finger all the way around her face—"is the only view I want to go to bed to each night, and wake up to each morning."

"Damn," she said, smiling. "Ten points for that one."

He laughed. "I thought so."

"I want us to make sure we're completely honest with each other from here on," she said.

"I agree with that. Although as it is, I think you know everything there is to know."

She quirked her eyebrows. "*Everything*? No dark secrets?"

He thought about it. "Okay. I've got something you may not know. I didn't just come to see you in every performance of *Grease*. I came to every single performance you were in. *The King and I. Oklahoma*."

She sat up, laughing and in complete shock. "You saw me play Ado Annie?"

"I did. I'll admit it, that laugh . . ." He grimaced.

"Oh my goodness. Wasn't it awful? I promise I won't ever do that again."

"That sounds like a good idea."

"Okay. *I* have a secret that's kind of dark," she said, needing to get all her dirty laundry out in the open. It was the only way she'd be able to fully move forward—if he had the whole picture and still wanted her for her.

He ran a finger over her bare thigh, his eyes on hers.

She took a deep breath. "I have ten thousand dollars in credit card debt." She made an overexaggerated worried face.

TJ winced, his eyes shutting.

"Don't hate meeeee," she begged playfully, hoping he wouldn't truly get mad.

He shook his head, his horror obvious. "Then don't hate me if I pay it off."

She rolled her eyes, but her relief was immediate. "I'll try not to."

Grabbing her hand, he yanked her back down on his chest. "What are you going to do for me?"

Her eyes went wide. "I'm a kept woman, am I? Remember what that's called?"

"I hope it's called Mrs. Laughlin. Someday."

That shut her up. "Do you truly mean that?"

"I do, Jen." He cupped her chin. "Don't think this is a proposal or anything. I'm smart enough to do that right. But that is what I want."

"Me too." She kissed him softly and then pulled back. "One last thing. I was going to make an entire presentation, but since you're here, I'll tell you now."

TJ's brow furrowed. "Okay."

Jen sat up on the bed, wearing only her panties. "I actually do not have any intention of you being my sugar daddy. So, I was thinking."

"Hold on." TJ grabbed a pillow and shoved it into her lap, covering her bare breasts. "I can't concentrate with those staring at me," he teased.

She glared at him, then stuffed the pillow against her chest. "Anyway, pervert, I have an idea. The up-stairs of the Stag sits empty almost six days a week. You guys only use it for weddings or other events."

"Yes."

"Well, it's a great-size room, with amazing acoustics."

"Okay," he said, a smirk on his face.

That was a good sign, she decided. "I thought maybe we could do some theater camps for kids there. Maybe a couple of shows a year. Just see how it goes. All on me. I'll do all the work."

He touched her knee, rubbing it gently. "You think

parents would bring their kids to a distillery for drama camp?"

"Of course they would. If I was good enough."

He chuckled. "You are good enough. And I love the idea."

"You *do*?" She almost felt like crying, knowing that he liked her idea.

"I do."

"What about Dean and Jake? What if they hate it?"

He shrugged. "I'll tell them too damn bad."

She frowned. "No you won't. They're your partners."

"Yes, you're right. But . . . they know exactly how I feel about you, and they also know how talented you are. And if I hit them with a profitable business plan, I don't see how they can object."

She bit at her bottom lip, grinning. "Can I help? I have lots of ideas."

"Of course you can. Does this mean you'll take Tara's job? Can you handle both?"

"I'll try. We'll just see how it goes."

"We *will* see how it goes. But as long as you're mine, that's all that matters."

# Epilogue

When the final number of *Grease Jr.* wrapped up, and the audience burst into applause, Jen let out a sigh of relief so intense, she almost fell forward.

Nearly two hundred people were packed into the up-stairs of the Stag for the first performance of a three-day run, and thank goodness it was March, because it was getting stuffy up here.

Jen stood up, beaming, as the applause turned into a standing ovation. She met eyes with so many famil-iar faces. Her mother grinned back at her; Terri was there; TJ's mom, who had sold at least thirty tickets alone to her ladies group; Lauren, Charlotte, and Dean. Everyone who mattered. Charlotte gave Jen two thumbs-up, then continued clapping along.

The past three months of their inaugural Stag Theater camp had been the most hectic, stressful, and rewarding of Jen's life. She'd found two seniors from Maple Springs High School to be associate directors, and one of the kids' moms had volunteered to be their choreographer. Along with the rest of the parents of their twenty-six sign-ups chipping in to make costumes and sets, and sell tickets, they'd actually pulled it off.

The kids took turns coming forward and bowing, and by the time her adorable little Sandy and Danny came forward, Jen was crying. Directing and teaching these kids had been one of the most enjoyable things she'd ever done. And as hard as it had been, she'd learned so much and was already aching to get busy on the next performance.

Her two young associate directors took the microphone and thanked everyone for coming before turning to Jen.

"And last, we want to thank our director, Jennifer Mackenzie. Without you, and the guys from the Stag, this never would have happened." They motioned for Jen to come up from her seat down front. She knew this was customary, but the past week had been so crazy, she hadn't prepared any words to say.

She took the microphone and everyone got quiet.

"What an amazing group of kids this is," she started. "I can't put into words how extraordinary it has been to spend these last few months with them. Theater has been a passion of mine for so long, and I'd like to extend my thanks to the owners of the Stag—and yes I'd like you guys to stand up—Dean, Jake, and TJ."

Applause broke out again as the three guys reluctantly stood up for a brief moment and then sat back down—except for TJ, who walked to the edge of the room and stood to the side, a smile playing at his lips. At her.

"These guys have put up with me—and that's not always easy!" She said, making everyone laugh. "But seriously, they've given me unwavering support for this endeavor, and I just can't thank them enough. And of course, my mother, who is so strong and inspiring. Last, but not least, thank you again to everyone for coming. Stay tuned for whatever we have planned next." She went to sit back down, but Evie, one of her young directors grabbed her arm.

"Hang on," Evie said, grinning.

Jen looked over in time to see TJ walking toward her. The room hushed as he took the microphone, paused, and then looked at Jen. "I apologize for holding everyone up, but there is one more thing that needs to happen here. I hope you all don't mind."

Jen felt butterflies flutter to life in her stomach as she watched TJ pass the mic back to Evie, and then get down on one knee. The room erupted into cheers, and twenty-six children began squealing behind her.

TJ started to laugh as their eyes met, and he held out a ring box. The diamond sparkled up at her, so perfect. So beautiful.

"I couldn't miss this opportunity," he said over the raucous audience. Jen felt tears pressing in on her eyes. "I love you, Jen. And I want you to be mine. Forever."

She couldn't contain her giant grin and then joined him on the floor kneeling, so he could hear her answer. "I've always been yours. So . . . yes. Absolutely yes."

*Coming soon . . .*

Don't miss the next novel in the Whiskey and
Weddings series

**MAYBE FOR YOU**

Available in September 2018 from St. Martin's
Paperbacks